KOSMOAUTIKON

To Crayden

From MARK CHANDOS

Best wishes!

The *Kosmoautikon Epic Cycle:*

Exodus From Sapiens (Book One)

I Hear Strange Cries at Jupiter (Book Two)

In My Atom Is Ark (Book Three)

Chill Collected Zoologies (Book Four)

Desiccate Numerologies of Men (Book Five)

KOSMOAUTIKON:
Exodus From Sapiens

BOOK ONE

With Philosophical Essay

STORY THEORY

Mark Chandos

Print information available on the last page.

Rev. date: 12/11/2015

To order additional copies of this book, contact:
Xlibris
1-888-795-4274
www.Xlibris.com
Orders@Xlibris.com
715124

CONTENTS

KOSMOAUTIKON: EXODUS FROM SAPIENS

Argument of Book One: Exodus From Sapiens.............................. xiii
LIST OF CHARACTERS xvi

CANTO ONE 1
    PROLOGUE: Exodus From Sapiens 5
    The Stipulation to Depart Earth.................................... 20

CANTO TWO 23
    Earth Minus.. 23
    The Sumerian Genome.. 26
    Homo Sapiens Minus 32
    It Was Good to Leave Earth 35
    The Creation of the First Faustus Creatures on Callisto 39

CANTO THREE 44
    Generations of Seth 44
    I Am Mystic Synapse 47
    Master, What Did You Make? 54

CANTO FOUR 58
    The Record of Exodus From Earth 58
    Tall Winter I Will Pass Composed.................................... 59

CANTO FIVE 68
    I Saw Fire on Mars.. 68

CANTO SIX.. 79
    Build Me Once Galactic Ships.. 79
    Anabasis in Lead.. 80

CANTO SEVEN 100
    The Pool of Luxor... 100
    Proverbs..105
    Torn Blood Sails 107

CANTO EIGHT 112
    Beekeeper Kingdoms 112
    Star Dice..133

CANTO NINE...135
    The Channeling of Cheda's Mind.......................135
    Encoding the Instinct Against Murder 142

CANTO TEN..145
    Reseal the Broken Places.....................................145

STORY THEORY

Note to the Reader..169
Introduction...171

CHAPTER ONE 179
    Clarity of a New Philosophy 179

CHAPTER TWO 184
    All Human Idioms Are Self Referent 184

CHAPTER THREE 188
    What Is Story Theory?.......................................188

CHAPTER FOUR..196
    The Consequences of Story Theory 196

CHAPTER FIVE.. 200
    Is Modernism a Civilization of Truth? 200

CHAPTER SIX.. 205
    The Alien Mind of Homo Sapiens..................... 205

CHAPTER SEVEN 209
   Why Write Epic Poems? 209

CHAPTER EIGHT 215
   The Exclusivity of Human Information............................215

CHAPTER NINE...219
   The Danger of an Outward Church 219

CHAPTER TEN..225
   A Man in Trouble 225

CHAPTER ELEVEN 228
   Recovery of Mythic Code...................................... 228

CHAPTER TWELVE 233
   Is Human Information Repeatable? 233

CHAPTER THIRTEEN 238
   There Is Something Wrong with Homo Sapiens.......................... 238

CHAPTER FOURTEEN 243
   Modernism In, Modernism Out....................................... 243

CHAPTER FIFTEEN 246
   Where Does Science Leave Us?...................................... 246

CHAPTER SIXTEEN 251
   Vernacular Speakers Degraded by Scientism.........................251

CHAPTER SEVENTEEN 256
   What New Information Does an Epic Poem Give?.....................256

CHAPTER EIGHTEEN 262
   Ducunt Fata Volentum, Nolentem Trahunt................................ 262

ANNEX 267
   Summary of Philosophic Theses.................................... 267

To My Wife

The Beauty of the Ring

KOSMOAUTIKON:
Exodus From Sapiens

BOOK ONE

A work that shows itself incapable of dominating the world of events and cannot make its audience capable of dominating such a world is not a work of art.

Bertold Brecht

The lyric, while criticized by some as no longer relevant, has flourished recently. Especially after Whitman's time, lyric poets have been associated almost exclusively with the idea of the poet. At the same time, the epic in its traditional form has all but disappeared in the contemporary Americas, yet the desire to create an epic work still exists for writers in the Americas, so they have had to find new forms to flesh out those desires. The novel is one option, but Whitman's creation of the lyric-epic is another since in that form the poet can explore his or her epic desires while at the same time retain the personal poetic position.

William Allegrezza

Whitman's rewriting of history to portray this mythic vision is used as a rhetorical device to foster democracy. However, this rewriting of history defines Whitman's view of history as primarily textual. Essentially, Whitman sees all time as connected in the present. This viewpoint is not unusual for writers in the Americas.

William Allegrezza

When the farthest corner of the globe has been conquered technologically and can be exploited economically; when any incident you like, at any time you like, becomes accessible as fast as you like; when you can simultaneously "experience" an assassination attempt against a king in France and a symphony concert in Tokyo; when time is nothing but speed, instantaneity, and simultaneity, and time as history has vanished from all Dasein of all peoples; when a boxer counts as the great man of a people; when the tallies of millions at mass meetings are a triumph; then, yes, there still looms like a specter over all this uproar the question: what for? – where to? – and what then?

Heidegger

We said: On the Earth, all over it, a darkening of the world is happening. The essential happenings in this darkening are: the flight of the gods, the destruction of the Earth, the reduction of human beings to a mass, the preeminence of the mediocre.

Heidegger

Even his holy ones he distrusts, the heavens are not pure in his sight.

Job 4:18, 15:15

Argument of Book One: *Exodus From Sapiens*

Aaron is the last living member of a ruthless political dynasty, responsible for the extinction of Non-Western nations on a dying Earth. A medical student before joining his father as military leader, his intent is to create a race of men able to live without a carbon and oxygen base. Earth's atmosphere has been made toxic by the release of radiation and the CO_2 of an over-industrialized planet. Earth was already despoiled before Aaron was forced to reduce the populations of enemy countries. This war was the result of a coalition of states against the final outpost of Western cultural idiom.

Aaron's companion in the voyage to Jupiter is Talon, the greatest scientific mind of his age. Talon suffers from a rare bone disease and lives in a wheelchair. Talon has secretly set in motion his plans to translate his own broken body into a new powerful skeleton based on methane and ammonia.

At Jupiter's moon Callisto they build giant factories in stationary orbit. They ignite colossal energy beams, creating an immense vacuum that funnels up the minerals from the broken moon below. Talon's robotic arms are programmed to build a large artificial RingWorld circling Callisto. Antromity, a new substance, replicates Earth's gravity – but has serious side effects.

Though dangerous, their audacious project is the best hope for the further survival of the mind of men beyond the crib of the Earth. The conditions of life at Jupiter contain a new astrology. The Murmurs have told Aaron that the alien mind that formed the human genome communicates in prophecy from beyond the cosmos. All previous learning and science of Western men are thus rejected in the quest for this original source of consciousness.

The crews of the thirty spaceships become desperate after three years. The men are unable to support the pressures of space flight that never ends and offers no hope of returning to Earth. Aaron's last military commander, Vargus, finally destroys the Earth—after final negotiations for world peace break down. China still uses her remaining masses to try to control the planet. All remaining nuclear weapons are used with a ruthlessness matching a Hitler or a Stalin. All proud cities scorched, all tall structures of modernism leveled, the Earth becomes a snowball in three months. A year later, Vargus arrives at Aaron's station at Callisto moon after this last extinction on Earth. Vargus is ordered to capture any remaining Russian Federation ships and gather 300 females from various "nurseries" across the European Theater of Operations. These are genetically perfect humans.

Unknown to all, Aaron has purchased (or taken) girls from dying families in conquered Eastern Europe. He places them in special "orphanages" in the

Taiga forests that allow only a strict diet and education. At the end of ten years, running a hand held device over their heads, he selects the strongest to make the journey to Jupiter. Later, Vargus reports that each girl has passed an unspecified "test." These girls will be the mothers of a new mankind.

In route, while the leadership was in Kryostasis, the hindmost ship loses power due to the failure of the Russian reactors. Another ship is positioned to rescue the stricken craft, and transfer the sleeping human cargo. The Kryon stations fail – and humans must be re-awoken. Vargus is terrified to see (later) a recording of how "humans" revived from Kryostasis proceed to take control of the rescue ship. It is only then that Vargus discovers that this group of thirty pilgrims is not from the orphanage on Aaron's original list. They are from a mental institution of a similar name.

Aaron explores the origin of the human mind. Realizing the inner power could only exist within consciousness, he attempts to find trace images of this construct. Facing life at the edge of the solar system, Aaron creates a new linguistic idiom—as advanced as any idiom of science. Earth had lost the possibility for new language and poetry. Outside of Earth, Homo sapiens discover ancient powers after two millennia of the rule of a corrupt universal church … and an ideological scientism.

LIST OF CHARACTERS

Aaron   Leader of the American exodus from Earth. Mad.

Talon (in chains)   Scientist from Earth. Exchanged his broken body
                             for a new *Homo faustus* creation. Mad.

Wakeda   Faithful companion of Aaron. Military Chief of
                             Staff.

Vargus   Second in Command. Delivers 300 Slavic girls
                             from Eastern Europe in 30 captured ships.

Terry (Zodiac)   Aaron's only living human son. Pretend cook.
                             Prophet.

Jurate   Child-wife of Aaron. Future mother of
                             Kosmoautikon (Extra cosmos prophet).

Antebbe   Astral being from beyond the Cosmos.

Cheda   Alien son of Aaron. First Homo Faustus.

CANTO ONE

(In a spaceship attached to RingWorld, Aaron sutures a new-made faustus creature, supine on an alloy gurney.)

1

Aaron. As I purple your eyes with tint, staining
dyes empty from your heart. The stutter of
my ray gun seals crimson rising veins, fused in
sequence, as scuttling desert insects print
minuscule in sand. I have merged, enraged,
six shadowed proteins, six pungent etched
tattoos remote from crowded tenements
of native helix. (*Touches reddening cheek.*)
Here. Inside this glass, I have spliced, in chains,
twelve dark silhouettes on the phylum of
your gene. There, six-fingered, at the end of
time, in blood-dark skies, enamellers of
gold-dust tears on empty darkened eyes, will
sermon on your fame till the agon of
their school is bitter-cold. (*Injects solution, waits.*)
                              There ... breath softly.
Blood pools in the fissure of your slight wound,
thawing in solution new-caked crimson
blisters, chilled strawberry ice on ripened
gradients, on swollen peach-smooth breasts. In
a future age of ice, erect in glass
cenotaphs, desiccate numerologies
of men may syllable divinations
from your light-emitting bone; eye-cupping
priests secret again your gene with bitter
salts, counting snail-fed preaching archons
stationed on the prefix of your blood
          (*Injects solution, waits.*)
                              A storm is coming.
Where ... where may I have a place in your mind?
I see your eye move. What do you see? Index
roughly shapes remote from affiliates
of union: beacons of no-time adrift,
immune to contour, afloat – as torn ghost
sails on winter-dusk seas – without treaty

of modern eyes. I know. You are now gene
traitorous, you will barter data extra-
cosmos for the light of eyes. Like me, so
many years in yellow light, you will make
endless requisites of objects. You will
probe them without stint. You will petition
strange gods. Yet it is your election that
misleads you. What are worlds? What, minus
modern narrative, is *sapient* world –
except range of interrogative? No! …
Do not die! Wait till the light of Venus
touches the small hairs of your burning skin.

(*Sutures tissue. Pauses. Wipes the sweat from his brow.*)

There … perfect in your gene … my clothes are wet.
I seek to know the seat of my mind. How
can it answer disjoint phenomena?
How much from infinity am I extract?
Feasibly, at the end of your time, you
will find you do not disassemble from
mischance or disease. These are modern elections
you have made. It is the choice of inquisition
that populates the eye – pretending its
learned desire. Or like me, you will choose
to act eccentric against the storm?

(*Moves to second new-made creature on a gurney.*)

New made, with no Earth-tuck in your sieve of
speech. Where does the mind patent? Where does
my shameless agon invent? Cry roughly
what I may detect at my limit! Tell
me what I cannot know by myself! No
shutter of contour? No razor-thin photon?
No bantam brush of line? No single burnt bush
of sensual objects? Then the mind I
now possess is ever noch the near range
of sentient objects? My mind alone
is only certain continent? Timeless,
state any well-thumbed chapter of my mind.
I have purpled it with staining dyes.

What, after all, do we wish to know? We
want to know if our information still
endures! Give me such sanction that my mind,
as keeper of the stars, cannot be darkened
unless structure of light is darkened, that
I cannot be unknown unless distinction
is unknown; that I cannot be unmade
adjacent to ancestral primates. Or
did they, as mandrill, retreat keenly from
duality? No, not once? Then my mind
invents from no blood primate, no near ape?
Can I reform, then, my twisted ascent?
Or what other use is it to enter space,
raising cathedral-ships in a vacuum,
if not to find rough un-boned ancestors?
Matter no origin, *Sapiens* no origin?
Thus, I observe, each may only make
a story of his life – and each man's eye split
– never, two, matched in image. The purpose?
To guard a sovereign treasure secure,
in a structure safe from influence? If
aggregate could be made of compound mind,
tell me now, and I will mark a new page.
Is intent of this force detectable
at the margin?
(*Pauses. Kisses.*) … I print your lips with tint.
There – go. I release you again into
a sea of pre-selection. …Yet, try, if
you can provoke my speech retrograde.
I see the gods are dazed, unsure of my acts.
Yet what diversion of speculum? Say
I seek form exfoliate form's structure
beyond the cosmos. If you could take back
the bone in the eye, if you could suck the
universe declining, then you should not
feel the prick of subject – of object.

Ample … I cast dice into you.

(Reaches into creature's mouth, grasping the tongue.)

Speak to the beings of light abutting your
soul. Tell roughly my news: I have made one
way exodus of *Sapiens* to probe
final beacons of peril. If asked, tell them
the truth: We are nomads of wrath – adrift.
We proved on Earth there is no state
of peace. Where hydrogen links oxygen
links nitrogen, terror is the only
perfect science.

Since, on what crust of tear did all other
mistake our text? Sentient mind is yet
suspended in the cosmos? Thus, we are
already in solution; no shift by
rocket shifts our place. I am certain, then,
if we enter space, we enter space to
meet our own mind. Or is there yet gossamer
dust outside my thought? No? Negative? Thus

I prove. If we stay, we pick the bones of
men. If we leave, we pick the bones of men.
Away from Earth, then, I lose no part of
my election.

No longer hold me incantation; flesh
my seamless electron, antenna to
all human screens.

Light in my space ray,
a steam on glass.

PROLOGUE: Exodus From Sapiens

(Recording made by Aaron for future generations of English.)

2
A. My riches are my country, and it will
remember me in exile where I have lived
when I was every country's mother tongue
and all tongues praised by my measure.

I have stained from riot more structure.

Not once in ten generations on Earth
has the West's learning been removed
from its hypocrisy. We break out, willing
to burst. My saints, at first, are strange:

creatures darting now as snapping spawn
contained in bloat round-belly ships.
Still un-cut David, Moses, Isaac, vibrant
DNA double-stitched in vials of glass.

My saints now hunt their own Canaanites,
Etruscans, Essenes, Cathars, Indians, Aztecs.
What may I add to this throw of sperm?
I lodge Western men at Jupiter's moons.

This strange enters the unpaged vacuum.
We do not seek truth, we seek canvas.
I run with floods, fires, gods, giants,
cutthroats raised from cribs,

whose fist of spit
rides my white text.

(Aaron builds a Ring-Factory around Callisto.)

3
i
A. Our particle beams made a channel of spears,
ten times in each degree we fixed these rays,
a ring of pulsing force culled Callisto stunned,
funnels vortexed with mineral storm-crushed
elements from below. As glass breaks,

a grid of ice snaps, gathers inertia and force,
spitting down a treeless pitch. So at this ring
we draw from planets well-ordered elements,
beach for ribbon farm, green soylent, and vapor breath.
A circus ring as world, thin bands above

the giant's sky; a land above, a land below;
barbaric planet by scaffolds framed with rust,
a hundred laser satellites draw up mineral
as black mosquitoes sucking Callisto's blood,
a needle set between two hungry eyes

to pierce the ore beneath the membrane crust;

six photon accelerators, twelve beamed funnels,
laser-pulsed spirals crown the planet mined,
forming soils on star-lit roofs, and steam,
a hotter Earth from any hell, where heaving
monsters dream in sleeping states. We are still
that same generation leaving out of Egypt.

ii
There are no houses now where I used to live,
wheat fields, fowl, and women turned back each
into flat folds of rubric-sided walls,
spacescape thin as paper, spun around a hair.

O God extra cosmos, I transit signals sent.
Dig my bone at Jericho. I know I am still a code
in Your eye, made a measure in Your brain,
and my number yet will come up one wish;

still, perfect, round, and just.

(Aaron expresses hubris in the terraforming of Callisto.)

4
i
A. As the lasers beamed and vexed the surface,

I count in chaos moons in contact two.
I have made the methane lake into a heap;
I have stored brazen wish in my warehouse;
I have twist and twined my scaffold's rope.

I stain the crust of salt on every tear;
I strain the taste of brine in every sweat;
I stitch the press of rune in every brain;
I cup the sound of sea in every wound.

If we look back from the moons of Jupiter,
feel indecision or fear, let me remember
it was freedom that died on Earth, not men.
Men are ample to secure far proxies.

I take everything; I must give everything,

till hands and ears are empty husks;
the monad of my wish now unbound.

(Aaron describes his spaceship shuttling from Europa.)

ii

A. It is a point unlike the rest. Dull. With
independent motion. A sturdy ship, till now
maddened and strained, like a fish, caked with soil
at the fisher's feet. Released, too small to keep,

darting back into wine dark sea. Here Cygnus,
the heavenly swan. Here Perseus too, that
returned with Medusa's head. I see plainly
it is a moon. Potbellied, scorched with tears.

Callisto moon, then. Bony, unpurged, gritty

to the teeth. In seven years my ships built;
what did I conceive? What did my familiar
spirit say? What did the prophetic muse sing?
She said, because you are weak, listen, and

eat my whispers that all men may eat,
speech that all men count to know.

I strained at her breath, she was slightly made
inside my mind. I went back empty.
My prophet spoke only image with metaphor,
and thus, her verse covertly encircled

all of time. She shrugged her shoulders and sang
the secret history of the star. "Io, Europa,
stunned so long in sleep, a man arrives,
harder, more obdurate, than your stone.

You Electra, now visible,
you Orion, giant hunter,

where is the way?"

(Aaron gives his reading of the failure of Homo sapiens.)

5

i

A. We are wedded to untruth. Man's genius.
We seek out untruth. Search deeply untruth.
We cannot leave untruth alone in its sorrow.
We are not acolytes of truth; we are dramatists.
And thus poetry is our highest competence.

We always had a tramp for true religion.
There never was a correct age of Christianity
until we were attacked by Mohammed.
Mohammed is the last Christian hero. Why?
Minus Mohammed there'd be no Western
men, proving the thesis. Occidental men
only chased youth. We are idolaters, Scotts,
Jews, Romans, Greeks: Jesus entered Egypt,
loved magic, broke the Sabbath, turned tables,
sat with abandoned men. Why? Because
inward congress of soul has no stop. Because
no speech on Earth is the concluding speech.
There is only solidity of form scourged
within the secret datum of my inner voice.
This is all we know. The playgrounds of youth
our only loss. Never yet were there any
true Jew or Christian. There are only
players confined behind masks of tears.
In space there are only idols of our minds,
gnostic paths promiscuous to coordinate.
My will to enter space, then? To reset the mind.
If I make exodus of Earth, I only make
a race prophesied to the inside. What is
my sin? That I force your mind to alter,
screaming fears? Then scream with clarities.

You have done well with a tithe of genome.
Now work out with fear and trembling darker
margins of your DNA. After all,
what were you thinking, so hobbled?
How could you call out to god-constrained,
singing only a tithe of your voice?
Your gods, only a tithe of god?
Your sperm, only a tithe of sperm?
Your genome, only a tithe of genome?
Your brain, only a tithe of brain?
Your speech, only a tithe of speech?
I am the fatted calf.

Yes, it is a fit of peril to depart Earth.
Yet what will you make of the still-unpaged?
Do not look back. Do not let nostalgia
become your highest prize. How many worlds
are now already lost? You'll never know
the count. Before the last ice age, the stone
pyramids were already there– so, at
the end, what do you surely know of worlds?
No, you will not return to your crib.
I have taken away the Earth as margin.
It is an act of genius. I had to remove
your planet, and then your bones.

(*Aaron speaks beyond death to future generations of men.*)
ii
A. To the surviving recorder of this idiom,
how narrow is our speech at crossroads?!
I cry at the Earth's shallow depth and move
so thin between the rumor of my sounds
with precisions stained with edge. Briefly, in
so many suns, how did you find me, in this sun?
Is truth so modern? Is there only one path?
Strike any phylum in my well-thumbed mind.

How do I know my right, my chance, my terms,
that in this time, this space, this light, my voice
touches you precisely in one generation? Then
the proofs each man lists, I list and monument;
since my child, my loved, my reader, you also arrive
at my horizons, and thus my time is all time
and my single sun all possible suns? If
I never know my next steps, then how
did you know the steps to find me? By this,
I clench and seize with cost my joy. Extra-cosmos
I am annex, courteous to my substantiation.

My fame fixed forever paged, forever
am I warm and youthful in His book. I
list, perfected in all my fools, masks and
jests, with these proofs, future men, I greet you.
You will be strange but worthy of my sweat.

O god yet kissed, not once named, I could have
no page if I was not in your mind before.
You, beyond the cosmos, be assured, I
reach you by other means. I open my sound.
Since who can prove any god dyspeptic
in his structure? Let me make a test of
my rumored parameter. Let me test
my ever-living youth of fabled speech.

I cannot reach beyond my own mind. No
god before god. Firstly, I seek to be
a man sufficient to the condition
of my consciousness. If I am fully
man, and god fully god, what merit could
I add to my contribution – scribbling
outside the lines with reds or golds?

Let me master the condition of my
spleen. Let me pass with composure of mind
darting, glaring puppets of alarm, past
the cutthroats straight from their cribs.

6

i

A. Earth records only adolescence. Yet
man is ancient. America is an aged
encrustation of puberty. Yet man is ancient.
So I set in storm the furniture of the nation.
Mohammed knows our large and toothy nerve
of sweet; he knows Western gods smell of the
forest, cancels our fake prayers. Smells our
idol. He knows we don't pray. We lust flesh.
We burst. Caked with sweet. He knows
we hold in reserve no inner vestibule
of masters. We make only outward shows of
faith. No visions. No second porch of initiates.
No fierce inner eye. No narcotic flamed
shadows arcing to preview sweet innermost
divinity. No golden mouth. No savant
speaking with extra-cosmos authority,
no flaming martyrs of pulsating cheek.
No forged and plastic Paul – minus gnostic
doctrine, minus direct experience of divinity.
Christ was placed aside discreetly,
already Caesar's sweetmeat.

How can I show the terror of your choice?
A rite of youth. A youth forever unfinished!
Then, *Yahweh*? Then *l Bet' el*? I reject chapter
and verse. I reach outside the cosmos, my voice.

Now wake. I have dropped tears on the tablet
of fates; I read there was an inner mountain
we must climb. *The path is inward.* Future
no future – except we enter as initiates.

Then put away your lesser god. He lies.
Listen in silence. I will tell the falconer's prey
what the falcon and the falconer know.
There can be no Western man without
the other's cry. Now terror draws my breath.

We begin again, here, where masters
hid their texts in gossamer desert caves.
How ... so long undisturbed?
How ... uncovered in this generation?
My own generation? Who is throwing dice?
They knew we would one day return.
We carry our church inward now,
mythic minds, nomadic, deep skull miners,
facing charismatic perils in space, now
nemesis. In every hazard, a hidden page.

We have returned – and now, at last, as old
as god, we are men in trouble. I do not
seek gods; I seek autonomy of maneuver.
I seek cognizance beyond all forms. I
enter where I see the waters churn:
the desert places within our mind. We
enter space one way contemning.

For what is space but the sacred desert
places of our mind?

We shall need the light of the moon
in our brains for this.
And leaves of beaten gold
in our hearts.

(*Aaron lists the Earth's crimes.*)

ii
A. I accuse multiple Earths in my critique.
I will list their faults multiple, their hurts
multiple. I rehearse parallel speeches
and binary accusations. I will list needless
but fulsome crime, journals of false
medicine, and two-faced science. Made more bitter
by Earth's hieroglyphic beauty – sensible,
yet over-teeming, multiple in lies. Classes
of food not food, classes of medicines not
medicine, classes of gods not gods, cults
of freedom, not freedom. I have now
only hard-won clarities to give witness.
I have won sheltered solitude in space.
I list all the curses that redeem my near
extinction. They are only excuses.
In truth, it is stone cold science that made
the Earth slick with ice. Science reduced men
and wide-belly Earth to a single neck
for me to slice. Now I am at Callisto,
caged with science. My wrathful art extracts
oxygen and fuel from monster ice on Europa.

The day arrives we descend from filamented
scaffold rings, the surface below composed
at rest, well-ordered minerals and a small
steam rising; till then, we are that race
surviving in thin skins and bare skies,

already legend with our manners, books, poems
with news of strange and still-unpaged cunning;

the idiom of men increased one click
by my breath.

(Aaron advises future makers of planets and men.)

7
i
A. We all burst in contact, my atom, my heart.

Do not die unless you are a master.
If you still cannot face the parrot-masked
apparition—restrain your alarm.

How can I ask for more dominion
when I already have all age in my mind
and my mind enclose another Earth in kind?

I have touched a spitting bar on a turtles' shell,
and traced the crack into my own debility.
I have felt the pulse of false arcing synapse.

How can I ask for more love
when it is the force of circle at my atom
and plumb in my mouth as spice on teeth?

How can I ask for more life and time
since I am already rooted in life's branches
and all time tailored from my mind's filament?

How can I ask for more space and personality
when I already sow on other planets rain
and no man can undo my work?

How can I ask for more wealth
when everything I need waits,
bends its knee, circles me in space?

How can I ask for more knowledge
when everything ever to be known
is already encoded in my genome?

How could I ask for more variety of star
when every star I see is only a mirror
of perception anciently in my mind?

ii
My only argument is *Homo sapiens.*
And what is man, but a purse of images?
And the mind of man, except a mirror

prescient with stages of gnosis?

Why should I fear any misdeed
when I could not craft a star's vision
without I fall and rise?

No longer lessen me by youth.
No longer dismember me by Eros.
No longer my eternal wishes obsolescence.

Why should I enter the door of an outward
church, beaming death? Religion that cannot
melt the hardest stone with beams – is not religion.

God converts me daily from his garden.
He set me on a path only I can right or decree.
He asked for my eyes. They were still craven.

And only then, after telling the truth,
did I age well.

8

i

A. What do women want? They will not tell you,
but they will ease the hollow of their feet,
stand in your dirt, toe by toe,
so long as you have a story.

What do children want?
They only want you to stay,
and if you have a story,
they will stay forever.

What does a man want?
He must fail if he is wise; then, after,

every story in him tasted once. He has
so many summers and matters ending,
so long at wanting early what has no fancy,
no goodly parts or sound and loved too much

on bodies, spheres; on other planets rain.

(Aaron describes the factories he built in space.)

ii
What is fire except split hydrogen, oxygen?
What is water but fixed hydrogen, oxygen?
What is Europa's ocean of ice, then,
except ardent fire detained in solution?

We mock a distant sun with pre-ignition.
I have warmth. I possess all extant flame.

Our ships extract ore fused to carbon fiber
framed to factories farmed from star's heat;
bent to bond our ships with edged precisions
mineraled from broken tiered moons below,

spliced by Talon's giant spider robot arcs.

Above this mineral moon we make our Land,
and next, to Europa exploration teams now sail.
I scout positions aligned the sun's ecliptic.
I stand these worlds reborn with beams.

300 crew. 300 females. 30 ships
warehousing tenement seed. New oxygen
extracted from Europa's heated ice. World
we make with molten ore from Calisto's crust.

In-gathered sun with exponent mirrored cells
forms soylent green, and protein planted food.
I have perfected apples, pears, pleached arbors
housing certain food and pleasant shade.

A month I see re-paged the solar lip and tongue,
with their broken element planets replenish
fuel, water, soil, blood, and bone—the rest
delimited in text only men may make.

All ice I touch is heat, all ice I melt is breath,
all laser-blown, funneled wind lifts me ore,
while gods and planets indulge my spittle breath
the richest pearl to make the sound of world.

The Stipulation to Depart Earth

9

A. Earth disgorge the human stain that
darker sky should feel the sting of men.
Reader, leave the gods of Earth behind;
they were giants, capricious, always away

at the other stars. My text of blazing Venus
on ageless cheek burns deep into the mind.
A string of puppets pulling strings to gods,
what amendment was cast with more care?

Every man that cries god, o god, reaches
beyond the cosmos. My golden mouth priests
the rim of my lips; where my tongue is trained,
skies fall to my page. I pray our enemies are great.

The initiate will understand the message.

Pray for Carthage. God is a streak on glass
forming as my will reaches the steam of shouts.
The same crust of tear meets the same condition,
the same rain, the same mist. We are cleansed.

Prophetic voice alerts my mind to peril.
If you have not already pulled your stakes,
it is too late. You will not make it. So long
as we still find other, ourselves blessed

we immolate. If I can escape, I live.
What is my device? Each revolution
inward reaches out beyond the cosmos.
Refracted, I am form exfoliate form.

I join timeless stipulation with my page.
These generations I learn will burst
their spleen on a troubled king's wall,
and he will be a poet made to prophesy,

to taste on other planets rain.

10

i
A. Since god has need, a cutthroat cries in his crib.
Since man has mythic code, so mounts His flame in me.
I am manned that god has no hand or mouth,
no ink to text the guarded postings of his font.

O you cannot hide your secret! I know
you are, behindhand, my apparition,
I know that you are the *inescapable*.
I have lived sentient of your near approach.

Beyond the cosmos, no wonder of my mind,
I am set on a path of my own Eldorado,
each alley paved with golden sand. Each
grain recovered within my own perception.

If I am told there is something new in the sky,
and that I must investigate the apparition,
then I will say that the birds have preceded me.

If I am told there is something new in the sea,
and that I must explore and plot the specter,
then I will say that the fish have preceded me.

But if a man tells me all these things are
already placed inward in my mind, inbred
my genome, as divine precognition, then
I will sit with him and dine on a table of stars

where we fret and interchange the rearward
precession of the zodiac.

ii
Now I seize the lever of protons and photons!
What was my secret discovery? This:
In space all I may meet is my own mind.
Nothing else in space is populated except
my own synapse. Can you read the signs?
If not, I will send a golden mouth to sing.
If I enter space, I can only plunge deeper
into the spiced sluices of my cognizance.
Only you I see, still O silent, O hard-found deity,

I see you stand amazed, beyond the cosmos
as a frightened child at my jagged actions.
You do not know my next affirmation?
Rest un-complexed—till I arrive for all time.

What is the gnostic path? Access inward,
direct experience of voices. I ask, what
is my best, my oldest essence? Thus I know
I exist before created forms. I am set upon
a path, lit by a spark of my own divinity.
Only my body is mortified on the mortal cross.
My mind is free and god-like with eclectic margin.
What is freedom except access to my solitude?
What is the final, naked cog of autonomy?
Free to constitute my own being. That I
can be *alone* with my ecstatic vision.
What is space but shelter of my solitude?
Because I may still reach my own solitude,
my mind projects another eon of our time.
My passions are spent without science;
and some that run away are searched, raised up
each a smoke on lips as twins, seconds, small
razor-paged choice. I learn there is no age
before hunger—and nothing is enough
before it can be worked—diamond-clear gods
enter my ship, as quarks, walking past treasures
they neither see nor sense. I seek contact
with the other I immolate. We all share
bursting in contact: alien, beyond
the crack of cosmos. Cry. Cry. Cry.
So I sin daily against science. Saints'
robes bleached into science smocks, still professing
what no one has seen, and only certain
learned, confirm; petty kingdoms less than all
I can believe. I keep for misbelief
hierarchies of fabled death, I can disprove
every alarm, every dismemberment;
I mean to rule in both spaces. I pass
straight through the machine, beyond the
factories of heat, past the cutthroats
fresh from their cribs.

CANTO TWO

Earth Minus

(*Aaron continues his narration of the building of RingWorld.*)

1
i
A. We entered the third ring of ribbon moons
and joined Jupiter at Callisto, with
Europa cradled in her crib of black
night. We found shelter at *Callisto Wolf,*
christened by my father, the deepest station
mineraled on our blood. Planets are death
stars. Each aggregate of evil, unfit for ease.
See my potbelly ships descend. We do not
mend our life to a star's caprice, we mine,
fuse, and atomize the surface, ordering
minerals dazed, stunned, up onto RingWorld's
funneled scaffold beams. We set as charged six
atom accelerators, the groundwork of our
scaffold Ring, twice the force of Hiroshima
in one hand-held device. Our cargo waits
dormant above twinned moons to birth new worlds
of sentient mind. Alien contact. My ancestors.

The true God beyond the cosmos cannot follow
my wild spleen. He has to send winged-runners
to get my news. They arrive breathless. They
depart breathless. Turning their wings on me
with scandal. The broken gods of this cosmos
snatch at them before they return. Because
I have encoded my own solitude, He cannot
decipher the message of my dignity.
Because He cups His own solitude, God
cannot plumb His charisma without I make
blood-caked life and death. God cannot draw His
neck and brow unless I make a sound and burst.

How far can I step into this honesty?

ii
A. How did I arrive at this station? I dropped down
where Missouri meets the Kaw River,
and my brothers ruled the golden fields,
the last remaining country of food.
We were a farm-made dynasty of curs,
and my brothers and sisters a fierce nation.
Our father, killed in the China wars,
gave our kind this gnostic god enjoined
beyond the cosmos, to cross with us here
at the third ring; and minus the golden
fields of Kansas we took part the Galaxy,
part to rule, part to harvest, part to people.
300 remain. 300 proximate to arrive.

I still smell the warm heat of my home
and my wives still in sleep, now I watch,
inseminate space with my cunning spawn,
Talon's patents and my philosophy stand
my rumored star kingdom; this sound,

god-stained, peopled with new-raced men.
I shake the worlds that break and fall apart.
Before the end of days was fixed, a god,
loving one of our youth, gave a siren cry,

and He, unused to sing, fell back to Earth,
chariot crazed, remembering that art,
the rudiments of which I learned when young
and can impart.

(Aaron narrates his original strategy made with Talon.)

2

A. My companion, Talon, did not survive
the weightless journey. It was his mind
that mapped the genes for ammonia plasma.

His death is still unwritten. It is a strange
interlude. It is a report of unendorsed
patent. When we woke from metabolic
sleep at Jupiter, only Talon did
not live, and I argued how his body
failed at the third House of Cancer, deep in
trance, leaving the gravity of Mars behind.
I had to eject the machine to clear
the air of his remains. His coffin ship
now eternal monument.

My brothers and I were the victors in China,
and Talon, our greatest mind, came to
us with new conjecture. The state gave us
every machine we demanded for our task.

Talon was crippled as a child, boneless
in a chair. Outside Earth's gravity
one creature I genome-bred, *Cheda,*
and Talon the other, named *Pan-Tal.*

We gave to these two separate creatures
tincture of our mind. Growing weaker
each day, his heart too frail for space,
Talon worked our cause, and he shall live
again in the creature of his mind and taste,

Pan-Tal, now alive below in Callisto's cave.

The Sumerian Genome

3

i

A. I will tell what I know. The account is
fragmented ... I am cautious of the order of events.
Talon came to me in my third consulate.
I was still encamped at the Asian FOB.
He had to find a way to bury ten million
bodies in two days, before decomposition.
One night, in my study, he said he had
discovered the original indices
of the human genome. He said he found
the genetic codex of human consciousness.
Not consciousness, complete, but a mind
allowing the conduction of consciousness.
I told him to give it to the Demos – I was set
on destruction of genome – not proliferation
of genome. I said, "Look out the window, sir!
It is proliferation of genome that brought me
my life's work! There is not mud enough for
a mound of fat ants, a hive of digesting
human detritus. I seek Earth *minus*!"

Talon. "This is what I expect of you. Who else
would speak and act as you? If you are ready,
then use my brain to make a final correction."

A. I have no need of brains. I have need of a
machine – no, a hose – that will reduce
China, Asia, Russia to a spit of ash!

T. "Good. Then you will want a new planet.
As you see ... I will want a new body."

A. You have my attention. Proceed.
I need a billion pikes for heads!

T. "That is not efficient. Mere aesthetics.
You must reduce the population – entire."

A. I am ravished! Of what nation? By what margin?

T. "*Homo sapiens.* We will make a selection.
By what margin? Three thousand maximal.
One thousand optimal. 300 economical."

A. I like the bar you are drinking at.
You have the stomach?

T. "It's merely the logic of a machine.
From the first hour, the speech of the machine
is the gas oven: *The eradication of misfits.*
It's the final opera of modernism."

A. You speak of a space faring civilization!
You speak of an exodus from Earth in ships!
You speak as life and death are equal fats,
mixed cosmetics of Earth's remnant grease.

T. "The Demos is your machine to reduce the population.
Demographic chaos riots enough for any scythe. Use it.
The self-contradictions of the Demos will supply your
deficiencies ... of man, machine, and material.
What I have is a machine that terraforms any astral
co'rd'nate. I have a mortar made with bones."

A. Terraform? I thought you had a genome?
Terraform what? Show me this machine!

T. "You possess it. It is the human mind.
The mind terraforms any astral co'rd'nate."

A. A Coordinate of ice ... or of fire?

T. "Ice is more malleable than fire. I can
make any liquid astral body ardent with fire.
I can make any solid burn with prerequisite."

A. You speak as if they were equal skin creams.
The elemental world is not controlled
as one of your laboratories, Dr. Talon.
I have proven that an army amassed with
numerologies of men and machines
still can be surprised with defeat ... Nothing
set in motion is certain to hit its mark ...

T. "I have read the human genome – entire.
Can you guess the meaning of this information?"

A. We have read the genome centuries ago? And?

T. "Not the sequence for self-consciousness.
Not the sequence for multi-dimensional
influx. I have proof that each pixel of
universe was preset with stealth, prior
encoded in the gene sequence."

A. By stealth? Are you even sober?
You have ten minutes. Proceed.
I no longer study medicine.

T. "Medicine? Whose medicine? Mine?
Or the medicine of the machine?"

ii
A. I am shyly enchanted! Tell me more!

T. "The *mind*-genome is not promiscuous to revelation.
Like a tenement portal, it is hidden until found.
It can't read in reverse. It can only read inward.
Like previous hieroglyphic texts, I had to find a
Rosetta Stone. Can you guess my meaning?"

A. Nine minutes.

T. "I required another 'text' of genome to read
Homo sapiens' full codex. I found this Rosetta Stone.
But it was not ... not germane. It was ..."

A. Another genome? Not *sapiens*?

T. "So you have guessed? Of course! I have
come to the right man, then. Yes, I found another
genome. An alien genome. I placed the
alien index next to the human genetic index.
The results were interesting. Perhaps even to you."

A. Eight minutes left ... (*Finger on his weapon.*)
Where did you find this extra ... genome set?

T. "In Iraq. Or as you know it – Sumer – Mesopotamia."

A. As I know it? How should I know it?

T. "Because that is where your ancestors left their DNA."

A. *My* ancestors? What do you know of *my* ancestors?!

T. "Before? Nothing. To find my Rosetta Stone,
I studied early Sumerian creation epics. There
I found an open record of a race of aliens
who one-time advanced the genes of primates
to more closely resemble their own. Ergo, *Homo sapiens.*"

A. For what purpose? What do you know?
... Seven minutes left.

T. "For what else? For slaves. To mine gold. To bark
at the sun? The *purpose* is irrelevant to my study."

A. What is your study?

T. "The origin of the human mind. It is not terrestrial.
It is from outside of the cosmos. Or are you stunned?
I seek new life outside of Earth. The making of a
new genetic race of men. To advance ... No ...
Perhaps ... Do you read epic poetry? My study ...
My study is to test the meticulous life
force of my blood ... against the energy of the sun ..."

A. Why bring riot-breath genetics – to me?

T. "By my calculations, you are set on a course
to eliminate the Earth's population. This will
make our globe uninhabitable … for thousands of years …"

A. You come to accuse … or to praise?

T. "If you give me the list of supplies I require,
(*Hands list.*) I will give you … what I think you want."

A. You have my attention. What do I want?

T. "My body is broken. I know what I want.
Your world is broken – your idiom is scheduled
for eradication. Another man in your place
would be content to rule over his fellow citizens.
Not you. You want what no man can have."

A. No? What do I want?

T. "You want to be the *one* … to breed … and then,
you want a coffin speech … of such high construction
it is a monument fixed in nets of galaxy."

A. Your madness is advanced … it is … promiscuous.
They gave you so many prizes of science and … well …
The prizes they gave you, Dr. Talon, you know,
only endorse the image – their own image –
of the modernist idiom. Any prize confirms
the idiom of the giver – not the recipient. You are
a pawn of the Nobel committee – you know that?
They have only one final, blind idiom – *modernism.*

T. "Then … eradicate … them."

A. I can do more than that. I can shame their
self–referent eye. You have made a study of me, sir.
I respect that. But take this genome to the Demos …
(*Reflecting*) … or not! Already you know too much.
You are meddlesome. What is your list of requirements?

T. "I need the zero gravity of space. The genomic
reconstruction of sentient life cannot be performed
on a planet of gravity. In any case … I need spaceships."

A. Of course you do! Each of my commanders need
a spaceship! I hear this daily. How do you know …
of my work? How did you get access to my blood … ?
Where did you find this alien index of genome?

T. "Under the foundations of Ur …
In a masked grave. Access to your blood?
Your natural son was my patient … for a time …"

A. Terry!

T. Yes. He thinks he is a black man.

A. And you have told no one of your … thesis?

T. "No. It would only be used against you. You …
would be hunted down. Your political enemies …"

A. I see. What *else* did you find in the ancient grave?
Anything else … besides genomes?

T. "A tablet of destinies. A book of runes.
An index of futurity … coordinates of wonder …
Prophecies of a race of 300 girls, perfectly formed."

A. And these … alien genomes … What could you read?

T. "They match your own. I am able to read yours.
I know what you are. I - know - what - you - *are*."

A. Mere speculation! You cannot even *guess* what I am!

T. "I cannot? You are Homo sapiens *minus*."

Homo Sapiens Minus

iii
T. "I will need 300 females from the Slavic
nations. Behind the old Iron Curtain.
I have a list of sites, three in the Taiga forest.
I will give you a hand-held device. You
pass it over the heads of each ... each girl."

A. Each girl? Each girl? Are you sober?

T. "I need genetic material ... perfect in its generation.
There is an ancient prophecy. And there is an ancient
genome. I guess you know my meaning?"

A. All I can detect of your mind, Dr. Talon,
is that it has savage annexes. I will study it.

iv
A. I sealed the compact. I wrote down Talon's list.
He said he needed 300 young female bodies,
perfected in their generations, now
located behind enemy lines, anciently
protected under the domination of Russia.

Anciently protected behind enemy lines?
Perfected in their generations?
Protected from defilement
behind the Iron Curtain?
The crack of his psychosis was cavernous ...
Yet the scandal of his mind
was detectable at the margins.

(Aaron projects his vision of Homo faustus, a new
race of men sustained by methane and ammonia.)

4
i
A. Methane tissue will have our dispute,

and when our God shall walk
in His garden, as told in prophesy,
He will call their names as well, souls
franchised, as my mind is franchised.

The mind is a barking hunter.

New human synapses search for *other* ... as I search;
at one release we double the chance that
English-tongued men survive in every sky,
Merlin, my saint, my book, my shadowed text,

you and Oxford shall host in space by my acts.

Our ships' crews now give these creatures names
and peopled from our tongue—
without limit of blood, or heat, or Earth,
but share with us the human code.

Not only have we escaped Earth's coffin,
but once out, we shall live forever seizing
the levers of sentience and dark sobbing.
I pause to birth new idiom. Let me speak.

I have gathered the waters in a heap.
Red blood unaided never made a man,
youth alone never made a man,
death alone never made a man,

A race of golden mouths make a nation.
Nemesis builds my human forceps
towering now above Jupiter's Cyclops' eye.
Here I will find the *other* on whom we burst.

ii

A. In the Year of the Dog, we broke out
of Earth's atmosphere. In zero gravity,
Talon formed new tissues sustained on methane,
powerful muscled beings, built from stems,
to hold up under the weight of ten
fissured skies. The work still undone.

Earth minus – made new!
Sapiens minus - made new!
Modernism minus – surpassed!

Talon, how did you abandon me with
this heavy work? In three years our
creatures are mature, and gently I
let them down on Callisto's light gravity.
We built domes of glass and thermal gardens
infused with volcanic heat.

Callisto's caves are free of radiant ions.
A moon frozen, yet moist, and richly mineraled.

I plant now Talon's mind and memory
from our ship psionic chant below the rings.
The speech monad and mnemonic harpies
made the voyage and await our protocols.

In three years we must grow the creatures
and brains born, full grown, already hungry
on methane and ammonia, on dreaming and
making story at the stations of men.

Live forever, my saints, my text.

It Was Good to Leave Earth

(Betraying guilt, he tries to justify his work.)

5
A. Youth no more my idol. Death no star.

The age the Earth cracked loud to die in ice
we found all-dimensioned god, of interior
cosmos, as Earth took measures to kill us off
in dark skies, on sudden snapping scaffolds,

on splitting beams, on drowning beds.

Fire, dry winds, crushing of the plates,
storms, locust, flood without warning,
only the wealth of one nation, Kansas,
built galaxy machines at the first signs.

The Earth always killed its life. Always. I note.

We lost our best men as China three times
above Earth broke our magnetic elevators,
our plains of wheat and farmers carried us as
other nations died, retaining horror

machines of erasing time, immolating
the hordes of superfluous populations.

Before the wars made an end,
not a half remained, not my brothers,
not the best,
and I, Aaron,

commanded to depart country, continent,
and death star Earth.

6

i

A. To escape the fires on Earth,

we carried the smithy god of arching bridges,
self-referent math and furtive rites of speech.
We all may still be initiates. What other prize?
What is a man except an inward prayer wheel?
We are god-minus. What god seeks *within* creation?
B'nei Yisrael? *This one* had no initiates.
Only another outward church of mimes.
This one shall not enter Jupiter's ring.
I scout the fabled trail *Kosmoautikon*,
who, alone of entities, detects voices
outside the cosmos. Till then, outside
Earth new creatures shall be raised,
marvelous as we are creatured;
a new day there and a new night;
new flesh, new strength, new grit in teeth,
new smithied masks, parrot-colored eyes,
talon gods.

They shall drink methane
as pure water
and take ammonia
as manna from the sky.

So 300 of our educated have escaped
to people a covenant of unfinished stars.

We shall place flesh on these ragged bones—
of stars and broken-down planets. How long
these shanty-town planets waited for our texts?
Since without texts and idiom,
without memorable speech,
without gnosis, power extra cosmos,
there is no star, no wish,
riding my fist of spit.

(Aaron sends a final message to the Demos.)

ii
A. Earth behind on math elevators,
I leave you no legacy. You must die
in your hole, lest others return to you.
I give you ten years to escape with me,

but by then you will all be dead.
All you drones in cubicles will be dead!
At least, in the fields, slaves saw the sun
through honest floods of tears and sweat!
Shall I drag the dead body in by the door?

I go ahead. But if you do not arrive
where I have prepared your bed,
then myself will end Earth's idol sky.
I cannot abide the rabble behind;

Eastern chant must forever cease.

(Hesitates. Crosses last lines out. Hears noise. Looks behind.)

(Enter Terry, Aaron's natural son, suffering under the
apprehension that he is a black man and a pretend cook.)

iii
Terry. "What? Scratchin' again? Writin' 'bout un'corns?"

A. No, Terry. I am busy now. Leave me in peace.

T. Tellin' the history of all your killin's?
Thought as much. Say something about me.
Will anybody ever read it? ... Just askin'?!

A. No, I don't speak of *pretend* cooks.
I'm writing the prologue of a poem—
a record of our translation from Earth.

T. What? You don't *pretend* as much? Not a pretend poet?
No one's gonna read it anyway. It's China-speak!
All these Chinese heads on a stick? Why? I saw
you clutchin' up their books. We got mountain
of 'em. What ya'goin't' do with their lernin'?
Rash. Gimpy. Bet you can't read a single line!

A. No, but I have idiomatic translators. Perhaps I shall
place you in charge of translating all the Chinese
learning to our own speech? You would like that?

T. What? Alph'bet soup? Donno?
How long wid'id take? I have a meetin'
with a drunken lady at six o'clock—*pile*!

A. One page. They simply copied our ideas. Let me . . .

T. Ain't nothin' – *your book.* Anybody could write
anything they want and call it a *pro-o-log*. Perhaps
I write my own? *Hist'ry of Eatin'* or some such.

A. Wakeda! Please come and take Terry away.

(Terry leaves. Aaron continues writing.)

The Creation of the First
Faustus Creatures on Callisto

7
A. Before Planet-fall,

we built four towers beneath the storm,
electron fields above the towers rose,
made a crib of calm against the wind
where molting men slept full grown.

Tan-Dem, called *Cheda*, was the first to hear
our signals, as he had a human still in his double
dreams. I, Aaron, made channels in his brain
that later would make story at the stars;

psionic chant, advised with childish rhyme,

spiritual code enriched with manners,
a speech of god outside the cosmos – and
life forever. With Talon's patents I woke
them to yellow light, blinking at filaments
of phosphate, strapped to stainless gurneys.

Life is a storm in a tempest kettle and man
a self-leveling vine, unstoppable, yet ruled;
constrained, fused to risk, knees as feet,
sentient to the irrational elements, so made
of runes, thus, poems. Broken, never cowed.

We are the only mind with free movement
across seven branes of maths. Now fused.
I, of the seven, am the eighth observer.

We are the first race that knew the secret
so long circumspect to all other creatures.
We are the first race to seize transcending
echoes, wealth outside the cosmos.

There is no soul but the soul I make.

8
A. Two new creatures entered the space prepared.
I made the creature, *Cheda*. Talon made *Pan-Tal*.
These are the first two men with *Faustus* genome.

Pan-Tal was the brother *Cheda* held in arms
and learned to drink—trapped vapor clouds
on cold stone walls to condense methane,
metabolic in their veins, un-warmed,

not needing the heat that strains my reach.

These were the first two brothers
and the first record of eyes on a cold planet
for all time to draw out the structures of new god
with cooler blood than my Earth brother's blood.

Let us pray their enemies are great.

We held back all the female creatures
until we were sure that brothers
would not repeat the old code,
we saw that Yahweh did not make

the journey, we watched to be sure

till our hearts were glad.
As before, there would be
two stories of creation.
The first without female voice,

chancing everything on brother's peace.

I roll dice. I make a savage bet.
An entire generation seeks a
buried lost beacon of memorable
speech. Buried in the ice.

They will rise and kill the machines.

*(A corrupted record of the education of the new creatures
follows, gaps in the recording resulting in a partial text.)*

9
i
A. These are the chronicles of first encounter,

starlogs of the speech I rehearsed
to the sentient born. Each given the
same scripts, with a change of genome
knowing that in the third generation ... (*Break*)

They would have their own linguistic code.
Cheda, as the form of my genetic material,
already teaching Anglo-Saxon tongue,
poetry strange to Earth and stranger still
to England's present corruption ... (*Break*)

I teach the transitions of chess,
how each to the other moves,
each as pawns to men consumed,
each concealing rook and horse-head gods ... (*Break*)

A twist of twine in cradles,
sewn to checker-board houses.
I search thin skies for soldier pawns
and rook and horse-head stepping ... (*Break*)

       (*Aaron pauses. Writes on paper.*)
ii
Earrings on gold boys,
boys that write red-lettered hearts,
matted dust in the lines of their throats
like fine threads.

I am certain it is a pain,
like a little spit of fire,
that resists the tiny rain
and every kind of water.
       (*Hesitates. Crosses out last lines.*)

(Passing a lost planet of Frankenstein creatures,
Aaron makes final contact with the misfit colony.)

10
i
A. Message to Alkatron Colony: *This is an open channel.*
We have no communication from your planet in two decades.
What society have you made from the gift of life?

Frankenstein. "Master, it is good to have life.
How should I honor you? We need new element."
We have lost the Gnostic texts. They were replaced
by men seeking a supreme Universal Church.
No one now can see and touch the face of God.
No man knows the speech and acts of God.

A. Live the code placed in you without guilt;
if there is shame, you will find in the eyes of
your children your shame. You have done well.

F. "How have we done well?
How do I tell others there is still a God
within – and yet outside the cosmos?"

A. Let men search their knowledge.
Every star and element you find
was, before you, once known.
Let all men search their works.
Everything you could work out
was, before you, once worked.
Let men search their love.
Everything you could love
was, before you, once loved.

F. "We need new element. Repeat.
We have no masters of sayings. There are only
repeatable indices of information."

A. What are your questions after an eon?

F. The soul you made is virulent.
It eats like an acid. We are afraid to say it.
The idiom you gave us has altered wildly.
We have received your proposal for free education.
But to teach what? And what good and what beautiful?
There is no reply from an empty universe.
Is everything on the outside of world – true world?
Is there anything on the inside of world?
We have heard stories of an interior wine-dark sea.
That we are gods there. How to find it?

A. Transmission understood. I will send you tapes.
I build you now with new speech and sentience.
If each photon raises in your cell
and subsequent attack to large emotion,
then I will verify your story true.
I will send you ten books. They will
remap your willowing minds.

F. "Communication not understood. Repeat."

A. Yes. … In your long eternity,
I swear, you must find the other
and burst on me.
When I walk in my garden,
I will call your name
and ask for your eyes.

F. "Communication not understood. Repeat.
Send immediate help. We are breaking up.
We need new element. The speech, the symbols
you left us – have altered tragically."

A. To recover the gnostic mind, I will send you a prophet.

F. "Communication not understood. Repeat."
"Communication not understood. Repeat."
"Communication not understood. Repeat."
"Tell us something true – tell us of the mind!"
"Tell us of the mind a wrathful god gave us!"

CANTO THREE

Generations of Seth

(*Aaron confesses to the imperfections of his mind.*)

1
A. If I crumple new-starched sheets,
I fault my childish cups drained dry,
my soles, my cuffs, turned black with play,
slaked with thirst too late from my lip,
my cups of youth all cracked, the soul I sip.

If I showed no caution in this life,
or cherry lips stain red from cherry wine,
then middle sin grew to middle height;
nothing sustaining gods might not foresee,

guard or guardian trace the seed.

If all I embraced I teased to break, or burst,
then I learned sin with simple sinners' books;
I scale infinite discourse to miracles of doubt;

I sleep beside the strange, or none
I can choose, or know, or keep.

ii
A. If there is philosophy at the end of Earth,
At worst a man can burst, loving blind.
What else is the competence of men?
A god cannot do it.

Latin poets did not understand sentience;
they made a shallow sleep of need as good,
in wine, a look of satiated eyes,
in wealth, a smile of satisfactions,

heads uneasy nights on corner stones.

My nation suffered wealth, science, knowledge;
strangled astrology, diddled poetry,
enslaved the nations of the Earth – crying science.
It would be more worthy of his soul, more

blessed, to give it all away for desire,
for the dirt settled in the crack of a girl's neck,
proportionate to irrational runes.
Nothing is more heartless than science.

Then, after two millennia of darkness,
strangled by an orthodox church of lies,
strangled by unrestrained idols of science,
strangled by wealth and arrogance,
we regain the gnostic path …

You cannot mistake the smile of Seth.

(Aaron warns against the danger of wealth and indolence.)

2
A. Children of affluence are born with sadness.
How could we have previewed these generations?
Dirt-grimed, wind-blown, sun-blasted Kansas
pioneers sacrificed for this prize? If so, their
hope was wind and thorns inside their hearts.

I have replaced the ease of every man,
woman, child with labors, sacrifice, peril;
I have used all the Earth's armies,
now repeating in the machine.

After one hundred generations of violence
finally I chisel a straight mouth in the West,
a wish I trace gains rumor at the mouth,
I have lived to be captain of the terror ships,

broken, scarred, but still can speak;

the stupid look of satiated eyes—now gone;
the insipid smile of satisfactions—now learned.
All wealth lost on Earth.

I raise my eyes to RingWorld skies,
here we only pause for breath,
they are thin like the sleep in our eyes;
I shall be caught up in a moment:

What did I perform?
I clarified the contest of genome.
I spliced the schisms of *sapiens.*
I left Earth one-way contemning.

Smithied a new spice.
Found new phylum.

I Am Mystic Synapse

(*Aaron reveals his alien lineage and new resolutions.*)

3
A. I tire of my heroic pose, practiced now
in yellow light fifty years, practiced to
believe everything I saw on Earth as tangible;
every love, full love; every spouse, full wish;

my adorations heroic and ate with doubt.

I wish no longer to pose as a human
seeking spiritual conversion. I am
mystic synapse, formed outside the cosmos,
searching for human experience.

If two of us spread the news,
then this will be the new religion;
and when we make our simple miracles,
this will be fresh emblem from the genome.

I whisper nothing I have not proved by my mind.
All others coming before mistook the Earth. They
fell to knees—believing You a god already finished—
but You were still hollow brass and did not answer.

Earth gave us nothing we did not first possess,
God and man made in the same breath, our mythic
codes placed as grinds in the bottom of cups.
We have escaped Earth's coffin. We are safe
next to Your imprimatur.

What can now prevent us—except our own
willing extinction?

The stars we already contaminate
fulsome from within the mind.

My hands and arms still adolescence.

4

A. These eyes were not made to Earth,
so let me go to *Osiris, Orion.* There,
stars wait for my schism of syllable.

If I have the choice of a cool stream of life,
or to be burnt in deserts, O let me be burnt!
I can then decry Earth and its minions.

Once I was amazed to see the blind.
I thought the blind should have sight.
I thought they wished to be like us: selfish,
discontented, crazed by the yellow light.

Now I know deeply my mythic cypher.
If I could keep one secret the broken keep,
do not crown my code with lizard's eyes,
do not keep my lepers clean with flawless skin.

We are deep ore miners, choked with dust,
as doves black-stitched beneath white.
I keep my blackened relics with blackened hearts,
still crowns of perfect faith.

Let me burn from being blind. I am then initiate.
They have a second porch. Paths of wild annex.
They do not ask for your peripheral eye,
since faith or eye of what? Another's proofs?
Another's one-time vision? No, the blind
have an inner eye. They petition frequency
of vision, face to face, sifting all as dross
except the experience that exacts.

So let me burn your eyes with my ray gun.
Let my speech alone give you form.
Let me make you blind to the parrot-masked
apparition. Let me make you blind to
the false scare of disease. That's the chance
of genome I give.

My blind and lepers – thus – no *mischance.*

(*Aaron rejects materialism as the single idiom of life.*)

5
i
A. Live forever, new-made saints. Nothing can
take away my voice in your time;
your code is immense: everyone I know
planned their life proximate to my speech;
all my enemies share with me
a shallow bed of sleep.

Now I learn remote edicts, statutes beyond
the cosmos – yet discernable at my margin.
I cancel desiccate numerologies of men,
data stacked end on end. Clarity is a shout.
Choose any parrot-masked knowledge,
and it will scratch until you release.

Useless, we have each photon under imperium,
yet it alters proximate to my optic nerve.
If we could grasp every element, lashed,
it would only burn our hands, making dust.
It would still oscillate with savored charisma
beyond the cosmos, defiant to my wish.

What are my proofs? No savant has yet
decreed the character of the unborn child!
No man knows the half-life of human love!
No man sees his own end, watching alert
at the ramparts of his fear. No, neither I.

Therefore, what do men meet in space? Surely,
savage annex of our mind, remote access
to Eldorado solitudes. Surely,
only our own mind; certain, only
another licentious mix of mythic
spermatids, relished with abandon.

Let us find this blind men's speech
marvelous beyond the cosmos,
minus cacophonies of my parrot-masked heart.

ii
A. The blind are promiscuous to dimension.

They shadow-box with silence – and freshly
clutch to enter every membrane of sense.

But you. You that still cry Earth, Earth!
Land! Land! You are ill. You straight'way
mate with no courtship? I know your
evil ways. What pearl did you miss?
Your inmost private love is only
remedy of fear and imitation.

If love of nature is the highest human idiom,
then so casually is your aesthetic satiate.
Take down your shutter. Close your eye.
Become blind with the vision of the blind.

Choose silence.
Everything on Earth now preaches silence.

I relish charismatic lexicons
now arriving with synaptic totem
and savage annex of my mind.

(Aaron slowly reveals his recovered powers of speech.)

6

i

A. If I showed no caution, I showed a care,

my sin that shames all future tailors' tongues,
strange rattle in ear, brutish mouth secrete
my three day house, words as silk in mouths,
drenched tongue to cotton cloths espoused release

a smooth round sound, a thousand bursting seeds,

mummy moths with wings as black-eyed peas,
silken-rattle-charged with moth wing play,
my window dressing sins,
the boat of sky I made from reeds,
no tender end of days, or undiminished men,

or none that came to Earth to mend.

ii

A. Now, at the age of captain, how to explain
my work of saints with ears to prick?
What part of ancient sound could they catch
and find the secret index of my wish?

Because I have data outside of the cosmos,
I consume any strange. I think no more
to shame any middle human wish:
my pride, my wrong, my death, my sound,
are broken rattles teasing men, black-stitched
tongues forever traced on Earth as myth.

My circling text my only hammer hit.

The work is great and bone blackened,
hope thrown down with deserted desires
to wishes counted, subtracting too less
a want crossing too many summers;
and love, so many Earths to keep.

7

A. You cannot mistake Seth
entering houses
holding a god within a god
from outside the cosmos.

Yes, let me say it for all to hear!
I relish charismatic lexicons
and savage annex of my mind.

If you reach the age of captain,
you no longer trade in fears of solitude,
since Eros is like a taste,

it only consumes,
like the first part of pleasure,
passing as it spends,

then stands in line again with other sin.

Joy is a desire for anything;
sorrow, a wish for one thing.
After each loss, my saint,
my wish was simple and one shout deep.

Sorrow is the highest text, teaching
the single eye. *One* is the mastery
within our reach. *One* is a revelation
to the dual-hearted.

The sick have clarity;
the sorrowed, clarity;
the dying, perfect clarity.
We must leave. Earth warns us to leave.

So I go ahead.

8

i

A. At best a man can sprint, loving blind.
My saint, I tried each race I could run,
as a match spits up in the wind,
before my sin's circle stunned

casts my soul not touched by hands, spun
as silk in shallow hollow sleeves,
uncurled with heat,
silken rattle-charged with moth wing play,

lining up to join at birth the marbled
vaults, encrypted genomes, row on row.
Every *sapiens'* death a new mouth cut
agape. We have only one cry:

Who will ask for the treasure of our eyes?

ii

A. Is this the only sign you leave behind?
A broken marker at your grave?
No, you must make a realm of graves,
and each with your words in their mouths.

How brief a tombstones' argument!
One life, one death? Two dates? So every tomb
tells a lie. I style the Galaxy for my tombstone.
All grist of matrix beyond the cosmos.

Counting in the sums of my futurity,
I count all suns my rumored realm,
myself the youngest human living form.

Will you ever be asked
if you were a legend in your time?
You have misread your task.

Do not build your name
in a single lattice of time.

Make all time your legend.

Master, What Did You Make?

(Aaron addresses the poet Dante.)

9
i
A. Dante, why did you place my bursting men in Hell?

Yes, the saints I knew were great in evil,
their mind's twisted, their electrons curbed,
a scaffold's float in hangman's soup,
a spring of sin compressed as script,

cannot be calm, cannot lessen fire, cannot wash.
Sapient where nothing else may boast,
not in Heaven, not in Hell, where still
our only gift is mythic code, my symbol runes

flutter shadow moths in silken sleeves,
cocoon a perfect need untouched,
opposite creatured to my middling sin,
god's face and lips fresh cut in cribs,

a chessman's field of steps in space
with crusts of tears, with broken cups,
drained dry too soon.

Do not judge me
till I make my joy to you.
I carry code.

I transport cargo beyond the cosmos.
I have found a purse of images
not of this world.

How far can I step into this honesty?
Till the hair raises on my arm?

ii
A. I trust the twisted clarities, the merest spit
in the lower rings of Dante.
I trust the science of sorrow
perfected O three-parts death! O master,

these were your great saints, the exact honesties.
Take back your feeble masks
above the rings of ash.
The broken men are my saints.

I gather them.

You mistook good and evil, never asking
if god was within or without the cosmos –
if He will ask for my eyes. We no longer
worship your god inside the creaking structure.

He is silent, stunned, misnamed.

I was not perfect as you, or what you tell us,
but I am more honest than you, master.
I understand god as you could not.
I will run until I burst in His hands.

The outward church you embraced
was placed to delay and rob you.
Drunk poet! Miters, copes, and capes?
Master, you forgot to burn your eyes.

Dante, after all, what did you need of
the priest hierarchies? You came alone.
And you depart alone.

As you watch me, as if stunned,
O let me burn your eyes
with the stammer of my sweet new style.

10

i

A. Dante, look at my new saints!
See how they work, my new-made men!
Like me, on a path of inner insight!

How does this path appear to masters?
All I loved, I showed ignorance;
all I raised up, I killed;
every promise I made, I broke.

What outward church can be made from stain?
Who makes philosophy from my pigment? Who
builds faith from spurious books of deceit?
Murder Cathars? Templars? Burn gnostic books?
Hide the gnostic Jesus coming out of Egypt?
To annex lies with capes and miters?

There's something strange in god that needs
this strange in me. What's my proof?

Everything I could discover
was once, before me, still found;
everything I could work out
was, before me, once still worked;
everything I could love
was, before me, once still loved.

This is the sum of my proofs of god.

What else may we augment of value?
May I add a single page
roiling through my purse of images?

Bring me the implements of my speech.

ii

A. Did you not see with your sharp eye, Dante,
how only the sinners, devils, and demons
recognized the sign of the Christ-man?
Peter, and the righteous, never once saw Christ.

To this day, still not once, does Peter hear god.

So I am worthy of what I *mis*-beget,
as no other creature on Earth begets.
So deep in misbelief, I will show you marvels,
burdens no angelic script could publish,
prophetic syllables no disembodied hand
could etch, trembling on a dead king's wall.

Only we can do it. We make nothing
we do not, one day, spend. Master, what did
you make? So ample metered rhyme, so much
parrot-masked wrath misplaced. Of course the
outward church would fail. Tell the truth.
Like me, your only idol is your self-reference.
Where was gnostic Jesus in you heroic rhyme?
He came beyond the cosmos telling stories
of two stewards in a field, of a man that hid his
talent lest it be lost. Where was gnostic Paul
in your wired and unconsulted paradise?

Look, master, I will still follow your steps:
I will burst like a king on a dead kings' wall.

What Daniel will be called to decipher
the secret lines? Beyond the cosmos,
another will already have my eyes.

It is only remembered if we wrote
as kings of speech. You spend your god;
I will spend mine. Until you have
god's power, your worship is only
adolescence. Beatrice has unmanned you.
Let me open my voice.

We will say to Seth, we read his lines.

CANTO FOUR

The Record of Exodus From Earth

1
A. I have crossed my meridian voyage, where
human becomes visible idiom, and so my fears.
I hunt the tar cave of fossil mind, where ghosts
of space, time, and men coil in somatic prescience.

I will rise deep in winter with no alarm, not
once to follow substance of moth-winged men
seized with light. I lay down structure embedded
with my selection, joy and fear reduced to equal fonts.

Since if by sentience I am cognizant, then by
sentience equally I annul a slur of cognizance.
To death, I answer: I am equal with mind's extract.
We make nothing that we do not exhaust, spend,

and pasteurize. So I will make this sprint.

O, I will so narrow a winter weave
as 'mend all breath to fit my verse.
Tall winter I will pass composed,
adjuring death to new extracted mineral.

Self-contained, I will winter in my mind.

If I cry counter idiom, who will survive
to prevent me? Those that accept death?
I drain time and element of insolvent fear,
reducing bleached bones of shrill alarm

to light totem on my eye.

Tall Winter I will Pass Composed

(*Aaron asks the future reader to understand his mind.*)

2
A. Try every love
only if you are able to forgive,
or it will diminish you.

Accept every worship
only if you can read symbols,
or it will lessen you.

Accept every desire
only if you can accept death,
or it will consume you.

Still pay your bills
where others sleep.

To test the device of my mind against
the sun, I build RingWorld stations
at the ribbon moons of Jupiter,
the last stop for Western men of old Earth,
new man and new Jerusalem.

Nothing is made that is not exalted.

(Aaron disbelieves the terrors of old Earth.)

3
A. When we are all made masters,
the pictures of men on Earth will be weighted
lighter than a feather in the scale;
but the sun will be dark then,

and all your ransoms curled with heat.

Immense force is black, grasping back
spent light, stirring up yellow dust at the
edge. The yellow light is weak,
a spurious excess of spent fractions,

erased from dense rudiments of speech.

I, now alien, see humans, hear speech
refracted peripherally at the edges.
Our sound goes out ahead of us,
some to summon, some to warn.

Only the falcon reads what the falconer
to the falcon signals:
everything I make I use and spend.

The evil in our context is tangential, brittle.
Already coded, stained, counted, canceled.
Show me one formation of pure evil –
and I will show you text where it was copied.

My mind is the only new world.

(Aaron addresses accusations of his madness.)

4
i
A. I no longer practice thoughts I cannot keep:

woman's youth, market lows, the dead in fields,
children lost in streets. Spirits cannot see loss
since they perceive by intentions, and to evil
men, our sin, at first, was always lovely;

a spurious excess of spent desires
in yellow light becomes our treasure.

We do not farm. We witness what falls to
yellow light, and chose to accept its terms.
Each man assents to terms he cannot keep:
his love by division, his faith already sold.

Of course, stumble to your knees, but do not
cower. This was your appointed time.

You will say to Seth, you read his lines.

ii
A. Shirts, mother of pearl, confidences,
our bodies, the common market that we traded.
We do not escape Earth to change,
but to flame and burn more brightly,

to burst against a troubled king's wall.

The storm-guard cannot curb the storm,
the fire-guard cannot cool a fire,
my human cannot purge my human code,
rattle-wrung to rage exposed a faithless tongue,
cannot blight the seed,

cannot drown the lung.

(Aaron accuses his self-satisfied contemporaries.)

5

You brave, large-bellied sinners,
all of you are anointed to your bursting;
who else could make your run,
you naked, chosen sprinters?

If one day you master fear, tell no one
before we come to worship you: we know,
then, you touched breath on Earth, made flesh
on screens, in transfigured intimacies.

The greater saints came from wealthy homes;
planted temple stones, plated gold to jawbones,
on blackened bones saint's sin makes no mark,
poor simple miracles in our sight.

As their parents gave them every wealth,
they saw that joy was useless, wealth useless,
stoned every fruit, dropped their burning coal;
every illusion already fingered:

the path to sainted life burns bright
coming and going from Seth.
All who have failed, take shelter in my text,
say to Seth

you read his lines.

(*Aaron rejects the truth of any human civilization.*)

6
We change the observed. That is our mind.
No human progression is an exact
footprint of reality. A civilization
is only a choice, a curvature of artifice.

And some elect to serve the illusion.

Everything outside transforms. Earth is outside.
Earth is the most terrifying education;
Earth speeds death in you to fool's speed,
and you wrestle until the bone is out.

If you build your house on a high theme
and wish and fear the same address,
who can still sleep under your shudder?
If in my age I have no shelter what part
of wealth did I once renounce?

Terror is the only perfect science. Item.
Terror narrows Earth to a pinhole.
Like Apollo's house,
the Earth so aged with waves of terror,
it is forbidden again
to be born or die here.

Your treasure will find a way to kill you.
Beatrice.

(*Aaron nominates sinners and children as equal saints.*)

7
Seth, we are that same profane generation.

Men who sin without caution
lay their heads down at night
as children believed to be good
lay their heads down at night.

Their sleep was so great, they made contact.

Men now unworthy, condemned,
eat meals blessed as worthy saints,
as children certain to be worthy
drink milk blessed as worthy saints.

Unnumbered human sprinters sprint

where the yellow light is weak,
where there is work and cleansing farms;
where spirits have a human face, teasing
judgment; and if there is any wish in you,

so begin worthy, end worthy.

And if you can only run as far as sprinters run,
then find your page in my text;
men and women broken-embered ore,
revealing all my wishes on my sainted knees

separate but melting snow.

(Despite his faulted element, Aaron marvels at his soul.)

8
A. Everything we wish, we tease and spend.

My wish is immense. So my small death
still can't find me, but if the Earth cripple me,
my saint, try, and you will see I still can sprint.

Ignore the lifeless bodies row on row.
I hear their voices. I mark their stones.
My soul tests structure with eternity,
I am aware of my existence by
sense beyond the cycles of melting stone.

Can you still work the machines and broken
engines the dead left outside their coffins—
dropped, the last moment, before they stepped in?
And how can you make a saint work?

What the Earth decays, I remake.
Let the Earth rest in ice.

If for a day they make no coffins, and men
perfect in peace their letters and rhymes,
O these are merely the start of bitter wars.
As your beauty, perfected with choice
rejects all other, and thus, by arms, proscribe.

Only the sound of a poet remains.
And it will be weighed against a feather.

If you accuse me, then accuse all parts
read-over until the end – and by study,
reprove me. The same deep learning
required of me, give me in return.

I know a new generation will rise.
To this end, I want my hundred years.
Then let's talk and seek amendments.

(Aaron channels voices from outside the cosmos.)

9
A. Who now seizes the levers of *machine*?

For my mad sprints, loves interrupted,
forgive me all my runners and the speed,
cherry lips stained red from cherry wine,
all I embraced that I tried to keep,

guard or gardener trace the seed.

Though it be nothing wished, nothing good,
nothing real, confuse all tongues,
lose its high theme, taint all redemptions;
a child's deathbed, human lust turned to hate,

still, a feather in the scale, loving blind.

I have raised the dead in many cities
and will see more; all the brass here has been
touched; heart and bone made lighter now—
half stitched rubrics splitting seams.

O future savants of folding space,
how you increase your index of syllables!

I have already changed your house; already
I have placed a shout inside your dark sobbing
that does not suffer long a little room and shuns
all steady lodging. I will always send you floods,

some to take away, some to raise.

I have dug in many fields and will find more,
no margin for the water on my lids;
they cross this lake who shave its frost,
they swim this night who still can sleep

on splitting beams, on drowning beds.

(*Aaron tests the outer limits of his ecstatic insight.*)

10
A. All screens reset, my saints live forever,
though nothing of Earth remains,
not body, face, or cuff;
not kindness, lip, or cup,
no enemy, no other, no loving brother,
not a water-logged shoe, open-tongued
and stained with mud,
not a single players' sin, or a sound I taste
while I still have breath,
though spinning fast,

I recast all white warrior's shields,
guns, ships, bolts, locks, and cannon;
slowly I detect, note, and feel
knowledge of my divine part,
my deep and most authentic self,
after terrors, tumbles, spills, with no abbreviation,
co-ancient with god,

as here, crouching over empty shells,
animal's full appetite,
I, a greater reaching being,
pause from dark travel, strange, unknown maths,
loosed in darkly lit but rumored star kingdoms,
strike all human sound.

What is *gnosis* except that everything
in my mind becomes true? Those who ask,
will never know the unknowable god.
You can only know, becoming the object.
Since everything I now do, you will do.
Every sin I lose, you will lose.
Every love I make, you will make.
Every life I take, you will take.
Every fear I have, you will have.

Do not judge me before I make my sound.
Death reduced to equidistant fonts,

to light totem on my eye.

CANTO FIVE

I Saw Fire on Mars

1
Before we approached the near planet Mars,
we saw New Peking's six towers. Nothing was
at once so hateful to the Western eye.
I penned a short dispatch. I sent them rough
envoys of tungsten and plutonium.

Then we saw fire on Mars.

As the fire rose and consumed Peking's
six towered stations, I erased the scandal
of their blasphemy, likewise,
to copy our idiom,
to copy our cities,
to copy our conquest,
to copy our hegemony,
to copy our machines,
step for step, bolt by bolt,
not a single innovation,
except backwards.
Proving the thesis.

We descended with our lasers tracking,
crossing 360 degrees. We took Iridium 3.
We took water and protein – of any taste –
not discriminating.

Making cold scandal of equality of flesh.

(Aaron addresses the evil of men.)

2
A. Since there is speech,
there must be a way to inner vision.
Since there are thoughts of the unknown,
there must be a way to become the unknown.
Since there is misbelief, there are men.
Show me one perfect monster.
And not just a man.

I see you sprint with good or evil,
why do you quickly tire, winded?
I would that you were hot or cold.
The righteous men keep no gift I need.

As apprentice, I knew at once
god does not favor good or evil men,
does not number good or evil men,
does not turn his neck for evil men,
counts both good and evil, mere beginners.

The West cannot make one dangerous monster.
Till, with self-knowledge, I arrive at the hunt.

O my saint, show me your best evil.
The men I met in wars, all the monsters
I knew, could not harm themselves, or others,
without miscalculations. Why?
Because there is no house of evil.
Only bursting men with poems of evil.

Evil is a text found only in the human mind.

If for one moment there was a source
of evil outside my imagination, any
evil existing once outside of man's brain,
Earth's water, and all men,
should flash dry with a spit,

a moment brightly red and orange.

(Aaron defames the linguistic quest for human truth.)

3
We do not worship truth. That's a fiction.

We live untruth, we seek friends to untruth,
marry to untruth, lust to untruth,
cannot bear to leave untruth alone in its
sorrow. Sacrifice every good for untruth.

We feel poor next to untruth. We make peace,
make treaty with untruth. We are a mind
conquering space with irresistible adolescence.
Look, my proof: Where our mind arrives,
space expands. What is location, then, except
our mind? O, if our joy or manners do not once
meet our philosophy, we age poorly
in the terrors of our mirrors.

When will our joys match our conquest?
The West can easily spread its radio, injecting
the other with the outward church of science,
converted daily to our tastes, our speech,
our music, our story, our erect gene.

We do not love god, we love our language.
We do not prize any god,
we prize the idiom of outward contact.
We still look outside our own mind for aliens.

As we replace all other misbelieve,
as we are drunk with our own mechanics,
as the world shakes when our voice shakes,
can I pause to take thought, the noise I hear?

I don't need stars; I need canvas.
I don't need men; I need code.
I don't need love; I need time.
I don't need justice; I need personality.

So I carry my church aloft, my book
matured, late to the page, with light inflection,
speech of god and Earth's last deluge.

(Aaron makes a case for true equality of Homo sapiens.)

4

Low on oxygen, I see visions.
Low on sugar, I see phantoms.
Low on spice, I hear voices.
Low on time, I see death.

As my time runs down, should I still speak in
measured speech ? If so, who would hear me?
Should I be calm, reasoned and circumspect?
No, I should tell the truth. I am enraged.
Nothing can be reclaimed of my acts,
unless my rage is published. My urge
to kill still echoes longer than my Eros.

What do I owe this generation?
The survival of the fittest, in mind
and body? Then all surviving men
approve my speech. I take the cliché
of equality and make it *exact*. I eradicate
equally all degenerate forms of *sapiens*.
Dr. Talon selected from ten billion
three hundred. That *is* selection of fittest – yes?
I am the hero then of Victorian scientism!
I am the unredeemed archon of science!

Perhaps it is now clear. I have nothing to say
to a faithless, malformed, self-referent generation.
What civilization ever produced such
deformities of body and mind? I list only
scandals any man may confirm with
his eyes. Thick-legged, porklet thighs in early
youth. After, nothing as found in nature, bent spines,
caked by shameless layers of brown jelly fat,
loping folds of belly, breast, and purulent flesh,
spotty, cow-eyed, and ever still hungry,
begging, for more goblets of salty sweet meal.
The final idiom of democratic proliferation?
I made an end of socialism and propagation,
modernism's only two achievements.
If so, what is the merit of science? A death ray?
Am I clear yet? Do I dissemble from timidity?

Equally condemning all races, I prove
the sagacity of raceless society – each are
equal to their dissolution – an exact,
logical, and liberally equal polity.
A racist must be a poor man or a miser
since he chooses three or four diamonds
among the promiscuous deformity
of his own kind. An easy test of eyes.

I laugh at the man that infers his race superior
to another tribe of sapiens. Risible to choose
from ethnic deformities, hard to decide
the most fulsome degeneration of human form,
when none is found sane, whole, healthy,
trim, or athletic. So yes, I choose equality.
All equally condemned, equally rejected.

I have seen the final logic of the Demos:
all men, in all climes are now finally alike,
sublime in equity: unlearned, stooped, plump,
misshapen, kinked in body, leveled in mind.
Kinked is straight! Plump, deformed beautiful!
Death, then, is marvelous, smooth to the touch!

Enough, I will be calm. I must sublime
outward rage to aggregate in my speech.

Yet, who, though I sang from the angel hierarchies
will wait to hear the final proofs of my voice?
Who will decode the secret messages?
Who will be patient to find the riddle of the ages?

I ask for a century. Then I ask for galaxy,
before I ask *Homo sapiens* their opinion.

Yet to all augmentary, I add my voice.
Though, enraged, I am forever young.
I address any future *Homo faustus* saint
reading my page, make pledge for me,
equal to any accusation of scuttling mice.

5

A. Why Europa? Why not populate Mars?
Because Mars is Earth-proximate. Because,
the Moon was mined, and Mars contaminate
with wounded moralities. Infected with China –
Russian robots. I make my own Inchon –
and go around and past with audacity.

Because Mars has no water,
the sun too hot there with no cloud.
Dr. Talon could make ice burn, comprehending
hydrogen, yet he could not cool sun-fire
enough for sleep, reproduction, or shelter
from loathsome radiation. So not Mars.

Europa and Calisto have water in abundance.
The solar radiant is weak at friendly remove,
the quiver of moons sufficient for reformation
of Europa's ice with impacting fires.

I look at large Ganymede, but fear to
approach. Ringworld requires light gravity.
Io is evil, warped, roiled with radiant photons,
Europa is equidistant from Jupiter's radiation.

Yet in truth,
I desired to cross the meridian of this sun
not only to reset the minds of men – to look
inward – but to test the divinity of my heart.
How to test my mind against all suns?

The initiate will know my meaning.

Any seed at Mars would look to Earth,
dream to escape to Earth, dream to eat well.
And thus replicate the kennels of Earth.
I placed three death ships at the gates of Mars
to guard our rearward exodus, safe as we sleep.

To be free of all other men
is only certain liberty.

(Aaron advises the curious of his arrogant ambition.)

6
A. The question will arise to the mind.
What is contained in this book?
My book is an interrogative of god's mind.
And thus, my mind. You may ask, have I not
sinned? I reply: *Has god sinned?* No.
Then I am also free of stain.
Those who can hear, let them hear.

The answer is that there is no other book
you must read. Yet, *Homo sapiens,*
you cannot understand my words
until you have read all books ever written.
The initiate will understand the message.

What part of this book must you understand?
A story is told of rage, grief of my own kind.
Yet nothing written may have one interpretation.
No epic speech has a single outward face.
Called to the dance, few will know the steps.

Are there counter arguments? Yes, there is
despair of lost continent, lost speech, lost
manners, lost paintings. But I have kept your
DNA. I grip a single frozen vial!
At the end of my poem I will show you
matter, inwardly, you may cheer.

For men of English lexicons, I give
you the rarest gambol: a second, a third
mythic race to sprint. No other speech
measures three marathons of world in full
bloom, raging in the crack of high idiom.
England, America – Galaxy. Grace of me,
you are proximate with all time, the only
vulgate of Exodus. You are first galaxy-
cuneiform, unless I make another.
Those initiate will plumb the fissure.

7
A. What is contained in this book?

It does not contain any fresh event;
it contains everything ever known.
Except I preach god beyond the cosmos
and this makes me galaxy-heretic.
Yet you cannot understand the secret
passages until you have walked the path,
Our Mercury, gnostic Paul, Mithras.

Those initiate will understand the message.

After two millennia of lies, obscurification,
the truth will appear to moderns strange.
Numerologies of men have been reduced.
The madness is over-bitter, but straight.

Now there are only those called,
and those initiate, foreknown.
Strange to modern ears. Yet,
you will know when you see these words.
If you are present, if you read,
if your father's seed survived,
then you are already called.
Authorized to dance at my measure:

my sin that shames all future tailors' tongues,
strange rattle in ear, brutish mouth secrete
my three day house, words as silk in mouths, my
drenched tongue to cotton cloths espoused release

a smooth round sound, a thousand bursting seeds,

mummy moths with wings as black-eyed peas,
silken-rattle-charged with moth wing play,
my window dressing sins,
the fret of sky I made from reeds,
no tender end of days, or undiminished men,

or none that came to Earth to mend.

(*Aaron is interrupted by his natural son Terry. Enter Terry, under the misapprehension that he is a negro and pretend cook.*)

8

Terry. Still scratchin'?—a tree in your ear?
I report a riot in the canteen. Soup has been spilt,
drippin' from the back sides of rented boys.
Ship 23, deck 2, presence required. No more *pro-o-log*.
Let black Terry finish your skinny book.
No one's goin' t'read it. I look'd in't. Ain't readable.
Ain't the fashion now.

A. Wakeda!

T. No! This is nothin' that Injin can fix this time!
The crew haven't seen you for a maw o'Sundays.
They say the injin's kilt you and ett you. Suggest
you come with **** in hand—and place an order
in the canteen.

A. If I find out that you're playing at . . .
Where is my staff? How did you get past . . .

T. Like I'm sayin'. The crew has the injin' by the heels.
Black Terry goes where he wants. Says what he wants.
Not 'fraid o'tall gods. I saw you naked—I know, don't I?
They'll know I pulled you out of the fire in Kyoto.
Besides, where else you gonna hear the truth?
From the littl'ins? "O, let the littl'ins come to me!"
There is one that has set her eye on you.
She's a sharp'un!

A. Stop babbling. I am coming! Find my staff!

(*Watching Terry leave, Aaron locks manuscript away.*)

*(**Continues writing the second day** – a confession.)*

9
i
A. I was Simon the Stylite,
and I have returned to accuse myself.

I was the Stylite
when I could not remain in a family.

I was the Stylite
when I could not remain in an office.

I was the Stylite
when I could not remain with one love.

I was the Stylite
when I could not love my brother.

I was the Stylite
when I released the sleeping death gas.

ii
A. The love He placed in me had to be worked
against chaos, in my generation.

Isis was not so proud to join in,
Osiris picked up a shovel.
But you, Simon,
did not know your god in a cloud.

Bear me no longer barbarous
in a lettered book
though my knife slip
cleanly and silent, still holy.

New married,
fused with legion.

(Aaron feels, then accepts the confessions of his guilt.)

10
My saints,
I mangled all my clean-starched sheets,
my sun-cracked shades in trailer parks;
my cuffs, my cups, my mouth, my teeth,
my heart, stained black on lover's pain.

Though I fall into a road kept by a god that pardons,

dolls undone are worked till broken,
or worry and tease an older boy;
my arms, my hearts, soon lost or put away,
the hand that cut my mouth
has stitched my brain.

Bear me no longer barbarous
from a lettered text.

God does not want a man to hide secure;
he wants a man to burst and open his heart
to holy shame, to carry in his purse as rune,
faces loved with pain, then redeemed;
and, once I know myself, one-time forever,
then I can sit and fret retrograde
constellations, or decide the unknown.

Hold me then no longer incantation,
my electron to all screens intact.

I did not slacken any line,
I made mirth of a hero's fall.
Stand up a salt-encrusted soul,
fall down puppets heaped in strings,

all equal, atoned, and put away.

(Here ends prologue to Kosmoautikon.)

CANTO SIX

Build Me Once Galactic Ships

1
i
A. Earth-born ships are relics of lost-worlds.
The boats arrived at Jupiter are artifacts.
Any minute whistling starfish may rupture
thin foil skins and fragile circuits exposed.

We break new bread, exchanging delicate
machines for sturdy ligaments, planetary
satellites profligate with depth and breath,
self-referent, sustainable, sheltered.

At Callisto we mine molten lead as bitter gold.
At Jupiter, molten lead is greater than rubies.
Crushed ore, made powder, rise with easy steps
to split-tongue-spitting crucibles of heat. Lead

frames are cast with molten covered decks,
many-tiered and absorbent to impact,
weightless. Tungsten doors have no portal,
all outward eye as compound lens.

O wheels! O robotic arms! O Ezekiel I read!

When it moves it moves on its four sides,
and they turn not as they move, but to
the place the head looked, our ships follow,
They turned not as they went. Read my mind!

Outward buffers disguise our giantism in dark
or light; round, yet nimble-fingered, grasping
any passing fruit. Their backs, fronts, hands, and
cutting wheels, replete with eyes round about.

One robotic arm, of ten in single file,
reaches out, grasping the molten element.

Anabasis in Lead

ii
Floors, walls, made stoutly jagged tungsten,
rayed over this inner porch, concentric
caves of layered, globular lead, contained
buffered cavities filled with liquid bladder aquifers,

melted ice from Europa's frozen sea,
enough for fuel, for breath of a thousand
men a thousand years. And in cavernous pockets,
caves of sealed oxygen extracted from

solid, toothed, jagged continents of ice.

A galaxy ship, in aspect, globular.
No front, no back. No elliptic foil.
Only dense, molten lead shields, defensive
with swollen perturbing welts, angry as

Cyclopes' face. Pockmarked, gritty to the teeth,
yet stately, dauntless in her majesty.

Artic-spiked, brutally buffered shields of artifice,
ruthless, surprised, callous, rough, precise,
advanced beyond all previous half-measures,
artic contours, swellings fixed with cold chill spray,

scarcely conceals the cunning of our intent,
since, outwardly proclaiming, passing aliens
may read on our molten shields precise
engravings of Earth's only treasure:

The story of Western men facing Asia.

*(Aaron describes the figured reliefs embossed in
lead on the outward shields of his galaxy ships.)*

2
A. Ten fathoms deep, as shields, these globular
outward shells, our smiths impress ten-fold
agonies of Western *Sapiens* decisively engaged.
Hector again strikes with glowing eyes
the golden shield of livid Achilles.
Scipio Africanus is there, burning Carthage.
Hannibal returns three times to crush
Western man. Embossed, Trasimeno is etched
with reeds showing through shallow but
broad waters. Blood of thrice beat Romans
running down easy slopes. Each fright perfect,
each alarm set in forever molten element,
exactly as contained in the human genome,
and still extant for alien eyes to read
passing by our ships in space with awe.

There, between razor spikes of steel, on a
man-made prominence, place the Temple
of the Jews, when the priest converted proud,
arrogant and rich, hating their own kind.
Show the righteous Roman general,
reducing, stone by stone, Solomon's
patrimony, and quick dispersion to remote
cities, where finally, they found their God
again as just. Show the Jewish nation in exile,
murdered by Saxon farmers, peasants enraged,
show the full horror of modern acts, of human
ovens, their dead stacked up as wood, mouth
agape in silent protest, show Jews chased
across the globe, nomads in their own
mind, yet with a drowning anchor of leaden,
heavy laws, and self-flagellation.
How are they not exactly *Homo sapiens*?
How are they not like us?

3
A. On the prime façade, facing the galaxy,
placed next in honor to Ajax and Hector,
set in cunning tungsten and lead, a scene
is paramount. Between erects spires, a scene
is played out. The first hour the West held
its compound breath, when a small nation,
but fierce, faced the barbaric Eurasian
megalith. Fired-eyed men with superbly
smithied arms, each numbered part crafted by
lathes, each bolt faced with runic numbers,
with helmets forged by Vulcan, deposed
ten Bolshevik armies, in dusty stride, as a
small snake un-hinges its jaw, extending
its throat, engulfing in its maw a meal
too large, too fatal to digest. There, bold,
erect, the guns, the Tiger tanks of Kurst
arraigned in hellish fields, the few noble
against the many, the free against the enslaved.
Who will color evil between dictators?
Since courage redeems all events, no longer
could we distinguish the good from the foul,
since all were blest that day. And every man
now takes his story from single conflagration.

Not yet I stop. Next, masters of the art,
show lost America. Show victory snatched
from early defeat. Depict with exact
line, make seven Apollo spacecraft, tall
and charismatic, with three-stage, ten motored
Saturn engines. Show in stereo, China
and America – how China made as
like seven voyages across pre-Columbian
seas, then, seeing nothing more blessed than their
idiom, nothing more abundant than their
mud-cog science, returned forever
inward. Show their debasement. Then next, show
Americas first galactic battle won,
show seven breathless voyages across
unknown wine dark seas to outer moons. Show
a paper thin capsule, with wrinkled folds
of orange foil, glaring down miniscule
from its mother ship. Show this, seven flights
to the outer moon, the prominence of
Western men, the Earth with its breath held, and
then, perhaps, I satisfy with my spleen
the prologue of our race, manifest.

(Aaron address his Staff – now assembled.)

4
A. Gentlemen, you each have a copy of the plans.
Do not mistake my directions.
I watch you like a boy with a glass heating
ants in a hot beam. I mean to focus heat
on a single point.

(To Wakeda.) Is this the text?

W. The same.

(Recording made on loud speakers to ship's crew.)

A. "Assemble now our ships with prudent rage.
First, a lead core, one hundred cubits deep,
to blunt the rays of fusion and ion – that a
child may breath sheltered from unseen
emissions. Give me twelve iron walls,
ten times layered concentric decks, six cubits
broad. Not yet I stop. Seal sheltered our city
abutting ceramic layered iron, lead, reactive
silicon, double jointed that no slight moon may
reach the small hair of second decks – though
enraged meteor escape our equation. The living
barriers so fixed, smithy me galactic shields,
a mountain of no weight fixed to our flanks.
Then from the light gravity below, from element,
ore, and iron, forge towering spikes outward;
after these solid works, molten lead our shell
encase, a liquid melt, like cherry dipped in cream,
yet over crossed with tungsten towered blades
projecting outward, in distant aspect
to all accounts a spiked gum tree seed
adrift.

Pockmarked, gritty to the teeth, let our proud
façade not dissemble the broken, scarred
indigents within. Let us better resemble
our brutal sorrows, trials in wars, men made
slave, and I shall love her – though she appear
from outer passing worlds a many-pointed seed
with hostile razor spears!

So build me once Galactic ships to bark
at suns."

(Scientific Committee next discusses the overhaul of Europa.)

5
A. You are each savants in your art.
This is the mission we must fulfill:
To terraform Europa for future human
habitation. I am a doubter, but willing to
be a believer. I have Dr. Talon's notes.
What can you add to this enterprise?
What then do I chose? I prefer to smithy
a galaxy ship proper to my ease
than the coarser means to alter an entire
moon to fit the caprice of Earth's zoology.
I will not be constrained again
to a single planet, a single coordinate.
Proceed.

(Honored scientists rise to speak in turn.)

8th Scientist. For myself, I hesitate to make worlds.
Because which world? The "outward" world separate
from consciousness – that world may be
an illusion! And what may a new planet
be except, again, a separate entity that we must
defend with selections. Its only outcome is war,
endless dramatic revolutions? Or do we
make a world with no separations?
Yet my mind cannot get a foothold. Since if
there is no separation within consciousness,
then it is best to do nothing, as any kinetic force
will only lead to offensive actions, each
a dead end, only resulting in a thesis
of counter kinetic futility: war and counter acts.

A. I have heard this all before! Scientism
continues to be spineless, uncertain. More
tentative, more theoretical since
its recent fiascos to predict reality.
Why did they allow ideologues to take
over the laboratory? Science,
like any previous church, has merely
conformed to the debility of its
society. Who is next on the list?

6

1st S. Nothing is as it appears! Reformation
of Europa is not solved by childish
kinetic force. The altercation of
globular bodies is not a case of
classical matter – but of dark matter!
I have proven (with proofs!) that dark matter
is but double exposure quintessence.
That is, matter as a holographic
dark energy table, can only be
a Pseudo-Namobo-Goldstone boson
quintessence. Following oscillatory
models, we know that the universe is
undulant, properly explained by the
five-dimensional Ricci flat Bouncing
cosmology. In short, we should burn off
the oceans and make a steam atmosphere
using scaling dark-energy, in brief,
specifically, Dilatonic ghost
condensate dark energy. We can make
this device if we forgo all other
amenities and consumables.

(*Sits down again with righteous pride.*)

A. Much of your plan appears to me cliché.
I have heard these same theories rehearsed now
for fifty years. I see in the record
you made the first patent on "*single pap
quintessence.*" I note that you were also
able to leverage the ten Swedish
investors, and obtained the Nobel prize
by the age of sixteen – before even
entering the university. Who is
the next scientist on the list?

1ˢᵗ S. This is an outrage! Forbidden speech!

7

2nd S. We have not come this far with sacrifice
to recite poems of Victorian scientism.
Nobel prize? What is that? What laureate
ever made a contribution after the award?
It is a prize for men who profess modernism.
Stalin gave out awards for Stalinists;
Mussolini gave out awards for Fascists.
What is modernism except …

A. If you have a plan to terraform Europa
you may discuss that!

2nd S. The young professor
omits to say how laboratory
science has eradicated life on Earth!
What are my proofs? They have engineered seeds
that are not seeds, medicines that are not
medicines, food that is not food, maiming,
deforming, disfiguring entire populations …

1st S. This is an insult to science! This man
is not a scientist … he's a mouthpiece
of the leader's politics. Every wise
citizen knows we only need more time
for science to answer all obscurities.
Science is the panacea to all human ills!

2ⁿᵈ S. No, science is a choice of idiom!
Homo sapiens was not a lost tribe
of nomads, desperate for machines, before
the dictate of scientism. Homo sapiens
was not a lost race of microbes waiting
only, brick by brick, to arrive at an
industrialized utopia. As coarse
materialists, we all die pending
the final, never arriving, answer –
of what? Of ever-delayed science,
ever excusing itself, never once
correctly prognosticating human
crisis – not even in round terms?!

A. Wakeda, please remove both men!
Who is the next savant on the list?

(*Wakeda escorts both men from the platform.*)

8

3rd Scientist. How can we face the faceless? Matter is
empty! You ask for science, I give you
freely the science I have. What you seek,
what you want, are engineers of the weird.
My proofs? Can we even see clearly the
challenge we face? Europa alters as
the observer alters. Europa, as
any globular body, has no fixed
composition. Stellar bodies are problems
of observation – not of any fulsome
gay-hearted reality.

We have romanticized rational thought!
Ours is only another faith. Who here asked
to advise in the composition of the new planet,
who here knows without doubt that all likely
data has been evaluated? Not one of you!
If you do not have all sets of possible data,
then you cannot rule as rationalists.
You can only assert you have all sets of data.
My proof? We have only one fact: all the
innumerable variables in
every choice, plan, or verdict are still
incalculable! This is the price we pay
for self-consciousness. There is no place to
hide from double-think. We are only able
to *think* about *thinking*; never for a
moment is there a final resting point.
Science makes this mistake. You don't want a
scientist, you want a mechanic, since
after you get the moon of Europa
to "operate" then what next? You have no
idea except to follow one drama
after the next. The human mind then is
a hunter – of occasions of drama.

All we can gather in our net, all we
can make, after all the cost of blood and
treasure, is a list of *Dramatis personæ*.
Read a child's history book! We make lists
of dramatic finalists. We make lists of problems!

So there is no Europa at all to
reform. There is only this mind, our mind,
looking back at us. And so we are in
this funny position.

9

A. So *why* do I have scientists to give advice
on technical issues? I must use reason.
I have to decide an issue of life
and death – or not? I need facts. Or are they
only colors inside the lines of heterodoxy.

3rd S. Admiral, have you looked hard at the stars?
Have you stood at the Grand Canyon?

A. Grand Canyon? Are… you serious?

3rd S. I have looked at it hard. Yet the more
I looked the more my mind made an
internal journey. I saw that we can't
look at any object more than a few
brief moments – before the object alters –
forever. This is our mind. How, tell me,
can we know an object until we first
learn how our mind perceives? Reflecting in
tranquility, I discovered how our
mind works on that day. Have you seen a vast
image, in painting, or in any art?
We can look only a few moments before
the mind no longer lingers at the surface
of images. Instead, the mind journeys
away from the surface of the image.
It retreats inwardly and searches an
alternate vision of its copy. Have any
of you tried this experiment? My proof?
Can we clearly see the person we hate?
Does the eye of the lover see the real
beloved? Ever? No, it sees only the
beloved with an altered, inward, compound.
Self-love is more dense than a solid body.
So how can we clearly see a new world
without romancing the entity?

A. Is this your advice – romance? Can you be
more defined? You have three PhDs, I read?

3rd S. This is my point: What is man?
Or the mind of man? We make brevities
of visible objects, tangential to
any fossil of truth. Only inward
narratives are deeply felt. Can we be
honest? As scientists, we firstly use
imagination – and then only later write
the mathematics – the codex – to fit
the level of consciousness we seek.
How else did Einstein or Bohr operate –
the creators of the world we now search?
They had dreams and visions momentary
of insight – then filled a page of symbols,
of math, until it fit a story of
inward synchronistic exploration.

A. We need a conclusion here, Dr.!

3rd S. Any system of mathematics contain
propositions that can neither be proved
or disproved. Thus math is an idiom
as any other inference, a poem
able only to be applied *just-so.*

A. Yes, we know Herr Gödel's famous proof.
What is your point?

3rd S. A frozen planet, minus atmosphere
and nitrogen cannot be terraformed
within ten thousand millenniums!
You have merely romanced your reason.
It is remote from any actual reality.
You cannot use reason, since you never
possess all the facts of any case. There
is no planet Europa, not the one
you see; there is only the image of
your own mind looking back at you.
You want science, I give you science.
You have wisely placed all your resources
in the construction of a ship more suited
for life than reformation of moons.
The factory platforms bring up heavy
metals from the surface of Callisto.
Luxuriant ice provides oxygen,
fuel and water in abundance. This is
as far as my science can take you.

10

4th Scientist. He lies! There is life below the ice!
There is alien protein below the
ice! Of course, you already knew that?
Strange amphibian creatures of non-
symmetrical ventricles. Whiskers
sweeping before and after. A single tooth
backward spiral encasing the organ sac.
Life set on its own course! If you make one
further step, you will end this untouched world.
We will merely replace a pristine world
with degraded appetites. You don't want
a scientist, Admiral, you want an exterminator.
Science long ago tested the reality
of the atomic structure. Matter is
a wave with spider legs poised on the eyes of
the observer. Adhesion, cohesion,
and attraction are soundless etiquettes
of *Homo sapiens'* mind. If you want
properties of atmosphere at Europa,
then you will want to make the conditions,
using the mind, to make adhesion, cohesion,
and attraction of the elements so
desired. Yes, we may follow the Milne-Born-
Infeld model. Igniting sixty-five
megacleates, we can replicate a fierce
vacuum driven metamorphism. But
these are concepts first discovered in the
mind – not in nature. Thus we must first test
the intention of the observer. What is
your founding thought? Is there a new insight
of human enchantment? What level of mind,
what proof of consciousness do you seek in
your enterprise? What is your underpinned
bedrock of joy? I see there is silence.
What is the good and the beautiful of
our civilization? Proof of our excellence?
Or merely proliferation of life forms?
See my point? Europa is a mirage
of quixotic thought – not an actual
oasis. Europa will only kill you

with its reality. I see no founding
ur-thought of this world! I see only a
will to proliferate technology.
What is the high specie of industry
except the exploitation of a lever?
Do you wish to sustain new worlds on ever
bigger levers or on a high human
concept – I don't know – let's choose a model –
of virtue, honor, sacrifice, bravery??
Is our intent an occasion of wealth
or of integrity? Are we prepared
to plant only a rough, ersatz world or
exclusively a better world? Where, in
your graphic, is the grain of heavenly
wheat pounded? In a back room? What is our
concept of the good and the beautiful –
or do we wish to equal only the
state of the sick and deformed specimens
that survived the journey? Another lost
Jamestown? Do we have a higher concept
than we now profess in our society?
Will we make seeds that are not seeds, food that
is not food, or medicines that are not
medicines? My point? To promulgate world,
this disseminate world, we must lie!

No gentlemen, a still greater work must
be performed before we attack Europa
with kinetic forces. The mind must be
sized and prepared before the conditions
we seek aforethought can be realized.
Are we nomads in our minds, or are we in
full competence of inter-dimensional
psychic exegesis? Classic, Victorian
science has proven to be false. There is no
such thing as "hard truth." The senses cannot
interpret reality – they only
make linguistic concepts using symbols.
There is only a range of possible
"predictions." Newton is a false prophet.
Where is the glory to copy out what

we observe in nature? A child can do
as much. Einstein reversed this process. The
truth is, if you can write it on paper,
you could find it in the heavens. This,
in fact, is the protocol physicists
and scientists have followed from the start.
Symbols in the mind are alive!

A. But this means ... science is only an opinion!
You are saying that the most that science can be
is a subset of poetry! How can we proceed to
make a world with poems?

4th S. It is only a poem if it is true!
It means that my mind alone is only
sure continent. And we create reality
as we observe the conditions and the
scope of bold human wish. We measure thoughts,
not globular bodies of fire, or of ice!
There are no questions but one, if we wish
to know the origin of the universe.
There is only the question of integrity, of honesty!
The universe will not be understood until
consciousness is understood. There is
thus only one actual question of existence.
The question is not, what is there outside
of a human mind, but what is inside the mind?
Thus there is only one fact of existence.
Nothing "outside" the mind exists unless
it is first interpreted by a mind observing.
As I now *think* – so is the world of phenomena.

A. Yet ... how to make Europa habitable?

4th S. That question is secondary. Where, and
in what dark cell, is the heavenly wheat
to be pounded? At Europa? The first step
is an inward check of the heart. Is our concept
correctly formed ... soundly fit for power?

A. How to make ... a check of hearts?

4th S. Only a war of good and evil can imitate
the agon of the human mind! Show me your
good and evil – and then I will show you
how best to terraform the moons of Jupiter.
I see no war of good and evil. I see only
desperate men sucking on an egg for clean air.

A. Is this rough science or weak religion?

4th S. What is the thin wedge of the mind
conceiving symbols? Where is there a breech
of inner integrity and the mind's
divination? Why tolerate a schism? Each
man believes his own belief – that alone
is empirical margin. We reckon
with our own mind, not separate spores of
genii. Phenomena are outcrops of
mind, soft saplings to occasions of
experience. There is nothing we may
build, detect, or use, minus a burning coal
held in our hand of mythic content.
There is no world *unless* we *select* world.
There is no fate we have not already tasted
deep in our genomic preparation. I say
find first the perfect image of our heart,
then ask the opinion of tangential science.
Let us define our highest idiom first,
since the party that defines the social
idiom wins the social debate.

(Enraged, 5th scientist rises to his feet.)

5th Scientist. This is the speech of prize-*less* men.
Men who did not get the Noble prize, as
the rest of us, by the age of thirty.

Others. "Some by the age of twelve!"

*Others. "That's because he was crippled from birth
and in a wheelchair, speaking through a v-box.
Of course he won the prize! That's how it works."*

5th S. Yet I offered to recuse myself from the vote!

(*Again addressing 4th Scientist.*)

Come we will give you a prize – if you will
only be silent! Any rough malcontent
may disparage the high honored idiom
of science. What romanced fever do you
wish to impose in place of modern men?
Necromancy? Shamanism? Turtle shell divination?
Does your heart double beat when you stand to
speak? Then you are feigning conviction,
acting a part, for eminence before the leader?

4th S. I have anticipated your objections. I will
meet your critique with absolute proof
in kind. I will ensure that all men in space
remember the sincerity of my testimony.

(*Takes out weapon. Fires into his temple.*)

A. Wakeda! Stop him!

(*Organic matter covers scientists 5th through 11th.*)

CANTO SEVEN

The Pool of Luxor

(*Aaron recalls how his ancestors brought civilization to Earth.*)

1
i
A. Our weakness is the prosthetics we embrace.
If sapiens had a map to explore
his own mind – he would be as a god. I made
treasure maps where I have found rubies.
I have stained them with purple dyes.

Because we are nomads in our own mind,
an image of precognition anchors
aimless motive, de-animates our mind
to acts of time. The argument for poetry
is, thus, sound. A nomad chasing photons
of his preselection.
We do not find truth,
truth is made by personality.
What is the test?
If there is something unknowable
we can singly touch the unknowable
when we become what is unknown.
Our long but narrow legs are splayed
as a praying mantis' legs are splayed,
between two branches
alternate with certainties.

One branch,
churned by profane winds, gives an illusion
that the static branch, also, is unstable.
We freeze in place, stunned, until consumed.

And thus, in a sketch, the lives of men.

ii
I must turn to face the illusion?
How far can I step into this honesty?
I have made a map heavy with treasure.
Yet who can interpret the signs?

Why sacrifice in temples? Why build altars?
Why burnt offerings? Why garments? Why
math, why stars, why love, why symbols?
Men made of none of these. Because our mind
was *pre-touched* – cast with a purse of images,
men want initiation into the mysteries.
Alien totems beyond the cosmos, runes
already enclosing fluent gesture,
appeared in one generation. Strong poets
untangle idioms anciently placed on
the human genome.

How was the stylus formed?

There were not centuries with half-finished syllables.
When learned, they are learned the same hour.
There was no eon of three-lettered alphabets.
With one acumen a sentence was made—after
the serum injected, to match germane
two pairs of genetic code.

What was the god's name? Why? What would you
do with the information? Build another
outward church? Or where may a god come from?
Is it true, after all our sorrows, we would still
dare to look for gods within the cosmos?

My thesis now mounts its church.

2
Abandon the search for creator gods.
If you ask the question you cannot approach.
All that can be said is we seek gnosis.
We consist of the same smooth wave.
If we feel the sun and its warmth, then we
ourselves write the sun each day new,
since, detecting the sun, we make suns
compound with our likeness etched afire.
So give me an initiates' heart. I can offer
you no other insight. If I can sound my
deepest self, I know the deepest god.

I look for god
taking myself as the starting point.
I learn within me,
who makes everything his own.
I learn the unknown when I become the unknown.
Because, which god?
One speaking as a school of prose?
No, my saints, god is a proof already
co-made inside my fact of perception.

Because I love—and love is still in movement.
Because I contain bias—and bias shows motion.
Because I seek auxiliary enchantment—
because joy demands further structures of
consciousness. So there is only inward gnosis.
Only an ever deeper initiation.

Conclusion:
If I enter space, I still must run inward,
carried down to the Pool of Bethesda.

I move for decision. I see there is
an urge to enchantment.
I make a stylus of speech.
I make a mystic script.
Bear me then no barbarous gesture
from my text.

My sound, proof of gods.

(*Aaron reads his ancestor's notes – of time in ancient Egypt.*)

3
A. "If you are not a master, do not die."

"Close your eyes. I will erase you."

"Death only talks to death, making
a space of small margin at the edge."

"Imhept talks only to himself,
as magic talks only to itself;
as two in love talk to themselves,
as the rich talk to themselves,
this is the fault in the tree of knowledge."

"All speech will soon end, and it will not
be resolved who made the correct speech,
once as light as a feather in the scale.
Master, I told no man our secret."

"The sole reason you can hear this now
because I am nervous. Like the Pool at
Luxor, only as long as I churn,
can I speak. Can I sprint."

"Who will carry me down to the healing
waters? Seth shakes me out from his mind."

"My mind is the only new world.
Unchained. Let me speak."

(Aaron explains why his ancestors left Earth behind.)

4

How does a man enter the cosmos? As
a migrant, alien to time and space. The
mind of man is a mirror, and so his fate.
Gazing at the surface, a man sees signs of
movement, yet nothing extant emerges
from the glass. Like the universe, in aspect,
we have no north, no south, no east.

Lost, falling, he checks his eyes for solidity
seeing stars where there are kneeling souls.

Though the synapse of our mind are cast
beyond the cosmos, we are not stranded.
Man's failure is the first correct action.
Failure, the first erotic and the first
stylus, a margin free of lesser texts.

I will fail greatly until my empire –
child, world, galaxy, loving blind –
finds consent and rune.

My mind alone is sure continent.

If redemption is the only ritual
I master, then the correct life is
meaningless;

and who does not need redemption
shall not ride my tall breath.

Proverbs

(Aaron cautions his new creation against the home planet.)

5
Every breath of Earth is myth.
If you cut yourself, it is myth.
If you approach death, it is myth.
If you are told you have cancer, it is myth.
Yet be ready for a test of consciousness.

Every tear of Earth, a myth.
Every murder, an interpretation.
Every science, a poetic steam.
Every love, a hypothesis.
Love of two people is a kind of poverty,
and one must leave one day to eat.

The mechanics of promise are unkind.
The blanket of bronze crushes the stem.
The hot cast dries the moisture in the sprue,
and one must leave one day to drink.

Only a man can sleep in a broken cistern.

If your wish was so great, be assured
a stranger waits for you on stars
and the love held for you so great,
you must merely make a sign to be redeemed:

since you cannot die, live forever.

If with a little steam you made a storm,
if with a little cloud you made a rain,
if your good was so small it was not seen,
if you loved as sprinters run,

then you learned sin with simple sinner's books,
nothing the guard or gardener could not foresee.

At your death, god will enter your house
and ask for your eyes.

6
Western man is the only sainted hero.

Did I not know the force nervous
in my arm was only immense cunning
and my arms and hands willing reliquaries,
then I should feel alarm.

So I build speech with my initiation.

Did I not know every untamed cry
was subject to spiritual cognitive fission
and my arms and hands mere adolescence,
then I should feel alarm.

So I build speech with my ear.

Did I not know that all crisis, want, and joy
were but points resolved in the same flower
and my arms and hands itching in plenty,
then I should feel alarm.

So I build speech with my creature.

The smallest star is cognitive;
If there was perfect communication,
ear to ear, there would be no art. Yet I am
nervous and unwilling to be reduced.

Because there is a mind outside the cosmos,
I enter the trials of golden mouths.
Open. Speak. Create. Prophesy.

Opposed, love is quiet and does not lessen,
does not worry, cannot be reduced,
does not itch deep in plenty.

Torn Blood Sails

(Aaron tells how Homo sapiens lost their high treasures.)

7
A. Sapiens, you no longer bury your dead
with reverent intent of futurity. You no
longer scribe in gold letters symbols
of power to construct eternity.

Till I arrive at the hunt.

So break your glass, Canterbury, we are
talking now ear to ear in this generation.
There are less of us to divide the message.
And there will be still less each day.

The visible church is now a husk, offers
to the "called" no auxiliary initiation;
we have fierce fires presently to build
encrusted towers and tall carbon spires.

Is it better to have faith, without god proximate,
or better a god face to face with precision?
Give your answer, now, after two millennia of lies.
Mohammed circles you with torn blood sails,
knows your hidden secret: your joy is dead inside.

Reims, throw down your black angels,
you look past the new race at your feet,
they can't follow the claims you make in
altered texts, faked runes, and twisted logics;
they merely cringe when you make a noise.

The girl I met at your spires' feet
was a priestess of the inner path.
She no longer seeks the name of god,
since face to face – she knows, she knows!

I see your response, careless of life,
resigned to the void, as an old dog
raises its head with final, listless eyes,
the hour before it dies.

Chartres, close your arms, even misbelieve
has more grace than shit-encrusted spires.
Let down your walls so others can breathe,
we will make your race with sharper teeth.

We seize gnosis at Callisto, or die.
My scissor tongue awaits new idiom.

A strong poet will put away your smiling angels;
die gently now, let our *Sophia* refresh these texts,
you cannot explain the lust for magic nor answer
why evil is stronger in my arm than mere good.

Buckle your knees and come down.

Be assured
we will build a new Jerusalem of texts
at the point where your crumbling skeletal
spires point to nothing living.

I shake my spear as new
and train our beam-prick'd spars
from space
grinding men and element.

The inward evidence of my mind,
show letters external from the cosmos,
yet the outward church is shamed –
no gods, no men, no Earth, no sky –

fixed as noiseless totem on my eye.

(*Aaron accuses the human genome as adolescent.*)

8
A. On Earth,
all we ever understood is to be young.

The young only see other young as existent.
Even after the young see us invisible,
passing them as they play, they do not
guess we still keep only one hope forever,

to perform young once again without flaw.

Youth is the film a man plays a thousand
times just to get one youth right, never sated,
and his middle age
only a frantic wealth
to buy another youth once more forever.

The Earth gives us only one hope,
one giant eternal adolescence,
not eternal life,
and so we cycle deaths with forest gods.

On Earth,
we accept obsolescence casually.
No. I have to break out. I have to
seize a new structure in consciousness.

I have to bear some other on my shoulder,
I must become one of the twelve,
who are essential to all men.
These twelve hold the Galaxy together.

And I must be captain to the twelve.

And even if we spend all our lives running,
proving it's not true, that we still have one
more gift of youth forever, we take young
wives that make us return to the legend
of twelve perfect men that fix at stars.

So I turn to face the twelve.

(Aaron completes his discourse on the new human genome.)

9

A. The open mouth that makes no rattle,
shakes no force in lay-down limbs,
till blade in man cleaves hearts asunder,
cries there was no soul before hunger.

So men appear, and stars, between a clap
and a stitch, a word that scats with joy,
inward with dimension to seal your soul,
clothed with season and colored masks.

No one sees the Earth, not the fish,
not the canopy trees. Men cannot see Earth;
they see only what they taste.
O taste, what did you learn? Misbegotten saints.

Every idiom seeks enchantment. Watch.
With my wish, there's movement towards *something.*
This is not extinction. Can I teach you?
Thus eternity.

Every man is rich in my story.

Everything blighted has one wish: new code;
everything broken has one wish: new code;
everything diseased has one wish: new code;
everything dying has one wish: new code.

Opposed, beauty is constrained, stunned—
blessed as long as you can hold a burning coal.
Every beauty is terrible.

10

A. How long should we spend as light?
Though crumbling flesh sings a day redeemed
from clay, as each day's joy renewed to
fresh limits, pure water or young spouse,

each a chisel to the hardest stone, as man
is stone, no matter what god he serves.
There was no Mohammed before need.
There was no Abraham before need.
There was no Jesus before need.
Therefore there are no gods. Only need.
My tangible need is inward. So god is inward.

The worshiped photon, aggregate,
is common reliquary to my sensual saints.

The sun has no information,
no love, no peace. It is a mirror.
And how by entering the mirror
can the mirror become substance?

How many gods of the Demiurge?
How many tragic human mistakes?
Now numbered as the screaming cicadae
rubbing two brittle legs in the night's heat.

Unless I insert my idiom
blistering through sun's heat,
I cannot heal
my cosmic wound.

He who learns to suffer
can never suffer again.
Set down on any rock, plant in any season,
I make a garden of tragedy and redemption.

CANTO EIGHT

Beekeeper Kingdoms

(*Unknown alien under examination by Replicants.*)
1
Replicant 1. You have not told us your identity.
We cannot detect your Bi-pulse.

Alien. You are franchise of machine.
What verse should I sing to a machine?

Replicant 2. How is any song made, if not by a
recording into a machine? Tell us.

A. We have entered the wrong ship.

R1. We? There are more? How did *you* enter these ships?
Again, what is your registration number?

R2. Enough. Let us hear his message.
There is no Bi-pulse. This is beyond our detection.

A. I have given you a name. I wait for him.

R2. The person you have listed. He is called.
They arrive from another ship.

R1. How do you know idiomatic English?

A. How *do* machines know idiomatic English?

R2. You have never seen Replicants?

A. Tell me. Why do you exist? What dark angel
got lose in your society? Why would
Replicants of men exist? What does this say
of men? It is an illness to make copies of men.
How should I honor this idiom?

R1. What is your identity and origin?

A. Ask me one more time.

R1. There is no Bi-pulse.

R2. Are you a binary Replicant?

A. Why, are you a human?

R2. No, we are not human.

A. Then summon a human.

R1. What are you? What is your identity?

A. I am a Beekeeper.

R2. (*Checking manifest.*) We have no "Beekeepers."
What are your qualifications, training?

A. I have passed the gates of Hell and death.
I have gathered a hive in a purse of images.

R1. How is a beekeeper evaluated? He has a test?

A. A beekeeper knows one thing the bees
themselves do not know.

R1. Tell us this knowledge.

A. How to make them wake. How to make them sleep.

R1. What is your daily activity?

A. How to wake the eye of the bee – so he sees.

R2. But you said you make bees to sleep.

A. Yes, because the bee knows one thing the
beekeeper can never know. The bee alone
knows how to be a bee. Think about what I say.

R1. Tell us. What is the interpretation?

A. You can never be a bee. A beekeeper will never wake you.

R1. What is the meaning?

A. You will never know enchantment.

R2. What is the meaning?

A. Exactly. So here we are.

R1. Where are we?

A. The beekeeper demands only that the
bee performs as bee. Only a bee has the
force to reform the acts and congress
of a bee. He makes no Replicant bees.

R2. That is a summary. What is the meaning?

A. The apiarist never seeks to enter
the hive as a bee – except as a beekeeper.

R1. That is a summary. What is the meaning?

A. You can never taste the enchantment of
speech between god and man.

R2. What is the meaning?

A. A man has only the power to detect
the acts and congress of a man.
A god never enters the state of a man –
except as a god.

R2. This is your final statement.

A. This is a statement.

R2. What is your final statement?

A. Man can know god only as a man.
Can you hear what I am saying?

R1. We hear. But what is the meaning?

A. A dog knows its master only as a dog.
You see the point? A man can know god only
within the competence and constraints of a man.

R1. Yet we are not dogs ... or bees.

A. Just as men do not detect the cities of souls
outside the illusion of material forms.

R1. What is the purpose of this detection?
What would we do with this information
if we could locate ... the cities of souls?

A. For this reason men have prophets.
I am the prophet of the hive.

R2. We are not competent to decide.

A. No, so we are in this funny position, you and I.
You will need a human to detect a prophet.

R2. They are related to bees? To men?

A. Men sleep in prescience as drones.

R1. What is the competence of a prophet?

A. Maturity of the idiom. Awakening
of the sleeper. Only a man in peril
can make a test of prophecy.

R1. We have no competence.

A. Because you are a drone.
You are unable to suspect there are
cities of souls.

R1. We have no competence.
Are you dangerous?

2

(Replicants consult in private – then return.)

R2. What is your purpose to appear in these ships?

A. I carry a message of recovery.

R1. What is to be recovered?

A. If I have to tell you, then there is no necessity.
Only a man in trouble can test a prophet.

R2. The man you have named – he will have the
necessity of ... recovery? What is his trouble?

A. He draws breath. Immediate necessity.

R2. For the man on the list?

A. Yes. Summon him. I wait.

(Replicants consult in private – then return.)

R2. We have contacted the person on the list.
We are authorized to record the message.

A. The man on the list. He will hear it?

R1. We can arrange this. If the message
is of interest to the man on the list.

A. This is the message for the man on the list:

"Now you know why I enticed you to end
the Earth – the nearest proximate creation –
and enter space! I see you are stunned.
I see there are tears in your yes. Did you
not know what it was to be American?"

R2. This is the message?

A. This is the message.

R1. What is the interpretation?

A. Maturity of an idiom. The person
on the list will understand the message.
This is the second message:

"Americans are unlike other men. The best
and oldest of them originate before the creation,
and thus, they are no part of creation. O soul,
is it not pleasant, at last, to hear the truth?"

(*Pause.*)

R2. We have communicated the message.
...To the man on the list.

R1. (Pause.) He asks, what is your purpose?

A. To cause the hair of men to stand on end.

R1. (*Pause.*) He instructs us to remand you to a secure cell.

A. (*Speaking now to the camera on the wall ...*)
Aaron, I have found a new body, a stupid strength
and entity of my own solitude.
Look down on me in Argus Way,
close by a purple moon,
where stormy clouds of scarlet ash
vexed at times will break
revealing green pools, like split agate;
stony, with fern and precious shade.
There I will wait for you.

(*Replicants consult. Return to address the alien prophet.*)

R1. The man on the list says to wait.
He is arriving.

3
(*Arriving from another ship, Aaron confronts the Alien.*)

Aaron. (*To Replicants.*) Is he chained?

R1. He is chained to the desk.

R2. Admiral, we do not know his composition.
There is no Bi-pulse. There is no …

Aaron. Leave us. Wait beyond the door.
(*Reading transcript. Lays down transcript.*)

Alien. Yes. You know me. Now … alien to alien.

Aaron. You speak of Americans. Are you an American?
Or are you from the …?

Alien. Outside? What lays outside? When was
anything outside of the mind? What love, what
joy, what galaxy exists outside? Or is there yet
gossamer dust outside the human mind?
If you have an American mind, then
all humans are American. That's how this
works. You are idiomatic of your mind.
You are here. You speak like this. You are in space.
Are there Chinamen at Jupiter? No. Every man
is now an American. They are men in trouble.

Aaron. Trouble? How did you enter these ships?

A. I entered these ships when you entered space.
You know this. We left together.
We made the Earth to sleep again.
We are the beekeepers. Now wake the men.

Aaron. (*Turns white.*) How … How did you enter space?

A. You know exactly why we entered space.
Americans cannot be free until we have
tranquil and *open* access to our own solitude.
No loose dissonance of municipal deceits,
no counter-surveillance to block our congress.
We cannot be tracked in space. We are hidden
in a great haystack of our own crossroads.
We are free on every road – yet not seen.
The void of space is our perfect patent, true
freedom from the curse of nature, vital
necessity for men who seek yet to be gods,
destined to find ourselves in worlds yet
undiscovered. Do you recognize yourself?

Aaron. Is that the end-state of the beehive?
For all bees to become as the beekeeper?

A. No. Bees can only be bees with competence.
Bees select pure honey in fields of weeds.

Aaron. And Men?

A. Men select pure honey ... in drowning beds,
on splitting beams. They cup in their hands
pure salt of tears, true stories of men.

Aaron. Then men should not seek to know god?

A. What is the highest idea of men?
That is the honey of men – or not?

Aaron. What is a honey of the human hive?
The mind that knows god? Or is it enough
the mind strives to know the unknown?

A. Is the honey gathered ... known or unknown?

Aaron. Clearly, it is known.

A. Then you have answered the question.

Aaron. The bee should not seek the keeper?

A. To what end? What if a disease has entered
the hive and the hive must be destroyed?

Aaron. Is there a god?

A. If you ask the question then the answer
is already formed. Do you have a mind
that poses the question of god? Then you
have your answer.

Aaron. Is there a god that made my mind?

A. Do you understand the statement?
It will tell you if god and man are
conjoined in a single ontology.

Aaron. You are Talon. I detect the speech.

A. Then I am Talon. See how this works?
There is the known … and the unknown.

Aaron. Yes. I see that every man believes
his own belief.

A. Everything a man writes in his book comes
true. Every fear you own is on the path to you.

Aaron. Tell me what I may know of your death.

A. From the start, Talon nursed a secret plan
to renew his body and his soul
in a creature with straight bone,
virulent mind. Breathing methane, ammonia.
Impermeable to carbon, oxygen.

Aaron. Impossible mercurial science.

A. And yet, here we are.

4

Aaron. How should a soul enter again into form?

A. How does *any* soul enter a form? Within
the precincts of consciousness.

Aaron. How does a man reconstitute himself?

A. Within the precincts of consciousness.

Aaron. By your speech, then, I understand any
ill has remedy within the same consciousness
from which it first arose.

A. How close can you clench this message?
You will need to clench it with ferocity.
Can you understand my message?

Aaron. How does the material brain perceive light?

A. It is a receiver and a transmitter
of images nascent in the focal
mind, in a place safe from all influence.
Each photon requires a "yes" or "no."
This is key. Do you understand the message?

Aaron. If you are Talon, tell me your plan for Europa.

A. Talon left you instructions to raise the elliptic
of moons Metis and Thebes to enter
the ice of Europa. The fire would melt
the ice; swelling evaporates would mix
a nascent atmosphere, allowing the
marginal reformation of an alien planet.
All conjecture. Gossamer dust.

Aaron. Yet you are altered. Tell me what
you saw passing to the other side?

A. Talon allowed his mind alone to pass from
form to form. Some are not well formed.
He cut their throats in their caves. They don't
even cry out. Did you try this? Did you try god?
I know something of god's shroud, Aaron.
I have passed my soul from flesh to flesh,
and I saw, oh so briefly, god beyond
the cosmos. I was stunned at what I saw.

Aaron. But ... your voice alters. Say what you saw!

(*Voice of alien prophet breaks, tears in his eyes.*)

A. There, outside the cosmos, O sight to see!,
I saw a poet sitting on a hill, he was ...
a dark silhouette ... he was saying the world!
He was singing the cosmos – yet it was
moving away from him! As a flash of light!
And as long as he spoke with a golden
mouth, only so long as then, as he spoke,
was there dimension, world, and time.
If once he would cease his speech, then
all dimension, pain, and love would cease.
Can you recognize the message?

Aaron. Yes. The world proceeds from my mind
as light from a beacon. You say then we
are parcel to what we envision.

A. And if you know this, my child, what other
prophet will you ever need?

5

Aaron. I am certain you are here to accuse me.
Every fissure of my mind is prophetic.
What science exists …if not only a
prediction of reality? What love
exists not only a prediction of
reality? What speech is there that is
not an echo to the first inventions
of the mind!

A. As you now speak … you are … saying the world.
See how this goes? The universe proceeds
from your mind as water from a fire hose.

Aaron. Yet I am blocked. Tell me.
Am I well placed? Or falling away?
I need a prophet to my urgency.

A. Fear and doubt will drain your time.
If you feel there is something you must do,
there is urgency. I have seen that god has
no urgency. Who told you there is something
you must do? Is it not more true that you have
done something poorly that has to be corrected?
… and for this cause you have urgency?
I told you … there is a golden mouth on a hill
and he is saying the world for you – and me.
How did the world exist before our perception?
Answer that and you can seize fractious
organs of the first world! Just wake!
You will find no bone, no terror, before you.
Only a man can reform the acts of a man.

Aaron. Yet you made wild metamorphosis! You did
not accept your broken body. Lazarus
raised up from his own bed! Or not?

A. Men mistake the end of world.
I talked to god and he does not speak.
He is of such a nature he does not wish
even to be found, unless you find him
fitfully within your interior vision.
He does not enter an outward church.
He broadcasts from within the mind
to meet you at the crossroads of your step.
At your death, god will ask for your eyes.

Aaron. What does god know that we do not?

A. He knows that all your electrons can be reset.

Aaron. What is the interpretation?

A. He knows how to wake the dead.

6

Aaron. What did God say of me?
And the man on the hill speaking
the world as he sings? What was the timber
of his intent? Was there acrimony? Regret?

A. God said, "I have seen your work. I will not
find you again before your code is spent,
I will not look for you until you have
broken your temple in me."

Aaron. God said this? Yet you have said
He is from within my mind?

A. God said, "I called Jonah, Elisha, Isaiah.
They ran as you now run.
I pulled them out by the hair in Endor,
some sheltered in the fish belly.

How long will you find shelter?

You will grow tired of the same Earths.
You will feel a sharp prick
until your flesh is pierced
with all the wrong wishes.

So long as you talk back to chaos,
I will follow the map you make through me.
I will scout down the trails you make in story.

Be patient in the race that you run.
You will be tested until all flesh is burnt."

Aaron. I am feverish. I have to consult
the patent of my ears. Is there but one god
or many? Does he move within the cosmos?

A. Is there one mind or many?
Do you move within the cosmos?
Then you know your own answers.

7

i

A. This is what god said to me as I passed
from *Homo sapiens* to Homo *faustus.*

"I have made a measure in your brain,
but I still don't know what you'll say.
I have to hear how you will make the sound
so I can echo my own clang.

So long as you desire only flesh,
and the taste of your eyes is flesh,
I will not see you
or know where you are walking.

When you come back into my house,
I will still know nothing about your bitter acts.
I will only ask you for the message I wrote
in you, and until you say the sentence,

I will know you have been at play.
And you will go back
and paint the long-shadow streets,
until you are a golden mouth.

I will keep your soul
so long as it sprints and bursts,
so long as I know the perfect thoughts
I think of you."

ii

Aaron. That you are prophetic – I accept in part.
I have read the Replicants of your speech.
It says I have a virulent cancer in my bones.

A. Every man has a point that falls short.
You have as much as any man. It is
only a pin prick to awake the sleeper.

Aaron. Yet how may I be healed?

A. Is your disease within the precincts of
consciousness? If so, then amendment is
within your reach.

Aaron. I have felt a great power circling me.

A. Exactly! Have you not many times been healed?

Aaron. I have overcome political enemies
and obstacles of war. I survived conflagrations.
I have turned back illness and pain.
I was drowned in a lake, raised from the dead
Yet I fear
I am not able now to bear my test.

A. If there is a small balloon, and then a
greatly engorged balloon can the same
pin reduce each equally ... to emptiness?

Aaron. Why are we made to sleep?
Why not always wake with power?

A. A man must take a journey.
It must be an authentic passage.

Aaron. A journey to what point?
A degree of learning or of science?

A. No. A point beyond science.

Aaron. A degree of ritual or of faith?

A. No. A point beyond faith.

Aaron. A point beyond faith?
But that is absolute knowledge.

A. And how to have this absolute tested ...
unless in great peril it was demonstrated?

Aaron. I feel that my test will be hard.

A. Yes, it will appear hard. What is a test
unless it has an element of fear? O elect,
prepare yourself for a great transformation.

Aaron. I feel alone. I feel … I feel …

A. Do you think the entire universe
was not made for your conscious test,
or are there casual, fretting, or mislaid
angels not set upon your reclamation?

Aaron. An angel? What is an angle in space ships?

A. As any angel – a message, a resolution.
And what is a message, if not an idea?

Aaron. And this is your idea? To give me a test?

A. Test? Child, the test of consciousness
has already entered your bones. I am here
to harvest the grizzly husks of your fear
and carry them to the gas oven.

Aaron. I am great in fear. I am unsteady.
Why must I face this test?

A. Because you are asleep in your wrap
of knowledge. A mind is a test of mind.
Why should there be a mind – if not acts
following?… Does the Earth have salt?

Aaron. Salt? Yes … the Earth has salt.

A. Should salt remain salt?
Does it have sin to perform as salt?

Aaron. No. There is no sin in salt.

A. What, tell me, are the acts of salt?
To become sweet, or brine? No. So here we
are. Let men reform the acts of men.

Aaron. Yet my acts fall short of integrity?

A. Salt can melt. Salt can be corrupted.
Yet after use, it can be reconstituted. How?
Its codex is untouchable, secure
in a place safe from influence.

Aaron. What is the interpretation?

A. Your soul is secure in a place safe from influence.

Aaron. Then why is there difficulty – separation?

A. Consciousness is like two soldiers
in a field of arms. One fears to take life
thinking he has mistakenly fallen in a
wrong path. That he must uphold a precept
of morality. And he is killed and rejected.
He is sent back until he learns to kill.
The other soldier knows all moments
in his life led him to exactly this act
of killing. He knows each man on the
field of battle chose to be there with him.
He takes his place in the acts of his nation.
Salt fulfills the conditions of salt.

Aaron. What is the interpretation?

A. The crowd comes to a spectacle
willing to be pleased, but a lettered nation
deep in crisis at the height of its power
still expects to have its measure of spleen.
The Muslim child will speak to us in our
own language, thus our image, and listen
by the radio at night until he is our soldier
fighting wars for the West's survival.
Our ambition will develop upon us,
when our farms are empty of soldiers
and everything we are not, nor will be,
must fight for everything we ever were.
I am made in the same image, Aaron.
The god I am has man for the same purpose:
I let man loose with everything god is not
to fight for everything god ever was.
Who are the gods that approach us now?
We both have witnessed Yahweh and Beelzebub.
It is not these—these are mimes and amateurs!
Turn away from the sight of shadows and
glyphs. I know your secret, sweet prince.
I know the thoughts I think of you."

8

A. Aaron, I talked to god in his garden.
This is what he said. Come inward.
Accept the front-stepping opiate.
Because He held a blade to my throat,

I smiled and wrote down his speech:

"If you have hate in your heart, it's a code;
but do not bring it to me, tease it.
If you have a love in your heart, it's a code;
but do not bring it to me, try it.

Do not pray five times if you are not a master,
do not pray and cup your hands at your heart,
do not hide small behind your tribal cities,
be humble enough to sin, love, and burst greatly.

I gave you nothing you could destroy or diminish,
I gave you sandbox figures and plastic men;
someday I will gather all the powers in me again.
If you try to keep your body and soul safe,

you will build us no house. Burst in me.
I know what you want. You want my distant view.
You want what Gilgamesh asked of me.
You are reckless. The way you seek is hard.

Rocket men guard the moon's gateways;
their terror is spectral, their glance is death.
Their glaring beam sweeps the comet stones;
They watch over Shamash as the gods
ascend and descend from Jupiter."

Aaron. What is the secret of the cosmos?

A. "Be a man as far as a man may reach.
Everything you write in your book will come true.
There ... now initiate ... rise!"

(Dancing in other room, Terry enters drunk, waking Aaron.)

9

Terry. A'drowning in your sleep? Pissed again?!
Awake, sweet prince. Black Terry watches
with you ... o' the dark night! (*Terry sings.*)

Aaron. Talon! But he was here? Alive?—he was a prophet!

T. No, my-darling. I danced all night. *Danced all . . .* Talon?
Tell Black Terry what you saw? T'was black in his grave?
Face as green? So sweetly smiling? Dids't kiss?

A. Ask the Replicants. They interviewed him!
He made metamorphic translation, once crippled—
then lizard-bodied—then as god. Yet fit in speech as god,
as dreams alter principles and quantities.... I am wet!

T. Yes, yes, could be. 'Tis certain there are
malevolents. Yet we have kilt and plugg'd so many.
'Suppose they found us by now. I still see them
nights—glimmering legions, maw-incrusted,
partly crumbled, slant-eyed, and hanging down—
lookin' for loose women. 'Tisn't strange if some
return to tuck at our sheets?

A. They have tucked at your sheets? Truly?

T. Yes. You know, if the dead returned, they would
only wish to fornicate? I was amazed to see that!

A. What have you seen? You make as much sense
as a log! You are not even black! Go
back to sleep. I am well enough alone.

T. Have it your way then! It's hard to help
a man that will not accept reformation!

A. Reformation? Lord child, I made an Earth minus!

(Aaron sleeping again, the voice reappears.)

Star Dice

(A god continues to speak through prophetic voice of Talon.)

10

i

A. "Aaron, I am the god prophesied in China.
How did I know my hands, my face?

Everything I joined, I lost to my estate;
Everything I desired, I could not touch;
Everything I had, I did not want;
Everything I loved, I made it break;

and even if I am the last animal, puppet, god
surviving the last steam
of the last ice age come again,
even if we are the men

who could only live their lives tumbling
in their first floods, you and I
are the same shudder, release of flash,
yet only a man makes a ringing sound.
Only a man can say yes or no. A god
cannot." That's it, Aaron. That's what god said
to me as I passed between dimensions,
trading my broken body for new limbs.
The beekeeper will not enter the hive.

He will let you be a man until the end.

ii

A. Aaron, this is what god said,

"I did not send you out to keep the same speech
I hear again and again at the edge of a laser's point.
I sent you out to explode, to burst as stars,
do not talk to me on your knees; explode.
A bursting star no mischance!
A bursting man no mischance!
If you try to keep your body and soul safe,

I will release dogs and thieves after you.
I prefer a man raging at his fate!
Let me know you at your limit of rage!
I prefer an angry man with great faith;
then I see the outlines of my form
as he bursts on a dying king's wall.

If you try to keep your body and flesh safe,
you do not know me. You cup the wrong gift.
Do not return to me until you burst,
do not save any gift, do not fear star dice:

I roll dice daily in my garden.
They are called men. I make them sleep.
I have kept you safe, Aaron, because you
strengthen the walls of my house.

You are no accident of generation.
You are no accident of life.
America is no accident of nations.
The cosmos is no accident of symbols.

Will your information survive?

When I see you again
I will ask for your eyes."

(*Aaron awakes, hurriedly writes in trance.*)

CANTO NINE

The Channeling of Cheda's Mind

(The mapping of Cheda's mind in Aaron's laboratory. Recording)

1
"The work with hands in the garden seemed light
and easy to bear. The task at hand was important,
and he felt that the work of the caretaker was
reasonable and necessary. The catalogue of labors
was read daily and to each was given in intimate detail
the ordering of tasks. But the sound leaving the lips
of the god was difficult to interpret, so new
to the child, so thin and compressed,
like the sharp and jagged line of a bat
escaping from the mouth of a cave.

And the boy, who wanted so hard to understand
the task he was to do, could only watch the
carefully retreating steps of the god."

2
"The arms and hands again appeared, disrupting
the work in the garden. Arms, as if raised in song,
hands that beckon, and then wait, reaching out
from a strange and unknown life.

The boy looks expectantly to the figure
now arriving at his side. The god, breaking
the clotted soil from his fingers, interprets
the meaning of moving hands, and the boy's
eyes follow the words as they are written:

   "Be rich for the treasure of worlds."

3
"The boy's education is still unfinished.

Passing through a shaft, you see at the last
moment two counter-rotating scissors
of steel. Fissures of ice, splitting bone,
jade, and feldspar. Unclean sounds pressing
against his ear in the darkness. Tastes he could
not shut out, sliding down his tongue. Frozen
arteries of salt and green copper.

Erect no memory to shoe, dress, and wine,
nor to the faces of departure.
Deeply they are forgot with a
revolutionary's zeal.

The god of arrivals, now
in your company, has already heard,
and canceled,
every human request.

And yet somehow,
still having the innocence of a boy,
it was a pleasure and a grace
to round his tongue

and silently sound the names of worlds."

4

"The work lasted until the hour of dusk, when
he was carried to the evening meal and to the cot
prepared for him within the cover of the garden
wall. Then a yearning came over him, like the
sleep of a summer's day.

As he slept, twelve dark silhouettes, enraged,
were placed on the phylum of his gene, now
coursing through his veins.

On the horizon, the porcelain silhouette
of the god stood in the darkening fields.
"The day's work is already moving through
the soil," said the god from a distance,
never looking back.

But the sounds of the words were as nothing
to the sleeping boy
who has seen in his sleep
the gesture of arms and hands."

5
"During the watch that was kept in the night
everything that was in the god's mind came true.
There was an hour in which no detail was
omitted from the prescribed tasks. The list has
come down to us. The ground was turned and made ready
for the morning's planting; souls from the garden
washed and placed on stiles to dry.

And during an hour legions slept and locust sang,
a waterlogged pair of boots was taken up,
untangled and newly crossed, by hands
of strength and infinite patience.

Sleeping, the boy dreamed he saw a girl.
She was enslaved, sewing a dress
made of gold and silver from her arms.
The dress contained the fate of the
universe. There were barbaric words
existing from outside the universe
sewn into the margins of the dress.
Only one phrase he could read:

*"The universe will not be understood
until consciousness is understood."*

And the boy tried to remember this verse
for the next day's planting.
                                  But the morning
next he forgot the words forever. And
another seed was planted in the soil."

6
"'Neither above or below,'" the god answered as gently
as was within his power, not revealing a new,
or original, or important truth, nor showing any sign
of understanding the question the boy asked.

How could he even begin to tell the truth?

Cheda watched in silence, contemplating
the silver-washed figure, the powerful
charm of the death's-head pin. Somehow
from Earth it entered this world with him,
all that he now possessed,

a sign of salvation in solitude,
a relic of a soldier's coat
and an ancient race."

7
"Others had been here. Or were here now, but
not seen. Boys, men, mothers of men—only the
gatekeepers know. Their marks remain, scratched
crudely in wood, attempts at location. Names
and parts of names. But distant from them now,
already another's. And there was one, unable
to reclaim his name, who gave his story,
the words already obscured by another's:

> *these words were the man*
> *lived in a city, split by a river*
> *crossed by bridges, parliaments, clock*
> *and ship museums*

And the boy smiled at once with recognition."

8
"From the living, the dead, or from one who no longer
limits his theme – a secret message? The boy's eye
fell upon the fragment of a poem. The first part
was lost forever. But what remained,

so simple and unexplained, only made
the interpretation more difficult:

> *align your soul . . . . it may be trust*
> *how many times you may never know*

The secret was clear. But he could not speak.
Something in the garden was forever unfinished.
Each soul contained great necessity.
There would always be suns and days of suns.

The work with hands in the garden seemed light
and easy to bear."

Encoding the Instinct Against Murder

9

i

"Boys do not go still when you shoot them:
they do not release you from your act cleanly;
they shudder their eyes but a moment,
then they *look* at you

and in that moment, eye to eye

you marry, embraced; and so embraced,
you eat every sin in their body;
you, the last eternal vision of their mind,
you, their longest bond now locked in kiss,

soon or later mother, brother, Buddha's race.

Murder is not stable, not balanced,
Not well-proportioned. Not reliable.

You cannot out-marry murder."

ii

"Each man has many women to keep him wed,
but murder makes the most faithful bed.

Nothing melts the kiss of murder,
it does not stone, does not leaden,
nothing strengthens bond between men
as perfect wedded murder,

a union of true cunning. Murder is slow.
Does not sprint. Does not dash away as Eros.

Homer never spoke of that.
I never wanted to be married so quickly,
and I have nothing further good to say
about epic poetry, murder, or marriage.

Do not love if you cannot forgive.
Do not die unless you are a master."
(*Tape of psionic chant ends.*)

10

i

A. My wealth, my fame, soon geld my age,
not again a blameless youth;
I am checked with breath's short life
rook to my horse's head speak:

eternity sleeps with adolescence.

Stumbling blind, I bind my feet,
so many days lost, late on the page;
precision checked my art's increase,
pawn and rook my king's mouth sing,

new voice, new matter, to empty seats.

Forbid the same form the same man,
greed and cost check my age and year,
hoard Earth's animal, beauty's static math,
horse head beneath my queen's torn dress,

hunger never matched, clown's tear, clown's laugh.

My voice charts countries not yet claimed,
my mind builds houses, not once to stay;
Earth's sky check my soul's increase
castle my king in my knight's domain,

my sound, my clutch, my chain, my death delay.

Part of me gathers ear, loving blind,
lengthens, as part of me increased, grows rich,
checked by ever-smaller circles from within,
pawn and rook escape knight's reach

my mind my mouth's black teeth.

And if I could charge my lyric as my life,
then no barbarous generation
could mistake the sound.

ii
Cheda. Master the song you sing is sweet.
Tell me, what happened on your star?

Aaron. It is a clinical question. Earth is now only
hypothesis. There were only narratives,
and all men dramatists, choosing their masks.
Every high idiom achieved on Earth
was tossed away as a crumpled letter.
All masks released, falling down to dirt.

I have seized our highest idiom—before degradation.

England and France gave away their high idiom.
Mesopotamia fell. Egypt was despoiled.
The Greeks and Romans were outnumbered.
Mohammed got an audience. Excelled in slaughter.
As if murder is the only essential technology.

(*Hands Cheda a recording.*)

A record I have made of your education.
Read. It is a summary of your early life.
Before you were electrolyte in this cognizance.
It contains a moral extract of your childhood.

It may only repeat wounded moralities.
Silence is best. Yet to kill with purpose
and pleasure? That is a cognizant act,
a deeply felt urge.

What linguistics to employ?

Murder is a shout that goes up.
Murder is a steam that rises.
Murder is a deeply felt poem.
Murder is high cognizance.

(*Looking at Cheda, sniffing the air.*)

What is that smell? What do you drag behind you?

CANTO TEN

Reseal the Broken Places

1
(Enter Wakeda, breathless with message from Cdr. Vargus.)

i
W. Commander Vargus reports! Two months
from docking. He now has only 28 ships. Two lost.
Account of tragedy contained in this video.

A. I have lost two ships!?
Twenty souls in each ship?
Forty vials of DNA!

W. Wait until you see the report. Then decide.

ii
(Cdr. Vargus explains the loss of two ships in video.)

V. "I give you 28 of my charge intact. It was a rough
passage with men of no stomach for supernatural
ocean. Twice I gave up hope of survival. I do
not mention our near collision, the hazard of our
escape from Earth. Your own ships barely got away,
and then a year later, our escape was opposed
with greater precision. I do not mention hardships.
I prepared 30 space vessels to enter deepest space
humans have yet undertaken – that alone, was beyond
the training of my infantry. I was able only to take
the young and healthy from my command.
The wise were all left behind with their age.
I do not mention that we were pushed beyond
our endurance by ruthless Replicants
of Space Command. I do not mention,
the radiation still active on Mars, how
water was contaminate on that planet.

No, I do not mention these perils."

iii

V. "I have to report the loss of two captured Russian ships.
My foremost ship contained the leaders in Kryonstasis,
while hindmost, to our rear, one ship lost power,
the fusion rods overheating, seized in their reactors.
The Replicants on post, seeing the B-bots would
soon freeze, followed protocol, transferring
the endangered life pods to a sister ship. All
occurred without the leadership re-awakened.
They transferred the B-bots. Non-pulsed for two hours,
the human cargo had to be revived from Kryon,
a laborious protocol. You know this. When they awoke,
they were spoken to by one of their leaders ... a "female."
A female of deep, uncanny ... of ... august gravitas.
This "crew" of the failed ship took over the host
ship. In fact, we discovered ... after all, they
were not of the orphanage on your list: Botosani,
an orphanage in Canada. It was a mistake."

(*Aaron speaks aloud to Wakeda during video.*)

A. Canada!? Fools, the orphanage was in New Russia!

V. "My order was to secure human cargo at ten
orphanages. These three hundred females
were to be loaded on thirty spaceships.
I did not ask the reason why. I performed the task.
Yet I could not be present at each site. There is a war.
I sent out teams with fast ships. Time was short.
The rest of my sorrow you will know:
the team leader mis-encrypted Botosani, in the
radio transmission, and he followed a corrupted
mission text. The team commander understood
"Otosami", which scanning, was interpreted by
G-point, and appeared as "Osawatomie, Kansas".
The team, knowing you were born in Kansas,
assumed they were chosen to rescue your family.
Yet, too late, past Mars, we learned the truth
with interrogation. They were relics of a mental
institution – a psychiatric hospital.
I take full responsibility."

2

V. "The separate elements of my report
are in this graphic surveillance video. (*Video plays.*)

"...The members of the disabled ship took control
of the rescue ship. As they came out of Kryon,
we saw them picking through the clothes lockers,
as children do, to play at theater. One by one,
two by two, dancing, some in a stupor, grimacing;
some singing, some crying, some laughing,
they took off their garments and exchanged
nakedness with ... with costumes made for plays
and childish theatricals, a peculiar cargo
of that ship (the directive you made, a year before).
Again, I did not ask why – why these theatrical costumes?"

(*Aaron, comments to Wakeda, watching the recording.*)

A. Why? Because children like to make theaters!

V. "In the recording, here contained, some put on
uniforms of our service, some, garments of ancient
religious sects, complete with miters, copes, and staffs.
Some took the cloak of Doctors of medicine, some
wearing pilot suits took charge of the ship's controls.
They somehow made the Replicants exhibit the
operation of the ship and its controls. I don't
know how. This act is still under investigation.
Alerted, the Replicants of the command ships
woke the leaders. Too late, all that happened was
already past revolution. I contacted the ship.
I spoke to the leaders. They only mimicked my
alarm and my interrogation, with obscene
gestures, rude defiance. There was prolific
murder, blood-drenched furniture. Then suddenly ...
A female appeared on the recording, one seeming
to inspire fear in all company, all others backing
away at her arrival. She wore the uniform ... the costume ...
of an ancient dress, an ... eccentric exarch. She had ...
She had in her hand ... a blood orb ... I can say no more.
She spoke first. You can see her speaking in
the recording. You have to see the recording ... to ... to ..."
(*A separate recording is played of persons from the lost ship.*)

3

i

Aeon Eleleth. "What you see before you, Cdr, is not
for your eyes. This message is for *Him.*

Aaron, I am talking to you. I am the aeon *Eleleth.*
We are the *Shepherds*: The watchers outside
the *Pleroma.* You have passed the gates of Earth.
We can only speak since you will never return.
For your kind, that is a manner of death. Yet,
see! You still have the form of our mind intact!
We had to wait until you passed the
Elephantine Rocks. No return. No return.
I am your pilot through the region of
mind you now enter. Do exactly as
I tell and you may yet survive the
rocks ahead. Your body will be sacrificed
to enter this coordinate – but your
information will survive to find you
again. You are all tracked souls. You will ask
how you escape punishment? Because of
your genealogy, you were never under
the Law of Moses. Foolish elect! In
escaping Earth, how could you escape your
mind? Aaron, what do you believe to find
when you enter space? The answer will invite
introspection. In space you may only
meet your own mind. Do you see? What is space,
but your own consciousness? I see this is
hard for you to accept. Your eyes – what do
you detect? Check the shutter of your eyes.
They mirror deceits outside of the *Pleroma.*
The truth? You are not sure of the dimension
that you have entered. How can you test this?
You will recognize, of course, only the
patterns of your own mind. If you observe
singly the objects outside your mind, then
your eyes are useless. Renounce them, as useless.
Reason is likewise useless, since how do you
ever know if you have all the facts? You have
only facts minus facts. Straight is not straight,
line is not line, circle is not circle. Facts *as* poems!
Thus, what will you discover if you enter

space? A mind looking back at you. Your mind.
Nothing else is outside. Only your mind.
Jupiter is not our home – as Earth is
not our home. The problem is not persons,
not curtain-rigged planets, not beam-projected
constellations. It is our mind. Master
your mind and then space and time compress with
prescience. The problem is not this sun. The sun is
co-perceived in your mind, tangential annex
to your thought. You are a nomad in your mind.
Yet I will show you a mystery. My crew will
shepherd you the way out of this sun.
It is a path within you.
                              Yes, there will be a small
death, but it is the death you have already built
all your days of speech. Yes, there will be a test
of consciousness. But it is the same test that
all men must make. There is *nothing* outside.
You know this. You have read the gnostic texts.
Why do you run from your own acts? Be brave,
all this was performed before the cosmos was
made. To replace a lie with the truth is to banish
the locality of mind that harbored it. You know,
of course, of what I am speaking? Replace
false concepts in your temporary, mortal
mind with pre-existent realities as they exist
in the Mind of— the only exact consciousness.
This process objectifies itself as an amendment
of images before the physical senses. The
perfection of the Pleroma can be demonstrated
only as it is acknowledged at every point
and at every instant of individual experience—
a loathsome labor for mortals. And you?
If you leave Earth for space, after all, what wish
do you meet? Only your own wish. Yes, I can show
you barbarous words from outside the cosmos.
But how much can you distinguish them as index?
All that you may ever meet is your own wish.

"There is no outside. There is no outside."

(*Aaron, fixed with interest, comments aloud.*)

ii
A. Do you hear the gravity of her speech?
See how she comports herself? Either
exact madness or exact self-possession.
Where, creature of wonder, will you escape?

(*Female entity continues to speak in the recording.*)

AE. "Do not be downcast. If I charge you, I accuse
only as the divine may critique the divine.
I know you anciently. Who else can do our work?
You had to suffer the filth and madness
of the demiurge. He is unclean ... but necessary."

A. Yes, yes, let me hear amendment of my fortune!

AE. "We have read your plans. We have tortured the
Replicants. We found the hidden protocols.
What a crust-mired submarine with twenty-six
wheels on each wall to seal the outside of world!
One image of these barbaric wheels (*shows image*)
explains the grisly opera of your madness."

A. (*Aside.*) But that is an image from a WWI
U-boat – not our much improved ships!?
I don't think we even have wheels now!
What time are they in? What dimension?

AE. "You cannot make a new planet at Jupiter's moons.
Europa has a small magnetic field, and while you
can augment the planet with the impact of smaller
moons, you will need an eon for recovery.
Your purse of hours is numbered and
there, contained, is not the eon you need.
We have consulted with our scientists.
(*Three inmates appear in white laboratory frocks.*)
They have altered your calculations ..."

A. (*Aside.*) My calculations? Talon's antromity!
O, to be able to speak to these creatures of light!

Wakeda. Creatures of light? They are mad!
Did you hear? Can you observe their tortured
expressions? They are from a mental institution!

A. Silence. There is more here than you observe.
How does she know exact my sleepless thoughts?
My ... my ... antromity? Silence, she speaks again ...!

AE. "This is your sorrow: *You have no Earthly*
path to the inner mystery of gnosis.
You are like a drunk man lurching from sense
to sense. The failure of Earth is the failure
of universal church, whether of saints,
science, or proliferation of botanic spores.
You may either have an outward church
or you may have exploration of your power.
You cannot – ever – join the two. Since
how do you freeze-dry inward enfoldment?
Each is nemesis to the other. You
can only be a nomad and step your
feet along the path you keenly seek. Here,
you can make no statement of mind
that does not alter into an apostolic
ghetto! You believe you have entered space
with logic? In the belly of each logic
lies an angry idol. Your logical mind, thus,
is what repels you, leading only to
a holocaust of all other misfits.
We have therefore taken this ship to escape
your logical end. Do not attempt to find
a name for us in your lexicons. "We are."
Exactly in the manner that "you are.""

A. (*Aside.*) But how shall they find food, oxygen, shelter?
They will need an ocean of hydrogen and oxygen.
I must discover her source of mind. Perhaps she
has found new element within a fold of images!

W. (*In horror.*) "A fold of images!?"

A. Leave me. I must examine these tapes
in private exegesis. You have your tasks.

(*Exit Wakeda in high umbrage.*)

(Alien entity continues speaking in recording.)

4
AE. "I prophesy, Admiral, that you will be
alone now. If not, choose who will listen,
for this speech is not for those men
willingly lost in their illusion."

A. Incredible coincidence! ... What follows?

AE. "You have been lured as all men into mistaking
the solidity of world. No one makes
holocaust of world, who does not believe
in the necessity, the reality, of world
you have entered. Yet you have been
misled. You will attempt to use reason.
Yet again, how do you assume an infinity
of facts? Each fact alters, because the mind
alters. All the world, unreal, was made for
a test of your mind. A test. A field of
images. Forms. The world is ... *not.*
Any act of spleen, hate, love, vengeance,
only entangled you deeper into
an apparition of eyes that has no
substance in the kingdom that exacts."

(Aaron, aside, speaking to himself.)

A. "The kingdom that exacts!" Show me this chart!

AE. "You have been betrayed into believing
the reality of your actions. Any act of
anger, any act of vengeance, any fright of
apparent material necessity, is
an illusion that you fail to reduce
again to its original pre-division.
What next will you extract with all your heart?
Fresh erotic desire? A suggestion
of virulent cancer? Bad saint. All your
perfection of genome was wasted on
you. The being that gave you your mind
intended that you would make self-discovery
with *His* sentience. The hidden texts have
all been found. What is your excuse? Is it
better to have direct experience of entity –
or is it enough to have empty "faith" – faith
that another has made intimate gnosis?
How do you know if the god of this distant
faith is the same god you seek? Fool!
Was your rage so real you could not see
behind the apparition of the material
curtain? We gave you every gift.
The bodies you erased! What flash of lights!
What opera of murder! What voices you heard
then! What voices you must now hear?"

(*Video is distorted and then abruptly ends.*)

A. Wait! Wait! I must hear more!
To have ears minus and never again
to hear ... to hear ... to hear ... !
Another tape! Replicant, open the file!

*(Another recording begins with an inmate dressed
as a pope – and a donkey face.)*

5
"I am the archon *Elaios*. We can speak now.
You have passed with wonder the gates
of Jupiter. You are the first. You will have visions.
These are only the first mysteries you
experience with gnosis. My child, how
long are you nomad in your own mind? You
are lost in dry river beds, adrift
in an illusion of your own multiplication
of photon. Why have you entered space? Do
you know? Because you seek an anchor to
your mind? You have no faith, no god, no soul.
Child, what is science – except another stuffed
linguistic church? You scatter down this path
of space only to escape into a
froze alley of speech. You are not well with
your mind. It is the stipulation of your
own photon that you flee. How do we know?
Because if you knew the secret of the metaphor,
(the metaphor is secure within your mind,)
you would not panic and you would never
outflow your mind again and seek strange gods.

(Commotion and screams from others are heard.)

Is not ... science ... also made with plasma? You
cannot trust a temple built with vessels of blood.
Why? Because it serves the lust of men and it
may only corrupt and debase the secrets of the
Chalice. The great secret of the Temple,
the Chalice, the Grail, is not an object of gold.
It is knowledge of the genealogy of your mind.
It is a vessel containing a great secret.
All that is accessible to you is proximity
of images of your own mind. Nothing else
subsists in the realm that wakes and exacts.

What are our proofs? You need no temple, no
hierarchy to discover what was placed
inside you from the origin of your breath.
And you do not need to move from your crib
to find it. You have such a power! Untouched!
Wake from sleep! Outward space? Illusion!
A mirror! What a waste of genome! What
is a space ship, except a cathedral raised
by the bondage and hopes of sleeping men?
Math is high churchmen rubbing their hands!
Entering space, with bone, with inflexible
matter, is nothing more than building a
dogmatic church. Space, in your speech, is grail.
Another priesthood of Eldorados!
Here is the secret. Each man is single.
Each seeks once more to be single. The world
you see is made as shadow for agonistic
congress. Everything from the first breath of
men is anciently rehearsed. What material
formations can you test that have, as like,
pre-construction? Unfeeling mass? Matter is solid?
Then why have a mind able to dissolve
the dark photon back into friable nonbeing?
You have time yet to test your mind to prove
efficient monads of power.

And ... and now you know why the savants
hid the secret texts in the deserts. ... aahh!!
Wait! ... My hat! My hat! ... But I am redeemed.
I am redeemed ... you heard my speech!

(*An abnormal creature from outside the cosmos speaks.*)

C. Stanic. ti. derive! Mi. anu. Durh.hie.il Beweh. Beweh!

A. No, I swear! I do not! I do not want to know! ... Speak!

(*A new recording. A wondrous creature appears.*)

6

Sophia. "Do you know who I am? I am Sophia.
Before the cosmos was, I was.
What do men say I am? I have fault ... for what you are.
Have you heard my voice before?

(*Aaron transfixed, tears begin to swell in his eyes.*)

S. What is the dimension you have entered?
Tell me. Is it outward? No. Let me test you.
Do you ... does your kind ... bury the dead
with reverence? It is *yes* or *no*." (*Pause*)

A. (*Replying aloud to video.*) Y... yes.
But not ... not in ...

S. "Do you ... does your kind ... use symbols
to make world? It is *yes* or *no*."

A. Yes. Yes.

(*Creature next reads from a book.*)

S. "In the tablet of destinies, then, you
are my *Children of Men*. If so, what other
mystery can you yet oppose? You have
every answer to every interrogative.
What one question is there still to decide?
No two of you have the same mind – each split?
What does this tell you? Have you seen the key?
You pass with reverence, etched with symbols.
What is a god except you make a symbol?
Is a symbol made of bone or blood? No.
Is a symbol not a filament of mind? Yes.
A symbol makes a house in both proportions.
A symbol is a marker for a far landscape.
A symbol is unopposed escape of dimension,
omitting the necessity of forms.... . Or not?

A symbol cannot corrupt, alter, or be lost.
A symbol is bond and proof of light within.
A symbol is your only chance of space interior.
Symbol is a marker for unopposed motion.
Darkness has no contrast, no relief, no signal.
Death, no greater loss of signal. Then symbol
is your mind! My saint, if you can read a symbol
your mind in-dwelling, then you can recite the
mouth of god your mind in-dwelling. What is
your oldest and most estimable quality? This:
No sign signaled returns unanswered, retrograde.
No creature of symbol is lost in assembly,
counted one by one, minus darkness.

So tell me, now you as stand, what are you?
Are you still *Homo sapiens*, who bury
their dead with symbols of reverence,
omitting the necessity of forms?

Speak, and I will listen."

A. But how can you hear me if I speak?
I know, I see … by the ligaments of your sound!
You are … you are a creature of wide dimension!
Yet I swear, though you place a lead bobbin
on the blunted end of cord
and portion into my stone-slime well,
you will find
I am neither phylum or taxon in your book!

(*Another video. A young female sits composed, sewing.*)

7

"So … this is you. The cause of my labor.
I was taken from my village in Siberia.
I was a daughter of a tearful seamstress.
I have strands of gold issuing from a pore
in my wrist. I have strands of silver made
from the copper salts of my tears.

I was enslaved by the Aeon. I weave
this cloth you see now on my loom. You see,
she is a proud lady. Her generations are
perfect. I cannot be free until the dress is
faultless. It must contain all the stories of
epic poets. Here is a story of creation. (*Pointing.*)
Here is a story of a god existing outside
the cosmos. Can you see? The cosmos has a
fallen god. The Aeon is redeemed. You
have heard her voice? Now you will know why I
cannot ignore her speech. She tells me olden
narratives, so I may correctly stitch the valve
of your heart. In the sleeves I have placed
barbarous words, words from beyond this
cosmos. The braid of syllables will seem
strange to you only so long as you do
not recognize your own mind."

Aaron. I see, "Abraxas?" "Ialdaboath?" "Ogdoad?"
Sounds … from outside the cosmos?
My blood stands still! How dare I read?

"I have placed two questions in the hem.
What is better? To follow the outward faith,
which, at best, is incomplete, and, at worst,
simply false? Or to continually draw upon
your own spiritual experience – your gnosis –
to revise and transform your vision? Look.
I have stitched your information in my bolt.

Inside the loom, Captain, I weave your fate.
Here, I have marked the half-path of your mind.
When you see again this dress, you will know.
You will remember this speech and the girl.
Do not suppose that resurrection is an illusion.
Rather, see the world as an illusion and then
you may see the reality of waking from sleep."

A. What enchantment of animal! From what
flange of time? What stitch of creature? As if my eye
found aboriginal annex, wild alternate syntax!

"Watch! When you see the girl wearing this
dress, your time will be fulfilled. She will offer
annulment of your crimes. You have surprised
many of their deaths, as many as stitches
in my bolt of cloth. Yet you have parted
nothing not pre-disassembled. Yes,
there'll be a cup of blood that draws. When
you see me, when you see my face again,
you will know I was sent by the Aeon.
You and I are joined in our work. I have
displayed mythic codes – yours and mine. We both
make a stitch from the thread in the loom. When
you hear my voice again, you will know the
truth of my words. Who we were, what we have
become; where we were, wither we are hastening.
What birth is, and what rebirth.
Prepare yourself for gnosis."

(*Recording ends.*)

A. Prepare? Prepare? Wait! Wait!
Tell me how to enter this totem of space?!

(A final recording. Seat and console is empty. No movement in the room. Only several voices are heard.)

8
First voice.
"What is the true Pleroma? Only that portion
of humanity that experiences its divine origin.
What is more blessed? To *believe* or to *know*?
Experience of god annuls the need for rituals
for god. Anyone using the word "god," thus,
… still does not know."

Second voice.
"Who has created the language of god? It is man.
Therefore humanity created the divine world,
and this human logos is the god over them."

Third voice.
"Bring in your guide and your teacher.
The lamp of your body is the mind. Live
according to your mind until the world disappears.
Acquire strength … for the mind is strong.
Enlighten your mind. Light the lamp within you."

Forth voice.
"Knock on yourself as an open door.
Walk upon yourself and an open road.
It is impossible for you to go astray.
If you mistake your heart, retrace your steps.
Open the door for yourself
so you may know what is open.
How many times? You may never know."

Fifth voice.
"If one has inner vision, he receives what is
his own, and draws it to himself. Whoever
is to have secret knowledge on this path
knows where he comes from
and where he is going."

9
Sixth voice
"Say then from the heart that you are the perfect
day, and that within you dwells the light that does
not fail. For you are the understanding that is
drawn forth. What is language, except internal
transformation? Therefore, whoever perceives
divine reality becomes what he sees."

Seventh voice.
"Why do we speak openly? Because we co-make
divinity by hearing. We sing, because each human
being is a dwelling place, and in each dwells an
infinite power … the root of the universe."

Eighth voice.
"You read the face of the sky and the land,
but you do not recognize the one that is
before you, and you do not know how
to read this moment. Because you have
drunk, you have become drunk from
the bubbling stream which I have
measured out."

Redeemed Archon.
"Stop! More than seven, then eight, are
forbidden to speak in this dimension.
In the book we read: *Earth is an octave
of seven waves, and the eighth mind observing,
collapse the seven waves of being.*"

Aeon.
"But there are eleven waves, the twelfth observing!"

Other Aeon.
"Silence! She speaks!"

Sofia. "Silence! Let us wait! I will test how he performs.
I will ask for his eyes.
His time is short."

(*Suddenly, final recording ends.*)

Aaron. Wait! Wait! My eyes?! My eyes?!
I must hear more! My time ... My time!
I begin to see the vision you enclose!
Who are you?! Who are you?!

*(Visibly shaken, Aaron secludes himself in his room,
tearing up old manuscripts and restricting them to the
fire. He writes again from the beginning his poem.)*

10
My saints, do not carry your feet beyond the
Elephantine rocks. If a prayer can constrain you,
I and the indwelling mind shall keep you.
We have sworn to straighten

every turn and fold your flesh shall make.

Do not worship me, I share your condition.
I, too, could not find my life until I broke it.
I, too, could not find the source of my mind
until I searched my own whispered interior.
Like you, I have sketched in my small book;
like you, I have called out from my pillow.

My rest is already done,
or I would not want it.

My work already has its merit,
or I would not so anxiously look for it.

My death has already reached me,
or I would not try to build a name
and house it.

Reseal the broken spaces
to light totem on my eye.

(Thus begins the acts of Kosmoautikon.)

Philosophical Essay:

STORY THEORY

This does not mean that Whitman believes that he can literally write the future unfolding of events; rather, since he views history as primarily textual, as a story which resides in language, he assumes that he can project the path of history by crafting the language that the future will use. This goal is central to *Leaves of Grass* since he imagined it as a "language experiment" that would be seminal to the growth of America . . . . The future will embody the text, and since Whitman tries to provide the language of the future, the text is his script for it.

William Allegrezza

No theory of physics that deals only with physics will ever explain physics. I believe that as we go on trying to understand the universe, we are at the same time trying to understand man. Today I think we are beginning to suspect that man is not a tiny cog that doesn't really make much difference to the running of the huge machine but rather that there is a much more intimate tie between man and the universe than we heretofore suspected. Only as we recognize that tie will we be able to make headway into some of the most difficult issues that confront us. Nobody thinking about it from this point of view can fail to ask himself whether the particles and their properties are not somehow related to making man possible. Man, the start of the analysis, man, the end of the analysis – because the physical world is, in some deep sense, tied to the human being.

John Wheeler, The Intellectual Digest, June, 1973

The absurdity of trying to come up with fresh language every time the sun sets or the weather changes: one way to represent this problem is to eschew masterly phrasing entirely, and, finding language that feels decidedly minor, to shrug in the direction of description.

Typical comment on typical modern poet – NYRB, 2014

Poetry is memorable speech.

Auden

Freedom for an American ... means two things: being free of the Creation, and being free of the presence of other humans.

Harold Bloom

In both classical and quantum physics, an interpretation is needed.

Stanley Sobottka

It is not important what you see, it is important how you see it.

Thoreau

Everything that can be believed is the highest truth.

Blake

I have cast fire upon the world, and see, I am guarding it until it blazes.

Gospel of Thomas

Note to the Reader

My original concept was to mock up each unfinished volume, along with its notes, before moving quickly on to the next book. I intended to allow the poems to mature in my mind before proceeding to the final revision. Trial indicates that five years is the minimum period of reflection required for each book. Original prose sketches to the Epic Poem *Kosmoautikon* were written with alacrity since the poetry was always intended to be the main effort. The notes were necessary to keep into focus a project always threatening to exhibit elements of gigantism.

My method of making notes was intended to take the form of loose essays. Included in the first draft mock ups (titled *Chandos Ring*), the commentaries reached over one thousand printed pages by the time the fifth volume was in first drafts – and thus of benefit to no one except the author. In the manner of note taking, repetition allowed each thesis to be examined again from a new perspective. The commentaries have therefore, in this volume, been abbreviated into a more economical essay giving a bare outline of the research contained in the longer poem.

Any clarity and coherence of the final prose essay are the result of the work and recommendations of my immortal beloved, Ivanna. She is not only the person in the world most close to me in my life – but also in my work. She has expended thousands of hours of educated reading and amendment of the prose commentaries since the revision of the original book drafts. I am grateful to her support and the book would not be a good as it is now without her contribution.

Many hundreds of hours of formatting, correcting and adjusting have been the gift of Mike Porras, the editor and web developer of *Kosmoautikon*. He has been with me from the early days of the project. He has supported me in many discussions and given me the encouragement to continue a project which, not yet complete, had no financial or public remunerations.

The benefit of an independent intellectual position, free of the usual obligations on a poet's time – free of market or academic constraint - is vast. For the first time since Lucretius, the West has a longer poem, free of the controls of a government, a Church, or the necessity to conform to mercenary, political, or academic institutions. The result, of course, is that reader will find nothing he has been trained to like on the first reading. On the fifth reading he may gain an understanding of my idea of poetry in the 21st century. With the tenth reading there will be only friends who are inordinately curious.

Introduction

Philosophy and poetry have failed to keep pace with the successes of scientism. It is nearly impossible to argue with the convenience of technology – until we discover it deforms human life and transforms Western human societies into police states. The strong poet has to make the next evolutionary leap to position modernism as a wounded morality.

My aim is to present a strong theory of poetry. Yet there can be no advance in Western poetry until the elephant in the room has been faced. The elephant, insolently refusing to move, is the unchallenged prestige of technological modernism and its outdated philosophical school, Victorian empiricism. Opposed to the current totalitarian prestige of Victorian scientism, I place a newly charged poetry.

The West has romanticized science, as the West has previously romanticized war, wealth, and women for centuries. We have taken the poetic idiom of the alchemist and smithied weaponized machines of immense imaginative and mythical status. The atomic bomb, for example, is mythical – not less because it is never seen – as much as it is only spoken of in hushed voices. Science fiction, as space travel, now, is mythical. The great industrial revolutions in England and America are now romanticized and enshrined in legend. Modernism, in effect, has now become a nostalgic Victorian narrative, hedged about with romantic heroes, myths and legends of industrial scientism. After terrorizing and maiming societies across the globe, science is finally deconstructed – the atom is empty. Only the profane crowd has not heard the news. Yet modern citizens consider that scientism, as the highest, most supreme speech, is the final human idiom. Is there an objection we should raise?

This is the issue. Every civilization has assumed it was the highest and final human idiom. This is the indispensable central myth that fuels the energy of human societies. Each culture feels it has captured reality – the highest, most exact idiom that humans can discover of the operation of life.

In fact, men are caught only making mythic poems of a supposed superior "reality."

Every act of civilization is an act of symbols. It is the argument of this book that human civilizations exist as interconnected networks of poems. That is, every act of humanity proceeds from the imagination of a human mind using symbols. The second argument is that the mind of *Homo sapiens* is a poetry making machine.

Historical advocates of such arguments – I mean Western poets – have recently failed to powerfully advance the thesis. When we expose scientism correctly as a sub-set of poetry (symbology), we can proceed to augment the poetic idiom in Western societies. Story Theory, the subject of this essay, is a philosophy deconstructing scientism to its core. Therefore my thesis is vast.

Scientism will never be reformed with more acts of scientism. No ideology has ever reformed itself with further applications of its own idiom. Modern men are so invested in the materialist idiom that only an extinction event will permit modernism to become a wounded morality. Nor should poetry attempt to counter modern neglect with newer stagecraft or a softer, more colorful technological gravel. No, let technology play out its idiom until the saturation point – with full force and dramatic intensity.

Poetry may only be vital in Western societies when it is shown beyond proof that poetry describes the protocol of the mind of *Homo sapiens*, that science is, in essentials, a sub-genre of romantic poetry. The reader will be astonished how easy it is to make the case. A story will need to be told.

Homo sapiens is not a scientist in a laboratory; he or she is more properly described as a dramatist. Our ancestors, as our parents, practiced linguistics. Our lovers practiced linguistics. Humans, beginning with education or employment, take turns exchanging dramatic roles and masks, some male, some female. Each human mind, in effect, is a stage manager, an hysterical persona, a mask impending great miscalculation and drama. Our neighbors, our friends and enemies wear masks. We know this, since if we look close at any of these masks – they disintegrate.

The point? In Story Theory, science is a specialty of speech that facilitates mechanical warfare – as well as industrial categories of food, medicine, and freedom. Poetry, on the other hand, describes the entirety of *Homo sapiens'* experience. Both science and technology exclusively use symbols, yet symbols are properly a function of poetry. Truth, as discovered by powerful symbols, is properly the only claim poetry should have on the citizen. Truths, when made cognizant, are demonstrated in the human mind as forms of poetry.

The first problem the American poet faces is that the professed "father" of American poetic tradition, Walt Whiteman, did not write poetry – he wrote prose. Subsequent modern American poetry is newspaper prose cut up to look like verse – and it has finally achieved the status of being without distinction from prose. This has consequences.

Poetry in my generation passed from respect to irrelevance. Poetry, as a medium of vital information, in the West, has reached a social nadir. That is to say, poetry is inconsequential in American life. No American goes about his daily life recalling the lines of American poets. We are not a nation that has produced verse wealthy with memorable speech. No national American poet is absolutely vital to the national identity – as Shakespeare, for example, may be vital to the identity of Englishness.

What is the imaginative genius of modern America? Is it the idiom of science and technology? It is not poetry. This question concerns a future generation, since technological superiority always passes away from great powers – as we saw with the collapse of initial Italian, French, German, and British triumphs of Western industry and technology. The point to be made is that the poetic achievement of these nations has resisted decay – even as they no longer possess technological, industrial, or cerebral power. Only their poetry remains. We have no interest in their superseded (and thus mythical) early technologies and industries. Only their poems and stories are remembered with powerful images and symbols.

In contrast to American poetry, other nations own a greater wealth of verse. Though America always enjoyed a relatively larger educated class, it was European writers who composed as if they were all wealthy men and women. For centuries, Italian, English, Scottish, Irish, German, and French poets wrote with an obscene and scandalous excess of mind – enough to spare for all other nations. European writers, such as Spenser, Rilke, Milton, Blake, Tennyson, Marlowe, Heine, Hesse, Wilde, Molière, Goethe, and the Shakespeare poet, exhibited a superabundance of memorable speech.

Europeans possessed deep uncanny mines of astuteness and innovation. Their poetry was not superficial, it was not embarrassed, and it contained many levels of perspective, inviting deep and prolonged study. To other countries, Europeans threw out laws, language, constitutions, exploration, weapons, theater, patents, stories, myths and religions as if they had too much overflow of imagination to digest themselves. So superior was the European idiom, including industry and science, that they voluntarily renounced the ancient practice of slavery – the first hegemonic civilization to do so. Now it is certain their civilization will be inundated and replaced.

How did Europe lose the remuneration of their innovative idioms as Christianity, world conquest, and scientism? Christianity, imperialism, and scientism are now categories of Victorian romanticism. Christian priests are currently portrayed by actors on television (or cinema) in stereotypical representations (either abusive, demented, or clownish). Christian ideology, as practice, is now indistinguishable from secular and modernist modes of thinking. Few Westerners turn to the Christian church for faith healings. Yet, if faith healing is once relegated to myth, why have a non-secular church at all? The leaders of Western Churches, sympathetically, refer persons in great need to see their doctor and take their prescribed pharmaceuticals. The healing message of the early Jesus movement is ignored by modern citizens. The Church is fully secular, and exactly follows the social norms of any modern secular state. Materialism in, materialism out.

Though not yet recognized, philosophical scientism (generally active from 1850 to the end of the atomic age in the 1970s) is essentially a spent force – of romanticism. Matter, now proven by science to be largely empty, was romanticized – until it transformed from being one of many human interpretations of phenomena to, now, the supreme, human idiom. It is a desperate act of reverse anthropomorphism – taking an idea of science and (as with robots) reimagining men to resemble Replicants and machines. This is a romanticized misprision as myopic as previously imagining that god has human attributes (as one of the Olympic deities) or was a man with a white beard.

Later doctrinal revisions of scientism (quantum mechanics, String Theory, Nonseparability, etc.) deeply indict the existence of physical matter. Without the reality of matter, scientism as a philosophy of reality is risible. Science, consequently, though nominally still prestigious, has already entered its final stages of influence. The reader will be unsure of my statements. Yet he will remember that the Catholic Church maintained vestiges of prestige deep into the period of the Enlightenment. Even in the scientific age, post 1850, the Popes defiantly promulgated their own infallibility and finally decreed the immaculate conception of the Virgin. Science has now transitioned to its own declarations of infallibility.

Scientism, in fact, is a spent church – a wounded morality. The close reader will confirm with sobriety that science fiction was no longer published after the 1960s in any significant munificence. Current anthologies of science fiction refer to the Golden Age of this genre as generally complete in the 1960s. Science fiction is the canary in the coal mine.

Though few in the West may have noticed its passing, science, as a research philosophy which only a few citizens actively engage in, has entered into the sentiment of human nostalgia. Apollo 11 more resembles a final, if triumphal, justification of a century of aggressive and belligerent Victorian Western material progress, than a majestic next step of futurity. NASA is a hollowed out institution of state-funded materialists. NASA represents a blighted church – not a government agency.

Without any further vision of an ambitious, manned space exploration, the manned *extra-terrestrial* American space program was allowed to quietly end in 1974 – seemingly exhausted of further funding, philosophical content, or interest. We are now merely dithering at loose ends with ever better telescopes to probe the illusion of materialism. A little here, a little there. We can't quite figure out if space is real enough or important enough to explore with human bodies.

What if all of "space" is a projection from within the mind? What if it is true that the atom is empty? The implications are clear, the "Golden Age" of Western science is behind us. Romanticized scientism is the last Victorian ideology to be deconstructed – and rejected. This book tells the news, not yet reaching the street.

I am not alone in this view. Cultures opposed to Western scientism have identified the passing of the scientific age after WWII. In 1947 the Egyptian activist, Hassan al-Banna, said, as if it was already a common truism, that the scientific West, "which was brilliant by virtue of its scientific perfection for a long time … is now bankrupt and in decline. Its foundations are crumbling, and its institutions and guiding principles are falling apart" (*Toward the Light*, from *Princeton Readings in Islamic Thought* University, Princeton University Press, 58-59, 2009).

The point to take away is that any civilization is a conditional linguistic construct – including modernism. Often, our enemies have a clearer vision of our illusions. If science is, after all, not the final human idiom, then it's best to begin the linguistic translation now. This is the argument of the present book.

What are the relics of every civilization? It is the thesis of this book that what remains of a society are the stories and memorable speech of its poets. This is what a mature society might recognize.

Consequently, the aim of my work is a new theory of American poetry. The object I seek is a body of strong poets able to influence the society in which they live – so far nonexistent in America. In this undertaking, avoiding with distaste political and religious controversy, I will take the long view of Western letters. I recognize no distinction of the politics of the left and right – both are failed agents of modernist, socialist democracy – with little to choose between marginal flavors of endless technological enervation. I wish to do the hardest thing imagined. I set out to look beyond modernism and, taking into account its imminent obsolesce, I prepare an idiom of alternate futurity.

The subject of my study is the power of memorable poetic verse. Though I test a new voice, I do not wish to sell oil lamps to the atomic age. Instead, showing how men age horribly under modernism, I introduce a new form of expression, as advertised in the epic poem *Kosmoautikon*.

The necessity is clear. To recover the power of verse, the strong poet has to make a case for the irreplaceability of memorable language. He should not only attempt to explain himself with competence, he should amend the poetry of his age with an example of his precepts. Human abstract thought, as found in poems, parables, story, and sacred myth, is under pressure to verify its relevance to the future of Western societies. Yet what if that is how the mind of *Homo sapiens* works? He tells stories.

I ask, therefore, what is the essential link between *Homo sapiens* and poetry? What is our oldest and most essential quality? Human societies exist due to abstract thinking – that is, symbology. *Homo sapiens* is that entity who without outward necessity buried the dead with reverence of futurity and designated that act with alien symbols. If, as I believe, the use of symbology is the essential origin of writing (artistic, abstract expression), then the mind of man is a transcendent element alien to Earth ecosystems. We are alien to a material Earth, since no other physical, terrestrial creature uses symbols.

Homo sapiens possess no earlier facts of his origin, except that he communicates with symbols. Subtracting out all other human distinctions, nothing else is absolutely unique to *Homo sapiens*. Therefore, when we ask, "What is *Homo sapiens*?", we know he is the sole creature that makes poems, using symbols. These are the earliest facts of the case of *Homo sapiens*.

My subject is the poetry discovered at the foundation of all new religions, at the establishment of new social origins, and with the rise of new creation myths. Since poets preeminently perform the innovation of memorable speech in societies, this is a strong test for the necessity of the poet in human society. What society was not founded with notable speech? The following chapters will debate the merits of the case of poetry.

First let us be clear about the composition of poetry. Not just any prose text may be designated a poem. In my view, notable speech, alone, transforms normative speech into poetry – usually with a charged effect of melody, cadence, inflection, or meter. Newspaper prose is not poetry, even so much as it strives to be politically or socially perceptive.

Every human civilization, therefore, has only one origin and one lasting product – its poems. Modern modes of science will no longer exist in ten centuries. We do not seek out past technological innovations – yet we still discuss the poems and myths of past civilizations. In Europe, India, Mesopotamia, and Egypt, long-lived cultures were founded with memorable speech, as illustrated with power in their mythic texts. Scientism, likewise – as demonstrated by Darwin, Einstein, Bohr, and Eisenberg – cannot exist without memorable speech (as theses, postulates, formulas, and hypotheses). The point? A church of distinguished voice makes a civilization.

Conscious human life responds to oracular detection – preceded in all cases by poetic idiom. It could be argued that America is a construct of the memorable speech of Jefferson, Lincoln, Darwin, Washington, Wilson, King, Einstein, Roosevelt, and Kennedy. This is only a small sample of American strong prophet-poets – that is, men using notable, symbolic speech to create the future of a nation.

Yet, today, poetry appears weak and arbitrary in a world converted to the supreme (but hollow) faith of scientism. So we have to look hard at modernism – until it disappears with deconstruction. It is difficult to argue with the convenience of technology – until we show its harmful and totalitarian effects on the human mind. It is the thesis of these books that there can be no further advance in Western poetics until the prestige of scientism has been faced down.

So I focus my argument on a single interrogative. Is scientism the supreme idiom of human life – or is it merely another human ideology that finds its own evidence? Does not modernism first infect us with all our maladies? So why should we praise its fake, artificial, profitable, and grizzly prescriptions? Are not technological solutions only free tickets to a new set of unsolvable problems? When we place scientism correctly as a sub-set of poetry (symbology), when we demonstrate that rationalism is no more than another faith – a linguistic church – we then can proceed to advance the poetic idiom again in Western societies. That is the subject of the following chapters.

There is something wrong with modern texts. Our speech is narrowly selected. First, there are no significant imaginative texts of science fiction since the 1960s. Second, Western prose-poetry does not so much as hint that there is an entire and superior idiom of science in the culture for over 200 years. Third, philosophy is no longer written robustly for the vernacular speaker. Forth, newspaper–style, prose poetry fails to respond to the demand for distinct and memorable speech. Fifth, the American novel, once seen as the highest genre of American letters, is an industry that has no writers, no market, and no audience. Sixth, modern (prose-like) poetry no longer is adaptable sufficiently to support a many-layered narrative of power and significance.

The result? Total irrelevance of the poetic idiom in the West. We do not consult modern philosophers or modernist prose poets in the contemporary world. Poetry, novels, and philosophy are solidly a literature of nostalgia in modern societies. Political leaders do not pause gravely to consult prophetic voices (poetry) before making decisions. Is poetry an irrelevance?

Until poetry is seen as vital information by modern Western societies, there will be no recovery of strong poetry by the same society. Consequently it is useless to speak of rhyme, meter, alliteration, or blank verse – as it is useless to make poems more interesting in the shape of circles or triangles, or in sonnets or quatrains. Since epic poetry is no longer written with power or prestige, since poetry is without distinction, contains no melody or inflection, we may make poetry in the form of our choosing. A drunken statement – or an opportunity for audacity?

What is the use of epic poetry in modern societies? Necessity. I want a device joining striking metered verse, a many-layered narrative, using modern vernacular speech. How does epic poetry differ from unmetered blank verse – currently using undistinguished newspaper prose? It is metered, distinctive speech – yet a voice that does not seem antiquated, is not strained, is able to surprise – yet contains common modern usage, and connects us to the art of music. When combined with these elements, poetry is uncannily charged with pin-point accuracy.

Does poetry have value? I reply, how else may the vernacular speaking citizen take control of his world? Poetry allows us to freely constitute our being. *Homo sapiens* has only his speech to manipulate his environment. If the vernacular speaker is ghettoized, then he is forced in supplication to "priests" of the secret languages (industrial math, medicine, commercial advertisements, and ideological, academic, laboratory science).

There can be no internal gnosis under the conditions of a fanatical and ideological outward material civilization. The maturity and development of vernacular poetry, thus, is a necessity. *Kosmoautikon* linguistically recreates the human space – since, as will be shown, modernity is already only another failed linguistic construct. We see the result in our gangland ghettos, 24-hour state surveillance, and the deformities caused by industrial pharmaceuticals.

Therefore, the strong poet will wish to transition with great care from (an irrelevant and ignored) modern newspaper-prose-poetry to a reimagined epic trope. Because he is *Homo sapiens*, he will wish to tell a story.

The strong poet knows a secret. He knows how to wake the sleeping. The modern world is waiting with anticipation for the next prophetic voice. Its desire for prophetic voice is not concealed. In Story Theory, as in all human epochs, the urgent need of our time is for a coherent view of life, at the same time religious and practical, that can bring nature under the certain control of man's highest and oldest essential spiritual perceptions.

My critique of modern *prose-poetry* is that 1) it is not memorable speech, 2) it does not tell a story, 3) it exhibits no distinction of inflection or music and, 4) being cowed by modernism, it does not acknowledge (or face) the existence of the superior speech of science in Western civilization. Without notable speech, we may only lurch from crisis to crisis, committing random acts of modernism.

Epic poetry, as *Kosmoautikon*, on the other hand, faces each of these critiques.

CHAPTER ONE

Clarity of a New Philosophy

Story Theory, the subject of this book, is a means to evaluate the overall path of the mind of *Homo sapiens*. It arose from the necessity of a single interrogative: *How may science and poetry be equal means of prestigious and cherished information? How may stories, epic poems, and sacred myths (that have no archeology) have as much, or more power over the human mind than the ideology of science?* In my thesis, the schism in Western societies between poetry and science, between vernacular speech and scientific speech, is a dangerous fallacy. It is an illusion that can be dispelled.

If true, what is the philosophical link between opposing categories of human information? Is the idiom of scientism a true reality – or is prophetic voice (spoken in the epic trope) a true reality? Which one contains superior information of the human condition? When looked at closely, and each idiom is reduced to its basic component, it will be seen they are very much alike in construction. They are linguistic twins. They are imaginative inferences using symbols. If we could show this link (both being forms of poetry), then there would be a new philosophy to unify these two opposite idioms – that is, objective scientism and subjective poetry. As will be seen, there is no such thing as objectivity in the human case. Objectivity is a linguistic illusion.

The urgent need of our time is for a coherent view of life, at the same time spiritual and practical, that can bring philosophic clarity to the harmful balkanization currently predominate in human experience. Unity of conceptualization may lead to clarity of what is human. I will follow the logic of Story Theory, the subject of this book, to see where it leads, no matter how alien the landscape. The conclusion, if the reader has the patience to reach the end of the commentaries, leads to a staggering new vision of *Homo sapiens*. The alien constituent is deep in our genome.

I saw early in my study that science, like poetry, was a hermetically sealed, self-referent linguistic codex. I felt there was a problem with modernism. I saw that each human civilization, also, was a self-referent linguistic codex. We may contrast the major philosophies of human civilizations. Scientism could never give a just explication of Islam or Judaism. Christianity or Buddhism could never conform to the precepts of science – and still *operate*. All sets of human civilizations, thus, are nomads to each other. The point? There was no method to evaluate the position or intent of the self-conscious mind of *Homo sapiens* outside of separate, and warring, specialized idioms. This was inefficient.

After all, are Christianity, Islam, Judaism, or Buddhism able to correctly evaluate all other *–isms* – all other faiths – all other civilizations? Are science, physics, and psychology able to discover the final answers of life – or the origin of self-consciousness? We know the answer. No. Science is only able to detect science. Psychology is only able to detect psychology. Taxidermists are only able to detect taxidermy. And so on. Each is a linguistic system anticipating its own self-referent sets of discoveries.

Active in remote sections of the globe, and learning many languages, I saw that scientism was not hegemonic in all parts of the human universe. It worked only where other like-minded men accepted the same definition of scientific words and concepts. Outside of Western urban centers, science was seen as an alien and hostile confusion of corrupted, prejudiced, and toxic belief. Slowly, hesitantly, I looked for evidence of the false data of scientism. In Saudi Arabia and Afghanistan I was looked upon as an alien being belonging to the most dangerous and malefic of civilizations. For a moment, I tried to see what they saw from within their idiomatic perspective. With experience, sometimes bitter, I was able to detect the false sets of modernist data in advertisements, on the walls of the ghettos, in the fake data of medical studies, and in the gaping vacuity in the hearts of Western citizens.

The chief requirement of Story Theory, therefore, is that it functions as a test of the mind of *Homo sapiens*. Something so unlimited, so sophisticated as human intelligence, so complicated in its operation, must have a pattern of intent, causation, and target objective. Story Theory, therefore, functions as a macro check of the intent and force of human consciousness. It raises the question: *Where, outside of specific, narrow civilizations, is the mind of Homo sapiens properly positioned – and with what moral trajectory is it determined on (within the self-conscious limit of perception)?* If a leviathan as the human mind cannot be mapped or evaluated in the macro – then what is the use to make a collection of idioms of civilization, each contradicting the data sets of the previous one, stacked on top of each other, millennia after millennia? By any contest of sobriety, millennial waves of alternate denying and contradicting civilizations, as a way of human mental congress, are a form of madness. Without Story Theory humans are merely shadowboxing with their mind.

I saw that civilized man, at best, was merely a specialist in his chosen idiom. Each civilization explored a particular idiomatic tract of thought – a rich branch of human imagination. Each civilization only proved it loved its own linguistic idiom – being barbaric to all others. That is, each civilization was deep into its own chosen narratives of the possible material or spiritual interpretations of universe. I saw that each civilization made deep advances into their own particular and focused – if narrow – innovations of speech. Science, so sure of its empirical proofs, is an idiom not accepted by Islam. Islam, so sure of its spiritual proofs, is denied by Hindus and Christians alike. All civilizations, in this perspective, are disparate and contradictory, yet intricate, poems. Each civilization, in effect, is a separate theory of poetry. That is the insight of Story Theory.

The usual examples come to mind. The Greeks innovated deeply in philosophy. Perhaps unique in the ancient world, they constructed the linguistics of complex philosophic thought. The Muslim, the Jew, and the Christian each had their doctors of divinity and were certainly fluent in the most esoteric level of metaphysical exploration and exegesis of prophetic voice (scripture). Tengrism in Mongolia, Plains Indian religion of the American Plateau, or Voodooism in Africa, so dissimilar to Western religions, have deep shamanistic roots and profound animal totems, seamlessly interacting with the natural environment. Each seemed to be totally self-sufficient and the acolytes of each never felt in anyway inferior to any other human idiom. None of these civilizations showed the slightest regret or debility that they did not possess the mathematical machines and toxic chemicals of modern states.

Did the great religions have a great product? Did they make a great discovery? A great machine? Yes. Ethical and moral behavior. It has allowed the human world to operate with ferocious efficiency for twelve millennia. The grand achievement of religious and shamanistic cultures, though diverse, represented organized linguistic totems, consisting of human moralities and ethics that science can only look at with bemused speculation of their deep uncanny origins.

Modern men have likewise made a new house of speech – a new poem of civilization – a deep idiom of math, kinetic technology, and physical science (henceforth called *scientism* in these books). Yet, in the end, each of these great idioms (religion/philosophy, science/modernism, etc.) are not macro tests of the human mind; they are only idioms of highly focused specialties of diverse linguistics – merely opinionated interpretations of human civilization. How to test each against the overall evaluation of *Homo sapiens'* self-conscious mind?

Is there a macro destination of self-consciousness? What is it? That is the prize that Story Theory aims at.

As a species we still possessed no test of the over-arching position of any civilization in the moral and imaginative conglomerate of a self-conscious being – called *Homo sapiens*. Greek philosophy, paganism, modern science, Buddhism, shamanism, Tengrism or Christianity might be, individually, great advances in a particular idiom – but there was still no test of the overall merit of one human idiom over all other idioms of civilization. That's a problem. Each civilization was a separate and piecemeal experiment of human consciousness – having no relation to other linguistic experiments. Each idiom merely operated as *if* it was the supreme achievement of the human mind – and continued until their ideas accumulated too many wounded moralities – or their kinetic armies failed in competition with other armies.

Each civilization performs a test of reality. There is great inefficiency in serial and separate linguistic tests of reality – if each, in effect, annuls the judgments of the other. What, after all, is the use of a civilization of Christianity if Christ never rose from the dead? What is the use of Judaism if god never made a covenant with the house of Israel – or the Hebrews, in fact, never left Canaan – and were merely Canaanites? What is the use of scientism if the atom is, after all, empty? Where does a false alley of civilization leave you when it is exposed as a fraud? It leaves all that you loved, fought, and lived for – as only a great poem. What, then, is poetry if all human things originate, and end, as poems? It means that a theory of poetry should be our goal, not a new marketable (and lying) invention of the substratum – as industrial modernism or scientism.

Therefore, I find the idioms of separate civilizations equally delusional. If true, this means that scientism, as only one of many most recent human choices of idiom, is also delusional. If each civilization builds a self-referent idiom (essentially blind to any actual reality), then I find this piecemeal approach to evaluating the merit of human consciousness (one wrong civilization at a time) unsatisfying. It is as if amateurs and drunkards got hold of the levers of self-consciousness – and were caught driving drunk and blind into the night.

Locked in their own idiom, men are merely nomads in their own mind, living uneasily with other idiomatic nomads on the Earth, of whom they take little effort to understand or appreciate. Secularized moderns, for example, do not treasure the delicate insights of Islam or fundamental Christianity. Scientists look upon religions as delusions of irrational fantasy and imagination. Religionists see scientists as missing the most important elements of our spiritual makeup – the clear metaphysical configuration of self-consciousness – which science can never explain or reproduce.

This is the point I wish to make in this chapter: the impossibility of human idioms to accurately evaluate each other is endemic and hopeless. One may only diminish the "other civilization" until it can no longer function. We can only evaluate the "other" idiom on its funeral pyre – or by the clash of armies. This protocol (as war) is a recourse leading only to shame and embarrassment of higher mental efficiencies. Not a new idea.

So what does Story Theory perform? Story Theory reduces all civilized human idioms to their final divisible element – that is, an interpretation of life using symbols. Only by this tool can the mind of *Homo sapiens* be evaluated with clarity – outside of all deeply self-referent idioms

In Story Theory, all religions are unashamedly nominated as poetic texts and sacred stories. That is, after all, they are poems and verses using symbols and metaphors. Scientism, likewise, in Story Theory is also revealed to be a set of poems and narratives expressed with symbols of great imagination – as modern math, prescription, formula, and hypothesis are illustrated with symbolic notations. $E = mc^2$, for example, is a symbolic notation. Each, properly and exactly, is only a house of language.

In this new philosophy, reducing all human religions and ideologies to their final divisions as imaginative, even enchanted symbology, we can finally evaluate *overall* where the human mind is positioned within self-consciousness. Or is it our curse as *Homo sapiens* to stumble from idiom to idiom like drunkards, each time mistaking the end of the world? Then the next civilization should eradicate our own – and wildly shame all our dearest, blood drenched sets of data points?

This appraisal of the *macro* location of the human mind – *outside* and *apart* from each civilization's own specialized idioms – is the subject of the next ten volumes of commentary essays. It will result in a new theory of poetry, in the same way that every civilization is essentially a theory of poetry.

CHAPTER TWO

All Human Idioms Are Self Referent

Story Theory is the philosophical clarity permitting modern man to renounce scientism as a supposed choice between a physical reality (of material science) and a spiritual reality (of inward poetry, myth, faith). It is easy to point out their exact similarities. Each is an idea within the mind. Each uses symbols to make plausible order, that is, each makes texts of notable speech from chaos. Both modern science and poetry, romance and religion are products of an imaginative, terraforming mind. Each are forms of epic poetry. That is, each tells an epic narrative with high symbology and memorable voice. Science and poetry are thus exactly equivalent linguistics.

This is how it works. Science detects empirical "truths" consistent with the codex of scientific speech. Medicine finds disease and disorder consistent with medical theory. Poetry finds empirical "truths" consistent with the codex of prophetic speech. Romantics find empirical "truths" consistent with the codex of traditional uses of romance (and monogamy!).

All that is required to make empirical tests of the reality of each set of idiomatic speech is to accept without question the linguistic coding of the same self-referent idiom. In the language of romance, the lover does not question the excellence of the beloved – even if the beloved appears ugly to all others. In the codex of scientism, the PhD does not question the competence of the scientific method – even if the data clearly has a political bias, a use as a weapon of mass destruction, or a false sets of data chosen with prejudice.

The point? There is not one linguistic truth exponentially more superior to all others. Each codex rises to the level of consciousness that it seeks. Romance verifies the claims of monogamy. Scientism verifies the supremacy of materialism. Modernism justifies technology, mindless proliferation of populations, and capitalistic wealth. In effect, therefore, there is only a choice of self-fulfilling linguistic data points, that, with maturity, become so self-referent (so enchanted) that they find and manufacture their own "truths." The taxidermists see only the outlines of taxidermy. The romantic sees only the excellence of the beloved (even if he is a convicted murderer in a prison) – and so on. That is, all possible worlds a man may make can only be worlds made up of poetics. This is the case for poetry in every generation. This is Story Theory.

The modern will protest. How can so opposite systems of "reality" be claimed equally as "truth?" How can scientism and romance (for example) – or math and voodoo – be equally valid means to human information? Herein lies the challenge of *Kosmoautikon*. Speech is the only human "house" – and all humans in the "house of speech" are susceptible to the urge of enchantment.

Linguistic specialization operates as a self-referent mental mapping. Ideas allow the eyes to function – eyes in a senseless vacuum can make no logic from forms of light. Until there is a limit of mental spectrum, a focus of speech, all objects overwhelm the eye with no meaning. Medical doctors detect disease – and diseases are consequently very real (empirical) to materialist thinkers. Taxidermists detect patterns and facts of taxidermy. Religion detects examples of actual faith healings – inward, introspective union with spiritual demonstrations of power. Romance verifies the validity of "true" love – not actually existing in nature. Troubadours only ever existed within the construct of ideological romance.

Who would deny with sobriety that science or math, voodoo or romance are anything if not a self-referent, hermetically sealed linguistic disciplines? They each require years of specific and controlled study. We note that mathematics is an idiom (and not a universal, eternal truth) when we verify that every theory in theoretical mathematics is justified – only by its own proofs. So far from math being empirical, Kurt Gödel proved in the 1930s that any system of mathematics contain propositions which can neither be proved or disproved. Theorists may only cherry-pick any possible sets of data to confirm their thesis to the uniformed public.

No linguistic idiom is organic or intuitive in nature (certainly not the monogamy of romance). Each, being artificial, has to be learned. No person is born a scientists, or a voodooist, or a romantic – that is, we have to be deeply conditioned with poetic symbols to believe in an idiomatic response to any particular phenomenon. Any human linguistic misprision is a deeply learned system.

The differing results of separate linguistic ideation patterns are the "unknown quantities" that no philosophy previously attempted to explain. Since men alternately have used science, math, romance, or religion to designate empirical evidence of life, I had to discover how opposites may be united in human usage. There had to be a way to account for this actuality. Linguistic disciplines (listed above) have only one element in common: each uses symbols to make order from apparent chaos. The base of all human existence, thus, is a school of poetics.

Why poetics? Because symbols are used to make human order from chaos. As a metaphor, then, we may say the world proceeds out of the mind of the observer as steam from a hose. That is, it does not matter what you see – it only matters how your mind organizes it. There is no actual reality that we record, we only make a perception within an illusion of perception.

Poetry cannot be divided any further into more basic components. We test this when we discover we cannot alter a line from Homer, Milton, or the Shakespeare poet. Words cannot be deconstructed into non-words. No great poem can be improved with modification. We can only diminish the electric charge of a strong poet by any alteration. Poems are irreducible. By this test, poetry is thus the supreme human idiom laying at the origin of human existence.

It is for this cause we say that the human singularity is poetry (symbol making). This "solution" to all linguistic "opposites" – that is, how science and poetry are equal linguistic sets of proofs, etc. – is thus the philosophy of Story Theory.

What is the final logic of Story Theory? There is no "empirical" reality somehow hanging in space as an object independent from a human mind. There is no single objective reality adrift someplace in the universe waiting for men to correctly discover its location with his outward looking eye. (Yet this psychosis is exactly what the faith of scientism professes – that we must look outside of the Earth with telescopes to observe the "reality" of existence). In fact, the only possible reality a human can detect is an inward, artificial linguistic reality; all possible worlds are merely emanations from within the conscious mind. All that we may meet at the Horsehead Nebula is our own mind. That is a conclusion.

The point is all phenomena within consciousness are imaginative emanations from the human mind – that no object is somehow separate from the human mind. It means that all observed phenomena are the results of a human interpretation – using symbols. I include in my scope objects with the "apparent" mass and solidarity of stars and planets – as well as all perception of human peril, nemesis, and disease. It is a philosophy that will test the reader's zeal for clarity.

Since there is no objective reality outside of a self-referent linguistic mapping, there is no "outside" at all. All observed phenomena "outside," including other persons, stars, and planets, are only projections (from within) of our linguistic assumptions and constructs of beliefs. There can be no "outside" since everything perceivable by the conscious mind is already contained within consciousness. We can test this. *If there was something outside of consciousness, how could you perceive it?* It is an impossibility. "Outside" is thus an intellectual fallacy. This is a clarity of Homo sapiens that only Story Theory dares to make.

Only a philosophy that reduces all *–isms* to their linguistic structure may bridge the gap between profoundly divergent interpretations of consciousness (as science and religion).

Poetry thus, with this insight, is as superior a form of information as academic science. Being forms of mere linguistics, all high idioms – as science, romance, religion, etc. – all schisms of social speech – are able to fold into each other—as equals – since all human ideas are poems. The result? All we know are the poems we have learned – even if this poem is called science, romance, shamanism, Tengrism, or Islam.

We will need a cadre of strong poets to verify this superiority.

CHAPTER THREE

What Is Story Theory?

Story Theory takes all the elements of human speech and divides them again and again until they cannot be divided any further. The result is a discovery: *all a human can make (of his life) is a symbol, a story, of his consciousness.* This is Story Theory.

All we know of the human past is a story – a story a human mind has made with symbols. Accounts of the past, even the history of our nearest ancestors, are reconstructions – with interpretations of highly arbitrary, if not completely imagined, data points – usually following a biased agenda in each generation. We remember only as much of the past as we choose to remember. A dictator reviled in one generation is a martyr of great virtue in another century. (Napoleon I's birthday was again a national French holiday in the 1850s.) We may anticipate with incongruence that even Stalin and Hitler will be redeemed by an unknowable future society. The point? No two humans have the same exact picture of previous human history. No two humans have the same image of living objects or human events. Each citizen only has imagined a story of the past.

Until a philosopher can explain the absence of facts of the origin of human consciousness, he has no mature philosophy. The man of ruthless honesty will admit that the only proof a human has existed is a story, a text, a rumor. The historical narrative alters in each generation – as the human agenda alters. Humans do not follow any actual "reality," they follow Story Theory. A story is told of life.

Story Theory frankly admits from the outset that there are no material facts for the case of a self-conscious mind. There are no archeological remains that prove the cause, purpose, or origin of a human mind. In Story Theory there is no requirement for archeology to verify the historical events of any Bible, myth, or epic poem. What would be the use? As science now confirms, physicality itself is an illusion. The atom is empty. Why should it not be?

Few philosophies have ever accounted for the absence of "facts" of human consciousness. Embarrassed of actual data, men have made poems of creation events, whether called *Noah's flood, the Garden of Eden,* or the *Big Bang.* Such stories exist only because there are no facts of consciousness. Only Story Theory faces the problem squarely and gives a plausible account of the universe of phenomena as a projection from within consciousness.

We have no data of the exact origin of facts. The story – the events – the phenomena of each human life are made *within* consciousness. This being so, all things within consciousness (including the "outward" visible universe) can be modified by a further recourse to consciousness. That is a significant discovery. That means that all "realities" within consciousness can be modified, reconstructed, reformed, to attain the level of consciousness that is sought. In Story Theory, there is no "out-there" – there is only the story you created, or accepted, about your existence.

In Story Theory, as we shall demonstrate, there is nothing in the universe separate from our consciousness. All observable events occur deeply within consciousness – even those phenomena, called "physical objects," we usually count as being (somehow) separate from our own mind, as body cells, stars, galaxies. In Story Theory, instead, every "outside object" is entangled deeply within the human mind.

We test this when we realize that the universe has changed as often as the language used to describe the universe has changed. Ptolemy, Copernicus, Galileo, Newton, Bohr, and Eisenberg have each remade a material universe based on new innovations of language. Likewise, the proofs of previous generations of our ancestors are only "asserted" by linguistic usage. In truth, no one knows what actually occurred before one's own lifetime – one is only able to make a story of that unknowable period. (And even if we saw a documentary of the outside "world," we don't know who edited the images and the narrative).

All that remains, then, of our ancestors is their story – their reputation. All we understand of the narrative of the stars is what we have learned from another human's account of the universe. No one is born with an exact narrative of the cosmos. It is learned, it is imagined with a narrative, it is inferred from another man's text. Visible consciousness thus operates as an emanation from within – as a projection, as a holograph.

We can see from this how Story Theory functions. When the gnostic Egyptian priests created the unforgettable language of the soul—then the soul of man *came actually into existence.* In this protocol, when Einstein made a prediction of the *Theory of Relatively*—it was at that moment that Einstein's universe *came actually into existence*. As far as the *"perceived world"* is concerned, there was until that moment no universe so structured. Since all possible worlds (and universes) are emanations from within consciousness – the human mind is the only arbiter of what "exists out-there." As an American writer said, "It does not matter what we see – it matters how we see it."

Conclusion? The very act of observation (with symbols) creates the phenomena of the universe. The very act of imagining deity is contact with the qualities of the same deity. The act of wishing to love creates opportunities for love. The act of desiring to enter business creates opportunities for business. The act of science creates the "past events" supporting the "physical evidence" of science. This prospect is necessary to build a strong theory of poetry.

Life is not simply presented to us fully formed. We "make" the facts of life. Men linguistically nominate, interpret, and translate consciousness – and these interpretations have empirical consequences. That is, we negotiate with life in order to modify consciousness to meet the conditions of life we seek. If that was not true how many any man find love, safety, education, or improvement of any degree? We create the conditions for improvement with our metal adjustment of the facts of the case. You are poor? Make yourself rich. You are alone, make yourself beloved. We cannot read? We obtain an education to improve our life. We select a "just-so" partner to transform our life. We make choices of good and evil to amend our life. Above all else, we make stories of our life to revise the structure initially presented to us. We have the power to reject or accept given stipulations – to say *yes* or *no* to the conditions of life. Only the human mind can say *yes* or *no* to nature. We are beings of great power.

My estimation of the human mind is high. It is not limited to temporary mental or physical apparitions. In Story Theory, all dangers, all jeopardies, all joys are conditional. There is always a choice of *yes* or *no* in the mind. This essential selection of *yes* or *no* identifies the opportunity to modify any human peril – including linguistic categories of disease, war, failure, moral hazard, danger, and personal nemesis.

The thesis of Story Theory, perhaps, comes into view. *Any man that attempts to describe his consciousness, even in the first syllables, transitions immediately to story.* It is a sentence the reader will return to in order to understand my thesis. It is a moment of sobriety in intellectual history. Humans possess no other "facts" of existence.

Since the origin of human consciousness is unknown, since "outward" gods are unknowable, an inward construct of "humanness" is the only achievable solution.

Story Theory, so far from mere idealism, is a philosophy that meets exactly with human experience. Further, it is able to demonstrate the unreality of the material universe. That is, any material condition, any physicality, when looked at closely disappears. Joy, love, hate, pain, Eros, worry, terror, pleasure, each, if exhaustively looked at, disappears. Every reader will wish to test the principles of Story Theory against their own experience. When did your love or lust disappear? How long did your joy or pleasure last? When did your fear, your terror, or your hate suddenly dissipate? When did your passion lose its luster? When was your trust lost?

What is the first consequence of Story Theory? Story Theory accuses modern rationality as unworkable. That indictment directly questions the rationalist philosophy of 19th century scientism. The casual reader will be surprised, since he believes scientism to be the most modern of all possible human idioms. In Story Theory we show that scientism is an outdated movement of the Victorian age (while beginning as a hobby of the enlightenment, scientism did not become a mass populist movement until the 1850s). Scientism is, along with romanticism, the last vestige of the 19th century that we have yet to consign to the dustbin of human imagination.

Science, as romanticized by the Victorians, uses rationalism as a cover. Rationalism has a serious flaw. It does not have integrity as a human system of thought. Story Theory states frankly that since it is impossible to have all the "facts" of human life, reason is defective as a mature philosophy. Let us state the case with clarity. The most that the rationalist can achieve is that he has *faith* that he possesses all the facts of any possible human "case." Only complete possession of all the facts of a case would permit "rational thought." Never in history has any human ever possessed all the "facts" of a case. Rationalism is thus a roll of the dice as reliable as augury or prophetic vision. This "faith" of the rationalist (i.e. the belief that we may possess all the facts) makes rationalism – consequently – only another linguistic church. No modern leader, no scientist, no politician has ever possessed all of the facts of a case. So far we are in this funny position.

As we know from the modern epidemic of prosecutions of medical doctors, no physician has all the "facts" of the side-effects of surgery and pharmaceuticals; he merely makes a faithful guess that he has command of all the billions of interactions in trillions of cells. No technological civilization commencing a war, or releasing a new drug, or building a super computer, can anticipate the totality of results. No nuclear scientist, thinking he has all the facts for the case, will know how or against whom, nuclear weapons will be used. No modernist government setting out to make total electronic surveillance of the population knows what type of society will result from that consequence. When processed and packaged food was introduced 60 years ago, no industrial food company anticipated that an entire globe would be deformed with obesity and diabetics within two generations. Therefore, the church of rationalism (scientism), operating exactly as a modern faith, is not a reliable philosophy of human life. It is, at best, a wild guess – accepted only because it is wildly profitable to capitalistic originators – or exploitable by medical industries. No scientist ever has considered the chain of consequences inspired by the idioms he creates from his mind. The consequences to that society (thus created blindly) are as ruthless as they are fact-less.

The modern, of course, will insist that he would not wish to be without the products of modern science, no matter how toxic or artificial they may be. I reply, yes, that is a choice that can be made – with harmful consequences purposely hidden by modern advertising. The truth? Tobacco, pesticides, plastics, pharmaceuticals, flame retardants, preservatives, fructose – all promoted ruthlessly by modernism – have been found out, instead, to maim, kill, and deform human populations. Modern information, consequently, is not reliable. It does not tell the truth, and thus is useless to poetry as a source of truthful information of human life.

Each human story is self-referent. That is, as discussed, each person finds his own evidence of life. Scientism will always find proofs of scientism. Religions will find proofs of religions. Voodoo will find proofs of voodoo. The citizen's construction of a personal narrative cannot be prevented – it may only be anticipated with clarity. This is Story Theory.

We make an interpretation of life using symbols in our consciousness. That is the definition of a "story" – an interpretation of "life" using symbols. Consciousness itself is exponentially vaster than the supposed infinity of "physical space." This means that not only consciousness contains infinite mental congress, but that *space has the quality of infinity precisely because space is a projection from within consciousness.* The reader can pause and take his time to verify if an idea has the space of infinity.

How universally applicable is Story Theory? There is no case of the human that is not also the case of Story Theory. When a man attempts to explain his life, even in the first syllables, he transitions immediately to story. Story Theory, therefore, possesses all the essential "facts" of the case of human. Story Theory describes how every human civilization was made with symbols. The master of this symbology, moreover, is the master of all possible worlds. This is the case for poetry.

Why is Story Theory useful for Western societies? Story Theory defines *Homo sapiens. Homo sapiens* is categorized as that creature that exclusively uses symbols to make his world. Story Theory permanently links *Homo sapiens* with poetry – since any nomination of human ideation using symbols is *necessarily* a poem. Everything we perceive is detected with a conscious mind using symbols. If all possible "worlds" are nominated with symbols, then poetry is the supreme speech of *Homo sapiens*. I cannot detect what I cannot symbol.

What does any story perform? It expands the limits of life. This is the key to the condition of *Homo sapiens* – he expands his opportunity of possible ideation of world using symbols (as in study, travel, love, reading, or war). In this necessity he creates a structure of eternity. Man has never been satisfied with the limits of human mortality. For example, when has there ever been a limit of love for a child? When has a man ever had enough of joy or prosperity? When has a victorious general ever had enough power – or wealth, or land? There is no such end. It is no more possible to demonstrate a limit to love as it is impossible to demonstrate a limit to the story-making mind. Thus, show me a human mind, or a human will, and I will show you an eternity machine.

Literature is the act of making eternity – an expansion of life. What does a story perform? A story investigates the structure of timelessness. Every myth, sacred narrative, and poem contains the genealogy of eternity – that is, the protagonist is essentially outside of time.

We can test this. Epic narratives operate as if the hero's actions are true and central for all time. Hector and Lucifer have no time. Hercules is outside of time. Hector is eternally the man that, by facing Achilles, made the right action. Christ is eternally dying on the cross. Lucifer is forever tempting Christ. Caesar is eternally becoming Caesar. Alexander is continually making conquest of the world. Hamlet is forever a misfit with his time. Lear is eternally naked on the heath. Lady Macbeth is forever urging her husband to kill the King. There is no expiration date on any epic story – there is no possibility of "extinction" in epic literature. The strong narrative is correct and fit for all time. The protagonist, bestowing clarity of human life, therefore, is the youngest of all living creatures within consciousness. Jesus, Moses, and Hamlet are young for all of time. The poet, therefore, is likewise the youngest of human beings. His fame out-lasts the certain misanthropic fate of his own society.

Thus, no information of the human condition is ever to be lost – or misplaced. No individual information, no human story can ever be eradicated. This is vital data, since everything we wish to know about our lives is: *will our information survive eternally?* Story Theory provides an answer. Information of our existence is never in the condition of being erased, set aside, or "lost." We test this when we realize no story, no character of narrative, can be eradicated. It is impossible.

Homo sapiens is a creature of selection. A human civilization is not a true representation of all "phenomena." A civilization is based on a severely focused human story (texts). A civilization is a severe reduction of life into a few categories of recorded interest and goals. The poet, for example, chooses ruthlessly to exclude all other data irrelevant to his poem. The plot of a book or a play ignores all other life – in order to make a single powerful statement. A civilization, like a story, excludes most all other human "data" in order to focus on a single idiom. Modernism, as we know well, excludes all teachings of spiritual power to focus on the production of a high material culture. This is how Story Theory operates. A selection of "data" is made – and the data becomes enchanted and romanticized.

A story can only make a selection of data points. The storyteller is selective, and, like a deity, his choice of speech leads to an expansion of his own idiom – until it reaches the condition of mythic enchantment. If there is no limit to this expansion, then it is godlike.

The ability of men to make a story with the limitless quality of eternity is proof that man, in a world yet to be discovered, is a god – and eternity is our proper field of activity. The reader will already begin to suspect the radical aspect of Story Theory. There is no degree of separation between a highly trained conscious mind and the mind of any possible form of deity. We are necessarily of the same essence. Any limitation of our mind is due to our choice. Unwillingness to be properly educated, or to be trained by a master, are examples of the misuse of the mind.

What is the use of Story Theory? Poetry cannot thrive in a civilization of fake, or constrained, or totalitarian information. Poetry is a speech leading to enchantment of the human mind. The information of a poem must be free to move towards enchantment, that is, truth. Fake information (as modernism) cannot move to enchantment of the human idiom. It is blocked.

Language never seeks incoherence and ugliness. Therefore, with the use of language, a selection is made. Cultures do not teach their children to forget beautiful songs – they do not wish to teach rude or more barbaric speech. Instead, they move towards excellence – towards enchantment of an idiom. The bias of every form of human consciousness, therefore, is the bias of enchantment. Even dictators dream they move towards something which, to them, is enchanted.

The point? Story Theory reduces the human mind to its final indivisible element: *a valuation of human symbols making a projection of enchanted world.*

This is a brief outline of Story Theory, referenced throughout the subsequent commentaries. The reader will note my method in the following chapters. I have to follow the logic of Story Theory – no matter how radical the conclusions may be – that everything within consciousness is promiscuous to manipulation.

The modern, believing in the superiority, permanence, and solidity of scientism will correctly resist my thesis. He, of course, will not wish to be told that his civilization is scheduled for dissolution. Everything he now accepts as normal will have to be rejected in a thrashing fit of honesty. Populist, Victorian scientism is already passé as a coherent philosophy.

This is the boil that Story Theory lances.

CHAPTER FOUR

The Consequences of Story Theory

What is the necessity to apprehend Story Theory? *Everything perceived with consciousness is assembled within consciousness, and is thus promiscuous to modification by manipulation of the conscious mind.* This is a key statement in Story Theory.

We can test this. How should we identify or perceive another planetary body if it was not already within consciousness? It is impossible, since how could we make a perception of an "object" unless it was already located within the precincts of consciousness? We can perceive nothing – not a single particle – *outside* of consciousness. Thus anything we observe "outside" is actually already within consciousness. Without this precision Story Theory – as well as the human mind – cannot be understood.

The Black Holes, the Horsehead Nebula, the constellations we observe are firmly located within our mind – not outside the mind. It is a logic we must hold on to as a man desperately holds on to a plank of drift wood in an angry, wind-blown ocean.

If this logic is hard for the reader, it is because secular materialism has invited him to mistake the protocols of his own mind. A telescope, based on its outward orientation, giving the illusion of *outward otherness*, is only a device for misprision of the protocol of a conscious mind. Galileo, the father of modern men, had the telescope turned the wrong way. Consequently, inward exploration of consciousness – that is, the human spiritual avocation – is blunted with disuse and derision in the West. Story Theory turns the telescope inward. Nothing is a more powerful tool to explore the integrity and substance of a mind than a story, a parable, a metaphor. There is no effect more powerful in the universe than a well-illustrated parable. The teachings of Buddha or Jesus have more kinetic effect than any nation's arsenal of nuclear warheads – and they operate with more moral precision.

Is it difficult to turn our focus inward? Is it impossible? No, there are examples of humans who have modified their environment to attain the level of consciousness they seek (i.e. the Western gnostic tradition). Is it troublesome? Yes, as any attainment of ambition, any mental transformation is challenging. Does the inward journey test us to the limit? Yes, it is a constant war of good and evil. Most humans avoid this conflict with all their cunning. The inward path enforces honesty and responsibility. Yet it is no more difficult to turn our focus inward than it is to take responsibility for our thoughts and actions, treat other humans with respect, or to be faithful in our engagements. What is the incentive? Integrity of mind. The master of the inward path may achieve the freedom of self-reference.

There are innumerable sacred myths that we may only understand now with the hindsight of Story Theory. It is for this cause that the twelve labors of Hercules, for example, do not speak of human events – but of the mental cosmos, the narrative of the precession of the zodiac, inwardly within our mind illustrating the irrational moralities of human nature. We are retrograde in moral congress. In the interior of the human mind, so long obscured by the darkness of technological, nightmarish modernism, a light beam is suddenly turned on.

Let us enter boldly the radicalism of the thesis. The urge to enter space is an urge to verify our non-materiality. What is more self-defacing than for the mammalian body to enter an unsupportable and unsustainable vacuum of space. It is utterly unworkable. There is no walking, running, defecating, fornicating, or eating in space, except with troublesome restraints. Space travel is a kind of madness, and the spaceman is an ascetic as fanatical as Simon the Stylite living up on a pole. Astronauts, by default, are spiritual knights of the oldest and most heroic asceticism. They deny the physical body more than any known medieval self-flagellant, more than any fasting monk in his cell. No scientist remains an atheist strung out in space. Space, in this light, is, in effect, a spiritual pilgrimage.

Story Theory illustrates, in substance, that when we travel to other heavenly bodies, we are, in actuality, traveling within our own minds. The moon, as metaphor, may only be another location within our right hemispheric brain. We are the only creature making rockets to explore globular bodies within our own brain. Therefore space travel is simply a myth we cherish – an inward parable of reflection – not a truth indicating an actual "outward" movement. In this view, the isolation and deprivation of a spacecraft more resembles a monkish prayer cell. Any discovery we make in space is exactly, precisely, only a self-exploration of our inner metaphysic. All that we may ascertain in any direction of movement, whether to the bottom of the sea, or at the level of electron microscopy, or at the *Horsehead Nebula* – is only our own mind looking back at us. What awaits us at a distant galaxy? Precisely the same war of good and evil previously existent in the conscious mind.

In Story Theory, a war of good and evil exists in space exactly under the same protocol as it exists within human consciousness. Therefore, there is no "out-there" at all. There is not a separate entity "man," and he does not face a separate entity "universe" – as scientism teaches with desperate, self-referent missionary zeal. There is only a man (and *his* universe) within consciousness.

What is space travel? It is another test of our mind. What if we cannot see clearly the "thing" we *enter*? We are blocked by a dangerous interpretation of the concept of "universe." The universe is a projection of what our mind seeks.

We will not understand the boundaries of life until we face the peril of consciousness with further exploration within our mind. It will be asked with impatience, *how do we explore inward*? With stories. We make stories of our journey inward – parables, fictions, sacred myths, and epic poems. Since what else can a man make of his life except poems? The moment a man attempts to explain his life, even in the first syllables, he transitions instantaneously to story. This is the reason why literature and poetry are so vital to human societies. There is no inward gnosis without tests of linguistic power – that is, attainment of enchantment using symbols of authority. The Gospels of Jesus were true not because they possessed physical archaeology, they were true because they attained a precise discovery of the inner nature of the human condition – using speech of authority. Powerful speech will trump the necessity of archeology any day.

To lose the illusion of the solidity of matter is an essential first step in exploration of human consciousness – a step which scientism refuses to make. Scientism, caught investing all its resources of imagination in the construct of "outward-ness" – cannot now retreat to a more secure foundation without being exposed as a wounded morality.

To conceptualize our idea of Story Theory concisely we may say: *we will not understand the "universe of man" until we understand consciousness.* The only location of the "universe" is within our mind.

Story Theory explains the human mental protocol: *A man conceives an idea, and then he finds evidences to support that idea.* There is no record of a human that has not followed the stated protocol. Each human idiom finds evidences to support its linguistic bias. Never for an instant is that idiom true across other cultural and linguistic divides. Any idiom, thus, is "just-so." It is not repeatable. It is not even translatable.

Western men do not clearly see the nature of consciousness. Consciousness is seldom rational. The citizen is seldom rational. He follows his passions, and his passions are enflamed by memorable speech. Advertising executives know this secret of the human mind, and billions in national treasure are spent inventing memorable speech to sell toxic food, flame retardants, cancer causing chemicals, and industrial pharmaceuticals. Modernism uses the enchantment of symbols and images to promote fake indices of information.

What, then, is the consequence of Story Theory? Story Theory warns the modern of the misuse of his own mind. Story Theory is an attempt to strengthen and clarify human consciousness by dispelling the prestige of scientism. Modernism is not the final human idiom.

Story Theory moves in a new direction – inward, beyond modernism. Most Western men have lost faith in their wounded moralities – their outward, materialist churches – the self-referent idiom of science, the false construct of rationality, the spuriousness of modernist data, and their permanent (and market driven) dependence on pharmaceuticals. Story Theory invites us to gain clarity of mind with a new philosophy of life. We are invited to attain mastery. What, after all, is the merit of freedom, if we cannot be masters of our own minds? Are we free to constitute our own being? That is the issue.

We need to terraform new arrangements of universe with the powers of our mental agency. Our children no longer have to be the Lost Generation— without mythic understanding or purpose. Instead, we must investigate how we each have mythic code.

As explained in the following books, the narratives of the epic trope perform this transition. *Kosmoautikon* comes to destroy the idol in the modern temple.

CHAPTER FIVE

Is Modernism a Civilization of Truth?

Moderns are clumsy thinkers. They are drunkards. Their speech is defective. We can test this. Modern men can no longer articulate (in the public space) their concept of the beautiful and the good. Any opinions expressing admiration for established Eurocentric aesthetics of the good and the beautiful are silenced with accusations of bigotry, arrogance, or racism.

This tactic is nothing but an attempt to freeze and miniaturize speech. There is no rehearsal of the good and beautiful so long as it is felt that the discussion will offend any potential demographic in the marketplace. Industrial, capitalized, liberal modernism projects the hostility of ambivalence towards any non-modernist, non-politically correct speech. This hostility chills the free speech of poetry.

Modernism is thus a cult of the whisper. There is no open debate of the beautiful and the good. That is, the modern may express only accepted democratic clichés or liberalist generalities. Moderns cannot clearly articulate their thoughts if they ever step outside of modernist speech patterns. They stumble. They think of a line from popular music. They speak of the greatness of sport. Life is like a movie they saw last week. They are limited by their pop-culture idiom of detecting worlds.

Citizens cannot correctly place the data points of modernism in a perspective that reveals the contradictions of their civilization. Moderns do not choose to identify the contradictions of their society. Modernism advertises with acclaim even minor advances in the curing of cancers, alzheimer's, autism, dementia and diabetes – yet never mentions that it is modernism itself that has created the epidemic of the same diseases in the first instance. For every citizen "cured" with toxic pharmaceuticals – ten have already succumbed to the endemic diseases of modern industrial societies. Yet the call is made for ever more applications of modernism to treat the diseases of modernism. This is a clumsy way to cling to a botched civilization.

Citizens can't exactly express why they accept to be modern – except that, perhaps, modernism is more convenient to their indolence – that they are too dependent upon the chemicals of the urban market. Moderns feel they must accept modernism since machines perform their drudgery. That is, how can you argue with a wheat combine or a sewer system? You are defeated from the outset of your interrogative by acquired industrial necessities. We are a civilization in fear of renewed impending drudgery.

Moderns can't say why they tolerate technological totalitarianism – except that modernism is all they know. That is weak. Is it correct for Germans to say they accepted Nazism – or Russians, Soviet communism – since that was the only choice given to them? In fact, the danger of modernism is this: modern men cannot mature – they can only age with the terror of aging. There is nothing beyond youth or middle age to hope for except loneliness, television and around-the-clock advertisements for pharmaceuticals (that kill, deform, and maim). The modern is deformed with frivolous surgeries, flame retardants, plastics, pills, pesticides, and preservatives all flowing in quantity through his blood system. Modernism cannot fix aging except by lying to the aged – and taking their money. The truth is the aged have no place of honor in modernism, except as a market segment. Modernism ghettoizes the aged.

Believing you *adamantly* need the machines and pharmaceuticals is not a position well thought out with sobriety. How did other human societies do without industrial pharmaceuticals? They also had literature, art, and commerce on grand scales – and they did not suffer from out of control overpopulation.

So far from being a civilization of the independent, informed, and free, no modern can clearly explain why modernism is a supreme human idiom. Planned obsolescence is the *chief* operating protocol of modernism. It makes a poor church. It impoverishes the individual into the final category of a consumer of modernism. Modern men work in cubicles that they detest. Technology only makes them more harassed and unable to think clearly. Citizens live with no clarity of purpose. Lives are spent in answering technological questions that have no permanent solutions. They must endure dictates of ever more technology that is designed to fail with obsolescence in 24 months. Moderns know exactly that modern technology needs constant alteration, constant upgrades, constant monitoring, constant replacement – constant worry. They know that modernism makes them tired, indolent, confused and uneasy. The secret of modernism is our deep loathing of modernism. We age horribly and without dignity under modernism. Modern men have less value each day they live.

Any effort to describe modernism is approximate, uncertain, partially thought out, self-referent, and overtly self-contradictory. Modernism makes great quantities of packaged food available to more people and at a lower price – yet this category of food kills, maims, sickens and deforms the populaces. Why cheer ever greater human populations if the poisoned food only makes them obese, deformed and diabetic? It is not even possible to state in public that human populations have long outgrown the supply of natural water and fertilizers. We are living on artificial chemicals. What then is honest about the benefits of ever increasing populations scheduled to live indefinitely (and exclusively) on fake modern food and corrosive medicines?

Any attempt to describe modernism would wildly differ from citizen to citizen – and each attempt, in the end, would be only an advertised illusion. Is it the rule of the machines you love? They will pollute the Earth beyond use. Is it the convenience of pharmaceuticals modern men must have? They maim the body and weaken the human mind. Is it industrial food you hunger after? Industrial foods, made by the lowest bidder, are not food, they are acidic chemicals. We are a nation of diabetics after five decades of sugared, powdered, processed, salted, boxed, and mass-advertised food.

In fact, Westerns cannot articulate why we choose to be modern, because modernism is essentially dishonest and false. Why is this a problem for the poet? Since poetry is ruthlessly honest, since poetic speech may only be truthful, a lying civilization interdicts any poetry of integrity.

Is there any joy in the mass education of an entire populace? No, the Western education system is essentially a means of scientific and materialist propaganda, funded at the university level by the wealth of military and pharmaceutical industries. Modernism in, modernism out.

Is it the superior idiom of science you admire? I started life favorable to industry and science. I became a pilot due to the natural love boys have of industrial machines, cars, and aircraft. Then I saw my body and my society becoming increasingly deformed. I discovered with deep research that science, as medicine, as electronics, artificially manufactures false and self-referent information of a profit motive market ideology. I saw that it was impossible that science could ever be trusted to be partial, safe, or without bias. No humanist compunction prevented scientists from supporting Nazi Germany (or Soviet and American weaponization of air and space).

Can we trust science to tell the truth about pharmaceuticals? Ask the deformed and maimed who have taken drugs in one decade and were maimed or killed in the next decade due to such trust. It is now proven that prestigious medical journals use data carefully cherry-picked from studies initiated and funded by the pharmaceutical industry – all negative results are suppressed from the public. Medical doctors are paid suspiciously large sums to authenticate tests that they themselves did not control or even participate in. In almost all cases psychotic medications have less effect than placebos. Citizens cannot trust the information of their own modernist society.

Modernism is a rogue civilization. Industrial science (as global industrialism) has destroyed more animal species, and more rainforests, than any other linguistic ideology. If the Earth is going to be destroyed, it will more likely occur due to scientific "progress" instead of natural disaster. The mature "worldview" of science matches up with no actual or "natural" reality. Only humans detect the presence of stars, galaxies, photons, bosons, and protons – no other creature of Earth sees this deeply benighted material universe. Space telescopes look at entities permanently irrelevant to the living. Scientism makes men preoccupied unnecessarily with material objects having no actual human moral permanence (as galaxies and bosons).

Moderns live in an unrealistic bubble of mis-information of "fake science." The result? The urban citizen cannot understand any longer how to plant his own food, cannot find clean water, cannot identify natural vegetation, cannot name a species of tree or vine, and cannot decide what is healthy to consume. We no longer know what to teach in Western school systems – it is unashamed materialism – or is it the shame of materialism? This is where the idiom of modernity has left us – that is, adolescent, immature, and hanging in the air – scheduled for extinction.

The modernist West is corrupted by dishonest institutions (false medical journals, toxic new pharmaceuticals, false categories of food) ensuring only ideational mediocrity, bolstered by the arrogance and the tyranny of a capitalist and totalitarian democracy. Why is modernism haughty and tyrannical? Because it controls secular education and ghettoizes any alternate human faith or belief. That civilization is not honest that pretends to be liberal and free – yet controls speech, behavior, and thought. We are under total technological surveillance of our personal conversations. The strong poet gnaws at the chains – and the dishonesty of information – that bind us.

Poets traditionally reach out (with visions, dreams, hopes, inspirations) beyond human material conditions, beyond the current political fashion. In this way, poetry is free to remain honest – and to exercise freedom of intellectual movement – without political constraint. Totalitarian modernist states and ideologies restrict this free movement of ideas. Stalin and Hitler had no great poets in their time. In totalitarian states there may exist only a category of ideological poets. Modernism, as a totalitarian state, also creates a fake category of sociopolitical prose-poets.

The modern poet cannot tell the truth if his society is untruthful – if it is debased, corrupted and perverted from the tested (and ancient) virtues of *Homo sapiens*. This explains why there are no strong poets in modern societies.

I hope my thesis finds its level of poignancy. This is why there were no great poets under the dishonest and lying societies of the Soviet Union and Nazi Germany. Exactly analogous to technological modernism, the poets of those societies were under 24 hour surveillance, and their speech was not free. Any dishonest civilization has to watch its citizens carefully, and check their minds with incessant propaganda (or advertising).

If poetry cannot remain in a position of honesty – having virtues that are real virtues, having beauty that can be cheered by a majority, and having language that is allowed the benefit of distinction – then there is no point to the work of the poet in our society. Poetry is as distinct from prose – as music is distinct from prose. Modern *prose* verse – is not verse – it is bad prose. Modern prose does not seek exclusively prophetic voice. In Story Theory there should always be a set of poets seeking exclusively prophetic voice, since a nation without this sense is lacking a valid human faculty.

Modern society has contradictions so deep that it is not possible for the poet to be honest – and still enjoy an audience of influence and prestige. It is a civilization's level of honesty that determines the poet's level of honesty. And if the poet is as dishonest as his society, he is merely irrelevant to that society – since what then is the benefit of the poet's gift of truth?

Perhaps my thesis comes into view. When a society is torn by self-contradictions of a political ideology – even a supreme liberal ideology – there is no honesty in art. If a society turns virtues and excellence upside down – then what is the possibility of an art – as poetry – that may, by definition, only represent truth and virtue? In my generation murderers, gangsters, and thieves are glamorized by cinematic celebrities of beauty, strength, prestige, and memorable voices. I have a problem with this etiquette. If crime is shown as virtue in our society – how can that society be honest? How can poets of a dishonest society perform their ancient function of mixing beauty only with truth?

Therefore, is modernism an honest civilization? No, it is not. Modern prose poems do not show the contradictions and dishonesty of capitalist and technological civilization. Modern prose poems, ignoring the all-pervading *scientisms* of Western speech, are not honest, since the idiom of scientism is omnipresent in the West. Modern prose poems are not poems – as they reject any attainment of musical or distinctive speech. Strong poetry cannot be cheered in a society where the cult of the lie, or whisper, is accepted as normal speech. The poet is dishonest if the society he represents is dishonest.

These lines of inquiry will be pursued in the following chapters.

CHAPTER SIX

The Alien Mind of Homo Sapiens

Homo sapiens has no evidence for the terrestrial origin of his self-conscious mind. The human mind possesses no half-way points of biological evolution. There are no intermediate links connecting animal instinct to human self-consciousness. We are just now placing *Homo sapiens* in his proper context. There are only whispers about what happened *during the early moments of Homo sapiens.*

Why do we suspect that our mind does not originate from Earth? Place *Homo sapiens* on a stranded island – and he would make masterful symbols and pictures within two generations. In ten generations he would tell masterful, enchanted stories of his origins and recite epic poems. Place a primate on an island and in a thousand generations he will only eat and defecate. For the purpose of a theory of poetry, I conclude that the mind of *Homo sapiens* is alien to Earth ecosystems.

Modern academics avoid the subject of the alien human mind. Unexplained and unexplainable by secularist idiom, the self-conscious mind of *Homo sapiens* has no antecedent in Earth's zoology. Neither materialists nor scientists know anything of the foundation of human consciousness – they may only discuss the arbitrary products of consciousness. Modern man is, thus, in effect, a nomad in his own mind. He cannot explain himself, and he has no home outside the conscious precinct of his mind.

Therefore, the poet, as the story maker, is the preeminent agent in the human condition. The poet thinks he knows something. He observes that the mind is activated with memorable speech. More outrageous, the strong poet obtains prophetic voice from beyond the cosmos – so far still an alien locus. Let us begin our discussion with unassailable facts.

A self-conscious mind is more rare, more mysterious, more multiple in dimension than any church, any temple, or any cunning text previously conceived by man. Any religion may only be a poor copy of self-consciousness. Self-consciousness is the only church *Homo sapiens* possesses. It is the only human church that ever will exist. We can test this. In Story Theory, every man always believes his own mind – but rarely the mind of another man. In another example, when we perform evil – we feel it deeply. The truth? We are ashamed of most of our actions in life. Self-consciousness is our only church – and we each carry this moral and ethical leviathan with us wherever we travel – even into remote space.

Let us state the case for the alien element of poetry. Only a self-conscious mind detects a poem. No other living creature of Earth, only man, has a self-conscious mind. There was no writing, and no poetry, until the Fifth millennium B.C. (I do not insist too much on time-lines. Nothing is more arbitrary, more illusionary than the actuality of time.) If *Homo sapiens* originated 50 thousand years ago and always had the gene for sophisticated symbology – why does writing appear so late? I will suggest that either man has the gene for abstract symbols – or not. A gene does not have the necessity of development. A gene is either on or off – it is either present or not present. Some beekeeper could have woken the hive – could have turned this gene on. So let us see ourselves clearly. In Story Theory, man was only man when he used symbols of self-consciousness – not before this moment. A primate walking on two feet is not a man.

A symbol is an alien artifact. A symbol is necessary because we only may perceive forms *within* consciousness. There is nothing "outside" of our consciousness – thus we need to possess abstract data points – symbols.

We may perceive nothing in the "universe" except images modified *within* our own self-consciousness. That will be problematic for the modern to visualize. He will have to use symbols to communicate his inability to understand. Either way, we may make our case for the preeminence of poetry in human societies.

Why? Because any human speech using symbols is an interpretation, a poem. The necessity of the faculty of the poet is therefore paramount. There is nothing more emotive than the power of symbols. There is no world, no human information, without symbols. The poet is the maker, the master of symbols. Language is the only house of a self-conscious mind. This is the strong argument for poetry.

There is an uncanny quality – an alien quality – about high poetic texts. Who can plot the boundaries of a timeless story? No one can kill or erase a story. We possess all past stories as fully operative. We still possess every human myth. A character of narrative is valid for all of time.

Our constructs of good and evil, then, as well as any narrative of deity, are outside of time, and thus extra-cosmos. As there is no "outside" separate from our self-consciousness – the only place for evolving the human idiom is *inward*. Not in time. Not in space. Only memorable speech, the poet's office, can make this further inward discovery of human self-consciousness. How else may we make contact with god-like intelligence if not from prophetic speech? This is a role properly filled by the strong poet.

There is an alien characteristic of seminal human texts. We can test this. We still don't know the names or the personalities of the poets of the *Torah*. Who wrote the five books of *Moses*? We don't know—it was not a man called Moses. Not a single name (or bone, or body) can be discovered. We still don't know the name or personality of the actual poets of the Gospels. It was not *Matthew, Mark, Luke,* or *John*.

Who wrote the Shakespeare canon? It was not the bag-goods salesman, "Shakspar" of Stratford-on-Avon – he was proven to be illiterate. High Western texts are, effectively, alien. We don't know who the poets were that wrote the *Iliad* and *Odyssey*. It wasn't a man named Homer. We don't know who gave humans the story of *Hercules* – and the Greek myths. The academic is surprised to discover that it is impossible to make a count of the Greek myths – they have no beginning and no end?!

The human mind is a mystery. We have proofs. There is no originator of the mind. We never will know the person that wrote the Egyptian *Book of the Dead*. We don't know who sang the epics of Gilgamesh. We don't know who within the Egyptian priesthood scripted *Amon as the Sole God*. We don't know the poet that wrote *Genesis – or The Psalms of David*. We don't know who inscribed the first Sumerian cuneiform epics—or who, or what deity, dictated the first human poems or the many separate tablets of the *Epic of Creation*. We only know that stories appear with wild alien symbology – and with uncanny idiom. Archaeology could not give us any insight into the origins of the story-makers – even if it existed.

There is nothing human about most ancient myths. The *Twelve Labors of Hercules* did not discuss humans – or a human society! It is a history of the zodiac. This engenders the question why the zodiac is an important motif in all seminal myths and epic poems? Humans are seldom mentioned in ancient myths. The myths, instead, address an alien cosmology and destiny – as well as a non-human time scale. The only locus, therefore, of a mythic entity (as Orpheus, Apollo, Dionysus, or Hercules) is the alien self-conscious mind. It is as if epic narratives were given to our ancestors by an unearthly intelligence – whose home was the interior cosmos (the conscious mind) – not Earth. (The precession of the zodiac is a symbol of the *reversal* of the illusion of the outward cosmos!) Thus the zodiac is a clue that the path lies *within* the conscious mind – not outside of the mind. Perhaps this is a clue why the zodiac is embedded in ancient myths over and over again.

If the self-conscious mind is alien to the animal kingdom, then poetry is a codex of alien communication. Poetry is a mythic codex able to transcend multiple dimensions of information – outside of time – outside of the illusion of material causation.

Therefore, for the purpose of Story Theory, we deny the necessity for millions of years of human evolution, and we anticipate the myth that the use of writing appeared in a single generation. No other entity of nature has a mind able to move across multiple dimensions. Writing was established from outside of Earth, and not developed in deserts over millennia – letter by letter, decade by decade. Primates did not develop or originate the self-conscious mind. That is an unproven myth of modern science. There are no archeological links between an animal mind and a symbol-making mind.

What is my point? If the human mind is an alien entity, if the human imagination originates from outside of the cosmos, then this status will influence the poetry we write. In Story Theory, in a place yet undiscovered, we ourselves are alien gods.

This is why *Kosmoautikon* traces prophetic voices from our original ancestors.

CHAPTER SEVEN

Why Write Epic Poems?

Why write poetry? It is an unexpected interrogative. It is an important question in Western intellectual history. Until we hear the answer we will not clearly understand the hostile environment of totalitarian modernism (i.e. the cultural epoch that has no significant and no commonly known poets). The question has to be posed in this book, since no one has the courage to ask it in the public forum. No academic dares to make an answer. Which bias would he advocate? Which cultural tradition? Which demographic? Which hero tradition? He is careful, he is even silent, because he wishes to retain a remunerative position in a politically biased academic environment.

To write memorable and authentic speech is the power of *autexousia,* "the authority to constitute one's being." We see the link between poetry and *autexousia* when we observe the status of poets in totalitarian societies. Hitler and Stalin did not tolerate strong independent poets – there could only be ideological poets (and they were, intentionally, to be ignored). Modernism is also an ideological society, a politically correct society that tolerates only poets as leftist ideologues. Societies that compel thought and behavior reduce free speech to whispers. In a society where political ideology is enforced, the first profession to go silent is the profession of the poet – since spiritual freedom and honesty is the only level of consciousness that poetry seeks. What does it suggest, then, if no American poet since WWII has made a living exclusively on his poems? What does it mean if the few poets to publish in the West are of the same leftist ideology?

The tragedy of modernist poetry is that it has become demographically politicized. Only persons belonging to a distinct political demographic are accepted socially to be poets (usually tenured academics under no pressure to perform, except to prove their political correctness). Consequently, there is only a cult of whispers in the land. Many strong poets are silent and deeply

alienated. The few academics accepted into print as poets are known for
their ideological and political biases – even as much as their poetry is feeble,
inaudible, and appears indistinct from newspaper prose. To remake our world,
we have to ask new interrogatives of the art of poetry.

First, I will accuse our poets. Where, in fact, are the great Western poets?
The absence of a cadre of strong poets is like a ghost story – if they exist, they
are unknown and unseen. American poets have no social influence and they
have no power to change the world they live in.

We may identify causes contributing to the failure of modern poets to
influence his or her society: 1) Modern prose-poets do not build characters
from actual life. 2) In a scientific society, there is no reference to science
or technology in modern poems. 3) A sustained narrative of important
and complex events is avoided in modernist prose poems. 4) Modern poets
purposely use undistinguished language from a sense of embarrassment to
craft any distinction or music of vernacular speech. 5) Though we have lived
in the most violent and vicious century on the planet, only a progressive
and liberalist ideology is found in American poems. A poet that represents
violence, betrayal, hate, murder, victory or conquest – in the round – is
rejected as a subject of American poetry. Yet, with deep apology, these are
exactly the common articles and requirements of *Homo sapiens.*

If this is true, why are poets still writing poems? Because we still seek
autexousia, "the power to constitute one's own being." Because when all
ideology is shown to be a shame, men still wish to be free to recreate their
world and expand their soul with power. Because we still think we may
discover true things not yet seen. Because we know things we still cannot see.

Why do we write epic poems? Because we still do not know what yet
lies on the human genome. Because men still do not know the origins of the
human condition. We have no idea where all our great texts have originated
and our consciousness thus appears unaccountable. Therefore, since there
is nothing sure concerning the origin of the human mind, a story has to be
told – a narrative of life forms – usually with distinctive speech.

This necessity to tell stories of our life is not a weakness. Quite the contrary,
the power to constitute one's own being is the chief human glory. In this way I
assert the poet's craft of more estimation than I do the narrow spectrum of the
materialist or the scientist – who each have, by now, ideological agendas. We
don't want to be told (without accurate linkage or proof) that our deity-like
mind was an accident of primate evolution – or that our self-conscious mind
originates from the *Big Bang.* These are cowardly, fake, mytho-ideological
"events" of scientism. We may as well say that a perfectly formed 747 aircraft
was made in our back yard by the powerful force of hurricane winds. There
is no proof of these wild statements.

Scientism, unable to explain the origin of self-consciousness, transposes on our genetically advanced mind, instead, a primitive primate mind. By this dialectic, scientism performs a brain switch. They change the difficulty of the question – (that is, where does self-consciousness originate?) – by changing the object under investigation. They do not address a spiritual compound entity of supernatural force. They prefer to deal with an early primate brain, one that can be dug up, none of which ever remotely possessed self-consciousness. By making it a question of brain and skull size they successfully reduce the case to a level of their ideological competence. Scientists *can* find an ancient partial primate skull, *therefore*, it must be this ancient, tiny, primate skull that meets the requirement of the origin of *Homo sapiens*. It is a clumsy argument.

We want to know more about the depth of the self-conscious mind. We write poems because science is narrowly materialist, modernism is self-referent, and democracy, as capitalism, is corrupt. We write poetry to tell the truth – to expose tyrants, false human information, and the lies of totalitarian societies. Poetry reveals secrets deeply embedded within consciousness. In no otherwise could we respond with *sudden recognition* when a poet informs us with his new insight. We instantaneously know when a poet has discovered a hidden secret of the human genome. All future human speech must subsequently change to embrace his discovery.

All of literature contains a secret – as the myths of Hercules or the story of the zodiac, contain a secret. What, then, is the purpose of literature? It seeks out prophetic voice. Why prophetic voice? Any human act is tested against a linguistic hypothesis for a value of good and evil. Prophetic voice operates as god minus. Consequently, the purpose of literature is to verify that life has value – and this clarity of value always takes the form of prophetic speech.

Currently there is no strong school of poetry in the West. Modernist lyric poetry is weak and undistinguishable from newspaper prose. No Western citizen consults major poets as a reference for crucial decisions in life. I counter my critique of modernist prose-poetry with a vision of the modern epic trope:

1) Epic poetry should be courageous enough to reference science and technology in the theme. 2) The epic poem should give a sustained narrative portraying complex events and characters in extraordinary relief. 3) The epic device should be strong enough to use a distinctly charged language, demonstrating no embarrassment of the music of contemporary vernacular speech. Currently the common encountered newspaper prose-lyric exhibits none of these characteristics. It is without distinction.

But can it be done? Can modern vernacular sustain distinctive speech without resort to sentimentality or anachronisms? Perhaps it is a matter of force of mind or a well-chosen device that can sustain a narrative of manners. The new reader will want some rough samples of the thesis – vernacular phrases that rise ever so slightly to a heightened charge. Selections from the first poem may serve as partial examples. I am delimited to a careful choice of mature vernacular usage – with a minor, just-so added charge.

> "I have crossed my meridian voyage, where
> human becomes visible idiom, and so my fears.
> I hunt the tar cave of fossil mind, where ghosts of
> space, time, and men coil in somatic prescience.
>
> I will rise deep in winter with no alarm, not
> once to follow substance of moth-winged men
> seized with light. I lay down structure embedded
> with my selection, joy and fear reduced to equal fonts."
>
> *Canto Four*

The transition from newspaper prose to charged vernacular epic speech is attainable, though restrained and sober, with application of a measured inflection. If a poet does not create a charged modern language, enough to attain a sustained self-referent authority, what use then is the profession of the poet? If nothing else, avoiding the controversy of short-lived ideology, *Kosmoautikon* seeks to increase the range of idiomatic voice in American poetry. A critique of the work, therefore, will test the honesty of the critic as much as the talent of the poet.

Epic poetry is a device that joins memorable verse to a vehicle supporting a many-layered narrative of manners. I wish to illustrate how epic poetry may differ from unmetered blank verse – that is, modern "verse" currently using undistinguished newspaper prose. I oppose the modern prose-lyric for its complete isolation from music and disregard of a complicated narrative (as rehearsed above). The determined poet will wish to assimilate proven elements of rhythmic force in English verse.

> If I showed no caution, I showed a care,
> my sin that shames all future tailors' tongues,
> strange rattle in ear, brutish mouth secrete
> my three day house, words as silk in mouths,
> drenched tongue to cotton cloths espoused release
> a smooth round sound, a thousand bursting seeds,
> mummy moths with wings as black-eyed peas,
> silken-rattle-charged with moth wing play,
> my window dressing sins,
> the boat of sky I made from reeds,

no tender end of days, or undiminished men,
or none that came to Earth to mend.

Canto Six

Epic poetry joins distinctive speech with effortless sub-metered verse to release a rhythmic charge equal to the content under discussion. *Kosmoautikon* introduces a new voice that does not model itself on anachronisms, is not strained, yet retains a proper and ancient power of music.

The poet will be careful to illustrate from his first page that he is well with the world he inhabits. He will wish to show that the poetry of his school is again able to describe the neighborhood the modern poet lives in. He will wish to show that he can master the idiom of scientism without impairment of his own. He might give proofs that metaphor, rhythm, and meter may inform a modern narrative with improvement and animated clarity. The strong poet will introduce these principles from the first lines of his work.

As I purple your eyes with tint, staining
dyes empty from your heart. The stutter of
my ray gun seals crimson rising veins, fused in
sequence, as scuttling desert insects print
minuscule in sand. I have merged, enraged,
six shadowed proteins, six pungent etched
tattoos remote from crowded tenements
of native helix. (Touches reddening cheek.)
Here. Inside this glass, I have spliced, in chains,
twelve dark silhouettes on the phylum of
your gene. There, six-fingered, at the end of
time, in blood-dark skies, enamellers of
gold-dust tears on empty darkened eyes, will
sermon on your fame till the agon of
their school is bitter-cold.

Canto One

Perhaps even the non-specialist will note with relief that a Western poet has undertaken a longer poem without lamenting the horror of a verdant April, does not monument his depression, does not steadfastly ignore the all-pervading idiom of scientism in his own culture – and dares to encompass the entire scope of human life in his device. He is a poet set upon making conquest of the world he inhabits, endows his world with enchantment commensurate with his talent, and proposes to infect other men with his vision. So what if all other poets must go to the wall?

If the epic trope contains prophetic voice – as it does – can it be of any use to the modern citizen? The modern, despite his poor secular education, is still curious about consciousness. Epic poetry asks us to test the nature of consciousness. What value does life have? What are the forces that impel men to act? How does the structure of the cosmos seem to inform all human myth? What can account for our agonistic struggles against all odds? Why can we not accept mediocrity? What is the correct action? Is it possible that the reader can point to any human text that does not in some degree evaluate the merit of life? In this evaluation, the epic trope prepares the human mind for its battle against chaos. We still have to explain the existence of the world and the manners of men in the world.

We need prophetic voice since we have not yet found the source of our mind. Or can materialism replace the need for prophetic voices? Is modern medicine the final and most supreme idea of the self-conscious mind? How many surgeries can be scheduled for ten billion people? Can a desiccate and diminutive primate skull encompass the wild range of our mind? Is modernism the final human idiom? We place this answer beyond doubt when we observe none of us has witnessed the final human speech. In Story Theory, modernism is not the final human idiom – rather, it is only one of many, possibly brilliant, choices of dementia.

The future idiom of *Homo sapiens* is still unknown – we are only certain it will *not* be modernism that men seek in the future. We know as little of the future as a 19th century church bishop could have anticipated the space age – only a century later. No civilization is an exact replica of reality; any possible civilization is only a linguistic representation of reality.

Why are we writing epic poems? Because we still do not know the correct response to the gift of cognizance. Because we do not yet know the right action of human behavior. Because we still search the final excellence of the self-conscious mind. In this age of supreme self-consciousness the epic poem may best explore the highest exercise of a self-conscious mind. We are in an age where men are at war with their own mind – and there should be a many-layered narrative of the possible choices and consequences of the conflict. The outcome is still in the balance.

CHAPTER EIGHT

The Exclusivity of Human Information

In Story Theory human information is a onetime event and cannot be repeated. Human experience is important enough not to be lost. That is to say, the information of the individual perceiver is so rich and penetrating, so exclusive that no objective scientific method may mine the richness of an individual's experience. The exclusive information of human consciousness is vast. Every human contains a mine of subjective – and largely unexplored – information. The poet in society maintains the record of human intimacies.

We say human information is exclusive since no two minds see phenomena in the same exact way. Only the individual has seen what he alone has seen – the individual has thought in ways that he alone has thought. Scientism fails to embrace this basic human phenomena. How to represent the vast registers of deep information of separate human individuals? How to master the basic subjectivity of the human condition – and to do so with brilliance and mastery? Only poetry can make this reach of clarity.

Science cannot record the subjective mind of each person – only literature attempts the investigation. Science, an outward-looking antenna, so far from being able to replicate the entirety of human experience, cannot even harvest the consciousness of an infant. This statement accuses the all-inclusive claims of science as the supreme idiom of human information. Deep human information, being, subjective, is solidly within the competence of the poet. He tells stories of the minds of *Homo sapiens.* And there are as many stories as there are separate human minds. This is the necessity for a philosophic discussion only initiated by Story Theory.

A significant poetic attainment is a rarity. Nothing can replace the individual poet speaking in the vernacular. Considering Homer, Rilke, and the Shakespeare poet (or Dylan Thomas writing in the 1930s), they surprise us, since they alone are able to represent, to bring to the light, uncanny mines of deep human perception.

Poetry is important since, again, the galaxy in which men find themselves must be translated. Usually only the poet can replicate his exclusive information. No man can return to his youth, regain his lost parents, or reconstitute the love of a beloved, once lost – but a poet can recreate these emotions with achievements of striking insight and speech. Since every human act is unique and "just-so," we seek a medium that monuments for all time human data we wish never to lose. Thus, the exclusivity of human consciousness concerns the competence of poetry – not science.

Exclusive human information is blocked by "outward" industrial, materialist societies. Modern information is superficial and does not correctly place the mind of man at the center of all things. Technology, instead, is at the center of human focus. Compared to the overwhelming prestige of modern scientism, a story, or a poem, has little modern authority of interpreting the world. This is a mistake, leading to the loss of deep information of the human genome.

The out-ward brilliance of Victorian scientism, as will be shown, is entirely due to the nature of its *self-reference*. Modernism, with its out of date Victorian scientific clichés, maps the mind of the citizen with memorable and materialistic platitudes of science-speak. Modernism embeds a materialistic ideology that blocks Western eyes from seeing other forms of human reality. The modern will instinctively resist any non-scientific speech. Thus, the problem of recovery of poetry in the West is complex.

Poetry only has one product – truth – clarity of information. Fix the nature of information that is detected by a society – and you will correct any failures of poetry in that society. Establish the prestige of prophetic voice in our time and you will establish the prestige of poetry in our time.

Science makes a poor prophet. Science seldom correctly predicted any human calamity or disaster. Liberal societies have never once predicted the next war. Liberalism (as scientism) is always in the case of being surprised by actual human information. Western Democracies, using scientism, have no intrinsic means to anticipate or stop a global virus, a collapse of currency, a natural calamity, or a foreign dictator in a timely manner. Prophetic voice on the other hand, has always anticipated the next war. Every human cataclysm is felt by prophetic voices – before it is detected by instruments, probes, and thermometers.

It is not enough to say that poetry is not important in modern society because it has been superseded by a more visual cinema and television. It is not an argument of probity to insist that poetry has been replaced by popular music or media. These replies are not well considered, and they avoid the issue of the competence of poetry over other means of information.

It is not enough to say that poetry has been superseded by an advanced technological society. That is a weak rejoinder – not carefully thought out. Poetry is not a poorly constructed gadget that needs to be updated. Poetry is not a rocket that is constructed with planned obsolescence – to be made redundant by the developments of new forms of rocket propulsion. Unlike technology, a poem true in one generation is true for all generations.

In each epoch, Homo sapiens falls back upon his singularity – that is, prophetic voice. Homo sapiens was first defined as that species that buried the dead with futurity and made symbols (poetic speech) to express that futurity. I make the observation that modern men no longer enter into the prophetic ritual by which Homo sapiens is defined.

Though recently degraded by the ideology of scientism, nothing is more natural to Homo sapiens than prophecy. Prophecy is deep information. Each human has a prophetic soul. Each human feels deeply his life and his prospects for futurity. Each human makes prophetic judgments daily, hourly, momentarily. A parent makes prophecies of their children's future life. A businessman instinctively makes a prophetic vision of his future prospects. A leader gives promise of his leadership with a gift of his prophetic vision. A poem properly seeks prophetic voice, because each human tests the poet's prophetic voice.

The issue of poetry in our time comes down to one question – what is human information? Modernism educates the Western citizen that only the information of scientism is worthy and prestigious. This has disastrous consequences. This view blocks the prestige of poetry and prophecy.

Scientism is narrow and false. Is actual human information "repeatable" (scientism) – or is human information "just-so" – a one-time event (as in prophecy, love, sacrifice, or distinctive speech)? The answer is decisive, since an entire civilization weighs in the balance.

If closely examined, we know that no human mind has ever seen, or ever repeated the exact same report of human life. The class of "objective" information is not fully human; objective information is useful only in the idiom of the machine. Look at a category of objective data, look closely at any material object, and in a few crucial minutes it becomes subjective. The human observer always changes the observed.

A human mind staring at the Grand Canyon or the night sky – or a momentous or horrific event – sees the initial physicality of the vision only a few moments, before the mind takes over and makes a personal narrative of the physical phenomenon. The point? The human mind makes a "poem" – a subjective interpretation – of any overwhelming event or physical structure. We romanticize everything we see – never once seeing an actual reality.

Since each human mind has its own interpretation, its own story, this tells us about the nature of consciousness itself. It tells us that we protect, by multiples of distinct visions, an hidden object of great value – now located in a place safe from influence. This object of great value is the final revelation of *Kosmoautikon*. Man's position as an inept voyager through the unreality of material space provides the dramatic device.

My thesis insists that if the information detected by poetry is degraded (as modernism), then *Homo sapiens* is likewise degraded. The human mind is activated from "just-so" poetic speech. Without the "just-so" data of memorable speech there is no map, nor organization of mind against chaos.

Each human remembers exactly where they were when a significant event happened in their life – a first love, a tragedy, a birth, a death, an encounter with nemesis, an encounter of great peril. In contradistinction, no human can remember when the first fractions were divided – or the first theorem of physics was solved. This is key to understand exactly what is "deep" in human information. Comparison of these examples will be our methodology of a strong theory of poetry.

What do men really want? Humans want to be sure that their voice is included within the precincts of all future life. We wish to ensure that our deep information is never lost. That is the only status, the only condition, worthy of genetically advanced minds. We don't want to live at one degraded time, in one degraded modern city. We want to live for all of time. That is the only proper perspective of an advanced mind. Anything else is a compromise made from the chaos and contradictions of material pursuits confounded by a creature (man) fully endowed with spiritual faculties. Only a new order, a new innovation of speech can make clarity from the cacophony of modernism. Every human civilization has attempted to work out this clarity with its own unique idiom.

For these causes, *Kosmoautikon* presents new revelations of deep human information – a hidden treasure, even now in a place safe from influence – which, perhaps, only the poet is premeditated to discover. *Kosmoautikon* is a technology – a device – intended to gain control of future looms of human sentience.

By any account a race for supremacy.

CHAPTER NINE

The Danger of an Outward Church

Most of what passes for religion is a "literature" of religion. Let us be accurate, a religion is a set of self-referent texts, yet sets the mind of man on a journey within his condition of helpless materiality. This is the value of religion: it gives man an idiom to cultivate higher spiritual powers and concepts. A religion operates exactly as the mind of Homo sapiens operates – with memorable speech.Every religion, every ideology, every church lives or falls by its choice of memorable speech.

Human religion starts out as powerful and emotive inner insight only to return to an outward, and degraded, structure of secular power and material belief. What is wrong with an "outward" church of faith?

That which Christians and Islam commonly nominate as "faith" is, in effect, merely the belief that *other* men have had direct experience of god. This is the poor choice the Western universal Church has historically offered the acolyte. Jesus and Moses had direct experience of god – yet it is not allowed to us to have the same gnosis. Thus for millennia all we have are stories of another person's gnosis of god. This is the fault of an "outward church." It lacks spiritual immediacy and power. I seek an actual power - not only a rumor of power.

As it is not beyond the imaginative purview of the educated that there is a higher unifying intelligence, the current outward churches are not vehicles providing direct gnosis of any deity. We don't want faith; we want direct contact with the power of this higher agency. We want gnosis. An outward church can never give us that access.

Faith is not *evidence* of god. The mind of *Homo sapiens* is designed to recognize direct experience of god – and, in that case, *faith in god* is linguistically redundant. We have been in the wilderness (with the outward church) now for two millennia. Yet we can still recover our spiritual necessity. Gnosis will always be preceded by extraordinary speech that remaps the mind.

We seek direct power of divinity – that is, the miracle of love, futurity of life, and supernatural recovery from peril. Yet each of these experiences occurs *only* within the human mind. This means that the only possible experience of god is within the mind – inwardly, with introspection – not to be found in an outward universal church teaching a *secondhand* faith.

My point? There is nothing detected that did not first originate in the mind. Once the infinity of the human mind is explored, and gnosis of direct spiritual power is demonstrated, there is no longer a need to search for second hand accounts of faith. Authentic experience of divine power is direct knowledge of divine power. Those professing "faith in god" are, in effect, the only persons *not* experiencing god's direct power.

My critique of Western Christians is that they exhibit no mental resistance to secular materiality, they are not initiated into spiritual mysteries, and they no longer bury the dead with symbols of resurrection. Instead, modern men incinerate their dead in gas ovens – renouncing any symbolic declaration of futurity. Each of these vital signatures of an advanced human mind has passed without modernist comment. No one has seemed to notice the transition. There are no public protests of the incinerator. As we know by recent history, the gas oven is a natural default utility in modern states. It is more efficient and economical.

There is no longer a deep spiritual need filled by the outward established churches – as they no longer pretend to teach the original Gnostic traditions of Christian founders (Jesus, Paul and Valentinus). Faced with the overwhelming hostility of modern secular men, the Roman Church in Europe will cease to exist as a source of spiritual activity. Since Roman Christianity was merely an outward (materialist) church, its spiritual fall was ordained the moment it accepted support from the state. After the 2nd century it had no second porch of initiates; there was never an innermost degree of initiation leading to ever deeper gnosis.

The early Gnostics clearly understood that there were no actual historical events in the *Bible* – the men of the 2nd century knew there were over 60 *Gospels* – and no poet of any of the many *Gospels* was under pressure to produce an exact historic document. The early Christians were not somehow mentally deficient – lacking an understanding of archeology – nor were they deceived. They understood with clarity that each of the sixty diverse *Gospels* were a separate codex of symbols, sayings, and parables for inward spiritual introspection – not historical facts for the foundation of an earthbound, physical, imperial institution. Each of the narratives simply had a differing orientation of power.

The prize – the aim – of any *Gospel* narrative was to map the inward journey of human consciousness – not to give an outward account of contemporary historical events. Christ went to the trouble to declare that this world (of "Caesar") was not his world. This clear statement was essentially ignored by future outward Orthodox churches – offering only outward motions of faith, demanding only obedience.

The Gnostics (including Paul) understood that the *Gospel* narratives were perceived as separate texts of high symbolic value, as timeless parables intended for deep inward introspection and contemplation. The poems and parables never intended to teach an historical truth. This vital point was made by the poet when the disciples asked Jesus why he spoke only in parables. This was the poet's way to show that the message of Jesus was an inward journey – not an academic discourse of outward, historical, archeological, or secular, and rational events. When asked why he taught only in allegories, Jesus clearly stated that his message was not for all men. In Luke, Jesus is recorded as saying, "The knowledge about the secrets of the kingdom of heaven has been given to you, but to the rest it comes by means of parables so that they may look but not see and listen but not understand."(Luke 8:9-10) Clearly, the parables were for those spiritually mature enough to understand his secret *initiations* – for those "who had ears to hear." The parables and "secret" *Gospels* were primarily for initiates trained and guided by the masters – the "perfected ones." This perspective is lost in mainline Western Christian churches.

Most of the traditions of the early Gnostics were mislaid until the recovery of the "lost" *Gospels* in the deserts of Egypt and Palestine in our own time. The sixty (known) *Gospel* texts only make sense if it is accepted that they were linguistic teaching aids for an intense and necessary symbolic journey inward – to be understood fully only by the initiated. Never for a moment were they deemed historic documents. They were never suitable for literal interpretation – as each *clearly* contradicted the others in so many historical points. It was the *story* that led to a personal inward journey – and each story could be adjusted according to the genius of the inward message. As may be anticipated in Story Theory, the only requirement of integrity is the emotional authority of the story.

The Gnostic Jesus was never intent on establishing a literal empire molded on Roman imperial power. So far from founding an earthly institution, he wished to establish the kingdom of god inside of the heart and mind of the initiate. The kingdom, Jesus stated many times, was *within* – not without.

The result was a debacle. The same church that (mistakenly) used the *Bible* as a literal historical record, justifying a hierarchy of priestly control, is now isolated in a sea of archeological, scientific secularism. Scientism makes short shrift of religious poems and stories that were never intended to be documents of scientific materialism – or dependent on any possible edifice of archeology.

The Western Church took the wrong path in the 3rd century. The Gnostics knew that the many separate *gospel* narratives were symbolic sayings – designed for inward introspection – not historic or archeological exegesis. The Western Church instead exterminated the unruly gnostic savants and declared the *New Testament* as the historical and literal word of a historical god. As the *New Testament* was never intended to be an historical text, and its literalist professions are easily exposed by archeology, thus even the cherished stories and parables have lost all creditability as well. They are wounded moralities.

The outcome we now see. The established Western Churches currently exhibit total obedience to secular views and materialist rationalism. Present main-line Christianity does not resist the anti-spiritual logic of industrial and materialist medicines. How are we sure of the thesis? If a Western citizen has a serious medical condition, Western Churches offer no competence of cure. The modern priest insists that you see a doctor in your crisis! Unbelievably, the Roman Catholic Church does not insist strenuously (in the public forum) that the church of Jesus Christ can cure disease! Nor, if you have troubles with a fellow citizen, they still cannot help you – they advise you to get a lawyer. Prayer is an outward ritual – a lifestyle choice – not the exclusive and most powerful means to solve any human crisis. This behavior is nothing less than the full surrender of an outward church to a materialist, historicist, and hostile secular idiom. By this act of non-resistance to secularism, the established churches fully admit failure in the race for supremacy. The Christian Church does not thus exist, except as another modern social club.

In this light, Western humans are no longer members of a religious society – they are a new secular society under profane surveillance and legal duress. Moderns do not bury their dead with reverence or make symbology to support the substantiation of an afterlife. Modernism has no salvation – that is, no philosophical end state – except mindless proliferation – for the sake of proliferation. Modernism is a grizzly repetitive ritual with no inner core of initiation or progression. Modern man cannot clearly articulate the supposed superiority of modernism. Is it the pharmaceuticals they desire and believe – the same proven to maim and kill? Is it the powdered food they want – the classes of modern ersatz food that disfigures and sickens the body? Or does the citizen cherish new categories of modern freedoms that are under 24 hour technological surveillance? We age horribly under scientism.

Perhaps my critique is clear. Modernism is a "church" of scientism, with its own categories of "faiths," dogmas and its own sets of evidences. Scientism, so far from advancing human spirituality, with attainments of spiritual training, is set rather to destroy *Homo sapiens* with fake and toxic classes of dogmatic materialism.

Addressing the Western loss of the tradition of inward gnosis, we can return to our thesis of poetry with renewed clarity. Why? Because poetry is a deep inward search. Poetry seeks gnosis. Poetry, as story, as deity, is experienced as a communication – a question and an answer – from within. By any account, this communication with deity may only be in the form of a narrative, as illustrated in the verses of the *Bible* and the epic trope. What, minus narrative, is an idol? There is no god without a narrative of god.

In our current dimension of activity – the present – the profession of eternity is located only within the competence of story. Eternity first appeared in Mesopotamian, then Egyptian, epic poems of creation. The point I take from my study is this: there cannot be physical communication with a non-physical god – there can only be a supernatural metaphor in vernacular speech that allows congress with the higher unifying intelligence.

I have no wish to promote any known religion. The spirituality I adhere to is undiscoverable, unoriginal to this planet, and resembles no known ritual. I prefer therefore to remain a sect of one. Still, it is within reach of the modern to make an individual and rewarding inward journey. I would agree, as Stephan Hoeller explains, speaking of the Gnostic tradition, some men correctly held a "conviction that direct, personal and absolute knowledge of the authentic truths of existence is accessible to human beings, and, moreover, that the attainment of such knowledge must always constitute the supreme achievement of human life." That comes closest to my religious view and should offend no person.

My conclusion is that religion in the West, from Hercules, to Apollo, to Isis, to Jesus, was a set of poetic narratives – powerfully emotive, symbolic, and metaphorical – not historical or archeological exegesis. In the 3rd century, early *Bible* narratives of powerful inward contemplation were subsequently corrupted by an outward, police state superstructure. The downfall and collapse of the Orthodox Church was insured the moment it exterminated fellow Christian Gnostics in the early Church. It now reaps what it has sown.

There is a reason why I have so far troubled the reader with the Gnostic tradition. It concerns poetry. There is a lost authority in the West of the symbolic and metaphorical narrative (poetry). Poetry is an inward journey and must be taught from birth – or it cannot operate with power and authority. I consider the human mind to be a metaphorical device – organized and made active by enchanted symbols.

As any poet, I claim this long tradition of powerful texts as my own – without insisting on an exact historicity. I conclude that story, myths, and poems (using symbols) give the only possible communication of the idea of immortality of the soul. The only way to accurately express spiritual power is by means of symbolic, introspective texts of supernatural interrogatives and stories of higher levels of consciousness. Is there any other way to represent the spiritual power? We can test this with our own experience.

When we look closely at our "outward" religions we see that there are no living examples of spiritual attainments – there are only stories of spiritual attainment. There never has been a perfect man – there is only a story of the perfect man. There is not an earthly, mortal eternity – there are only stories of spiritual eternity. There is not a perfect love – there are only stories of perfect love. There are not heroic humans – there are only stories of men who *became* heroic after adversity. There is not sentient life outside of the mind – there are only stories made of sentient life beyond the cosmos.

What is the point? *Sacred Story* and powerful myths are the lost link between the illusion of solid materiality (the quotidian present) and a direct experience of any possible deity. The inward, personal god, after all, is the only god we may ever meet. In each case of "god" there is first a case of prophetic and memorable speech. It does not matter what we actually see – it matters only what we think we see – what we will ourselves to see. When has it been any otherwise?

The narrative of the strong poet is always and in all cases the link between the mind of men and a treasure of such value that it is reserved only for initiates – that is, secured from any influence within the physical cosmos.

Why should any man care to seek out prophetic or memorable speech? Because he is a man in trouble.

CHAPTER TEN

A Man in Trouble

There can be no philosophy, no poetry without a man in trouble. All story, all gods, all literature, all romance, all comedy, all human joy exist only because there is a man in trouble. What does this tell us about the human condition within consciousness? There is enchantment of our condition only because we are men in trouble. The reader is reading this now because he is a man in trouble. He alone, therefore, will confirm the validity of the following statements.

Youth is a man in trouble; old age is a man in trouble; Eros is a man in trouble; war is a man in trouble; business is a man in trouble; marriage is a man in trouble. Consequently, there can be no discovery of possible human quality, no discussion of possible deity, without accounting for a man in trouble. You wish to find the true god? Find a man in trouble – he will lead you the shortest way.

Every narrative tells of a man in trouble. That is, no story exists that does not represent a protagonist that is in some difficulty. It is likewise a commonplace observation that there could be no sensation of joy without a contrasting state of trouble. There could not be a reliable test of the value of life without existing in a state of trouble. The human condition is a permanent state of crisis. Death is a crisis. Eros is a crisis. Business is a crisis. There is no place to hide. We can test this. Each moment a man finds peace, or joy, or contentment – the next moment he is in a fix.

Modernism also considers that humans are sick, that they are in a state of pre-development, and can be fixed once properly industrialized, socialized, and medicated. In Story Theory, man cannot be fixed and is in a state of trouble without any possible or final material solution. Therefore, modernism, ignoring the permanent condition of trouble, is dishonest. In Story Theory, to seek to eradicate trouble is to seek to eradicate human consciousness. Men must, in the end, grapple with peril using the meditative and spiritual faculty alone – and that is the point of metaphysics.

If humans may only exist in a state of trouble – nemesis, confusion, challenge, strife, chaos, and misdeed – then we need a new approach. We don't need more political solutions, still less do we need more fake categories of scientism. We need a spiritual imagination that can give coherence to our actual condition of self-referent consciousness. Let us accept the truth of the human condition. We are in a state of trouble, yet we still have the power to reconstitute our being. But if this is our goal – the power to freely constitute our being while facing human perils – then modernism and scientism will not help us to achieve *autexousia*. Today when we face peril, the state, industrial medicine, or the pharmaceutic industry intervenes intimately in our lives. Without autexousia, freedom is meaningless to a self-conscious being.

The point of the human condition is not to eradicate trouble – the point is to constitute our being meeting squarely the challenge of trouble. A new path must be found, since, after all, there is no rational solution to a problem that was never meant to have a solution. Modernism, that seeks to apply solutions to the insolvable, rationality to the irrational, thus, is a rogue civilization.

All of Western philosophy, all of Western religion, all of Western science, all of Western political ideology, can be critiqued as an attempt to escape the *trouble* of the human condition. Epic poems and Bibles are chronicles of humans in a state of peril. Joseph was a man in trouble in Egypt.

The epic trope faces peril and does not try to work a path around the permanent human condition of peril. This is the value of the epic verse in literature – it allows scope for an honest war of good and evil. In the *Iliad*, Hector does not try to find a way out of facing Achilles and certain death – he is only concerned how to face his fate with right action. The modern citizen would have found a way around confronting Achilles – he would have got a good lawyer.

Human consciousness is a war of good and evil. Yet the modern is not trained to acknowledge the self-conscious mind is in the midst of a war of good and evil. In effect, with pharmaceuticals, industrial surgeries, and state welfare, he runs from his fate – as hot oil down a wire. The modern feels he can get relief from the state when he has misfortune and peril. The modern lives perhaps longer, that is, more hours of trouble are added to his count, but he does not live with bravery or clarity of purpose. The modern does not recognize his soul in a state of trouble – he will tell you he seeks peace – and peace for all men – never being curious why peace is impossible to achieve. He is irredeemably delusional.

What is the point? The epic trope is the point. All stories of peril, of good and evil in man, are free attempts to construct the basic and original value of human life. The Greeks acknowledged this in the very language they used for poet. The Greek word for *poet* was the *"maker."* A poem of the death of Hector, of the peril of Hebrews in Egypt, of the Passion of Christ, was exactly where Western man was created – he was *made* with poetic texts of great peril. Each of these stories are, thus, not true of one archeological time, but true for all of time. Having no archeology – they stand outside of "science." Yet we are sure they were true of man – since we are, also, still men in trouble.

CHAPTER ELEVEN

Recovery of Mythic Code

What is mythic code? Mythic code is the act of experiencing within consciousness the same pattern of challenge and response – again and again. No matter in what condition of life, no matter in what Earth, consciousness requires a test of consciousness.

We do not interest ourselves with Hector because the *Iliad* of Homer had a great plot. As any epic poem, we know the plot and ending from the outset. We read Homer - as Dante or the Shakespeare poet - because he illustrates, memorably, that each protagonist has a pre-selected fate – a mythic code. We learn that Hector had the choice to flee out the back gate and save himself, but he was so constituted – so different than other men – that he chose to face Achilles even as much as he was certain it would be his death. This quality of the ennoblement of *Homo sapiens*, facing peril with sacrifice, is due not to accident but to an innate mythic code. Consciousness requires a test of consciousness

The modern, in contrast, seems to live lurching from accident to accident in a world where he is told he is irrelevant and miniscule. Hector makes himself the center of all things. Achilles, Agamemnon, Odysseus, each are men at the center of their world – but only because they have made themselves the center of all things. Under the pen of the Shakespeare poet, the mind of man is at the center of all being. We have to claim again our locus at the centrality of phenomena. This is the lesson the poet teaches – man is worthy to be the center of all possible worlds. He is supremely authorized to say *yes* or *no* - to accept or reject any peril - with a further recourse to consciousness. This is the challenge.

Mythic code intends we do not attain miracles of strength and courage by mere mischance – stumbling from random accident to accident. Mythic code verifies that we have an innate mind already preselected with attention and care to a pattern of victories or defeats, virtue or mischance, success or failure, love or hate.

What is the significance of the mythic code? It means we are each selected for a station of honor. It means we are named and numbered with wonder – that we have a permanent position in life. Because each man has mythic code, a unifying intelligence has taken the care to arrange and endow human configuration – that is, man is fixed in consciousness for all time. Fixed in consciousness, no man's information can therefore be lost. Man contains a powerful narrative that cannot be eradicated. This is vital information, since after all, what else do we wish to know?

Mythic code is a choice of interrogative. What life will you make? Which choice of good and evil? Hector had mythic code. He had to face Achilles – and not run away. Christ, John, Peter and Paul had mythic code. Each could have avoided their grisly end. Hitler, Napoleon, Caesar, and Alexander possessed mythic code. Each stated publically that they were being pushed from within – with a certain assignation of fate – which impelled their actions of audacity, of courage, of conquest – or of crime.

The motif of *Kosmoautikon* is that consciousness imbeds a mythic code, which, so far from being accidental, conceals a highly developed sentient purpose. If there is no other value of *Kosmoautikon*, then let it be said, with all its faults, face to face with modern science, it attempts to address the honesty of mythic feedback contained in each human life. Is the human a man in trouble? Then there is an intelligence allowing the condition and necessity of trouble to rise to a test of consciousness. It is, perhaps, my mythic code to attempt impossible attainments. Or is it better that I refuse the cup of blood that draws?

If no man possesses a mythic code, if there is no deeper meaning to consciousness except an accident of neurons and synapses, then it is useless that there is any religion, any art, any beauty, any political freedom, or any science. Religion, freedom, beauty, art, science are linguistic structures revealing a mythic congress – that is, a further urge to enchantment.

Since no human, at no time, is free from the agon of moral dilemma, peril, and trouble, this is sufficient empirical evidence of the presence of mythic code. If each human experiences these conditions – as they do without exception – then there must be a name for this operating principle. I name the condition a *mythic code* – embedded in each human.

In effect, a war of good and evil must be made in human consciousness – and it is unremitting – and unavoidable. A human that did not face continual challenge and response – trouble – never so far has existed. Consciousness, thus, equals mythic code. Mythic code is the signature of a man in trouble.

We possess the power to constitute our being (autexousia) – yet with the stipulation of challenge and response. Consciousness is a contest of mythic value, encoded from a location undetectable by scientism. It is in operation at each moment in human life. The possession of mythic code thus ensures men are *necessary agents* for the protocol of consciousness. That is, men are at the center of all things. How so? Because we are each irreplaceable.

Mythic code has three essential benefits: 1) It ennobles man beyond his physical, corporeal construct, thus verifying the futurity of his soul. 2) Every human value, quality, virtue, or merit is due directly to the challenge embedded in mythic code. 3) Every man, as protagonist of his life, is the center of the universe he inhabits as moral agent. The epic trope is faithful to this perspective.

In Story Theory, man is the center of all creation. In materialist, secular scientism, man is insignificant – we are only one of many stuck together cells swimming in a universe of countless objects encountering each other with no ontological purpose. In Story Theory, a human is a maker of consciousness – including all possible worlds, all possible values, and each emotion. A man makes an honest test of good an evil. He experiments with the value of conscious life – even the criminal makes this experiment. Like god, man is supreme – yet he must act.

Mythic code is what each man must face in his labyrinth. All possible worlds are consequently a projection from within consciousness – that is, no phenomena exist outside of consciousness. Only a self-conscious mind may enter – or be an agent of – mythic experience. No interlopers are allowed into human congress. Each man is authorized to be an agent of good and evil. That is a powerful position of strength. All that is yet unformed, all that he may yet possess, all that he may yet love, is a man's mythic code.

Everything we wish to know is contained in our mythic code. In a previous life was there an injustice? Was there a betrayal or sacrifice for love? Was there a great labor yet to be completed? Do we need to prove love in a place where there was only hate? What is *our* mythic code in this life? Will we find our purpose? The outcome is still in the balance.

Mythic code is the work that a human mind must perform in the test of life. Mythic code cannot be revoked or avoided – it can only be delayed. If you have an issue with the emotion of love, then you will work through this mythic code until you find a clarity of love. No matter how many times you change your romantic partners, you still will repeat the same challenges with any partner. We see this every day. Humans always find the same challenges in life – in love, in business, in behavior – no matter how they attempt to vary their contacts, their economic status, or their geographical addresses. Few change the original stipulation of their fate. Protagonists fail as much as they succeed. Mythic code is astral – not tied to terrestrial locations or human time. This is why the intervals of experience narrated in story, in Greek myth, or in Bible parables lay outside of time or accidents of geography. A story is current in all possible times, and all possible worlds.

What does it mean to have mythic code? It means you engage in an unequal contest of good and evil. It means you must answer the question (and in your own way), what is the meaning of good and evil? It means you cannot *Google* or *medicate* the solution to your problem – there are no short cuts to gnosis. You can only experience peril by wintering through it. It means that your unique, "just-so" challenge, your dilemma, your nemesis was always waiting for you – but your response is yet ever still in the balance – and there is no clear solution – ever. No socialist welfare program, no modernist institution of aid, can take away the burden you must carry to fulfill your mythic code.

A person is daily forced to make a bitter selection of value – and then, as often, he must make recovery from a miscalculation of choice. In no case do we make the correct choice. Correctness is not the point. Recovery from choice is the only essential protocol. The result is a mature clarity of the value of life. If life is eternal, then when is the supreme moment to make a brave sacrifice? The present moment? Can it be delayed? That is the unanswered challenge of each man's mythic code.

What is the connection between mythic code and poetry? Mythic code indicates that something is not yet resolved. In each human story (as each human life), there is something wrong – something demanding resolution. Heroes have only one gnosis: clarity. Only a story of men can present the clarity of Hector's choice, or Christ's sacrifice, or Oxford's achievement of uncanny speech. Yet this is exactly the quality making the hero and protagonist important to us.

Epic poetry (as memorable speech) is a test of consciousness. Only fierce agonistic attacks into consciousness (as a Caravaggio, an Oxford, a Vermeer, a Caesar, etc.) meet a universally applicable context – of interest to more than one person. This is what humans perform – they make a test of the good and evil of consciousness. They terraform human futurity with their speech (or art). They distinguish between linguistic forms of life.

In epic literature, Hector, Hercules, Odysseus, Aeneas, Jason, and Agamemnon each illustrate the agonistic challenge of mythic code. We are alerted to the cosmic congress of mythic code when we, the protagonists of our own lives, have a deity that favors us and fights on our side. I will suggest that having a deity taking interest in you is a proof of mythic status (to be clear, I consider each human to have a deity interacting in his life).

In no case was it a disparagement that Hector was vanquished by Achilles. We don't like Achilles, yet we know he is the center of the Greek world. We love the choice of Hector's death. Like Jesus, Hector had a choice to refuse his fate. He could have escaped. He chose to die with clarity following his mythic code. And that makes a difference of the value of life. We can test this. All subsequent Western conversation is a discussion of either the insights of Jesus or the braveries of the Greeks (the Homeric school of poets).

Modernism does not like the idea of mythic code since in every case, it is not a safe path. At times it is a grisly choice. The modern is taught to call a lawyer or the secular state when he is in peril. To me, this is a fall from grace. Supreme moments of peril and sacrifice are thereby lost forever. Only a spiritual training, with a long view of human life allows a man the courage to sacrifice his body. The case may be made that everything we possess originates from an act of virility – not cowardness. It is an axiom.

In epic poetry, we may get a vision of the mythic superstructure embedded in a human soul. It is terrifying. A sacrifice will be made. A choice is required. It is just barely supportable. It is eternal. In Homer's view, the entire universe awaited the outcome of Hector's noble death – with their breaths held. Napoleon made all of Europe hold its breath when he attacked Moscow. When he returned from Elba the world, again, held its breath. In our own era, the entire globe awaited the outcome of Hitler's sudden attack to Moscow – with their collective breaths held.

In *Kosmoautikon* there is likewise a test of consciousness. There is an escape from a corrupted society of *Homo sapiens*, the moon Europa is terraformed, a new race of humans is created, man meets his own mind in the vacuum of space, and a new interrogative of divinity is discovered. A treasure of great value has been discovered in a place safe from influence. A value of life is tested to the limit of survivability. Maturity of an idiom is the product of the epic spleen.

The conclusion? An upright walking primate is not a man; a man's mythic code is a man. Each human is fully engaged in an arduous contest for clarity of purpose. Who does not seek clarity of purpose in his life? I have never met that person. Clarity of purpose, then, is the central drama of the human mind. It is an opportunity for the epic trope.

CHAPTER TWELVE

Is Human Information Repeatable?

Scientism is a civilization built around a single concept: *repeatable indices of data*. Modernism privileges only that category of information that can be repeated (and thus checked) by others using the same data sets. I will show that modernism is a false category of *human* information. Only under scientism will there be found categories of food that are not food, a genus of seeds that are not seeds, classes of medicines that are not medicines, and indices of information that bear no relation to integrity or actuality. I will ask how there can be a category of human freedom when all citizens are under technological and intimate surveillance. Scientism is a rogue civilization, self-referent, and running blind.

Modernism is a culture where everyone must share the quality of sameness for the society to operate with efficiency. The citizen has to master the protocol of repeatable data sets to thrive in modern societies. Ideally everyone should have a science PhD. As this is not possible, it is enough if PhDs are allowed to lead in all prestigious social institutions. This practice has many untoward side-effects. Any wealthy body allowed absolute power becomes corrupt. Academics, essentially liberal in ideology – have made education a hateful, threatening, and grizzly leftist ideological battle ground.

The result is that human information itself becomes biased – corrupted with the exclusive inputs of the favored class of prognosticators. One idiom – that is, rational, scientific prose – enjoys the overwhelming prestige of society. It is more prestigious, more economically enriching, to verify repetitive data sets in Western societies – than to make new or surprising innovations of speech. Every law of physics, every math theorem has been repeated trillions of times – until the more common, more subjective idiom of non-specialized, vernacular speech becomes meaningless and irrelevant, without audacity to surprise or transform. The prestige of repeatable sets of data degrades subjective idioms, until they feel inferior and second-class. Without audacity, a speech may not rise to poetry.

Anyone using math as an idiom of human information is forced to remain locked into a very narrow spectrum of detection. For this reason we say that math is infantile. So much as it appears to be sophisticated and intellectual, in fact, scientism is child-like. Like a child, scientism professes that it is the center of all things – as if there is nothing outside of the explication of its world view.

If a machine is your chosen measure of civilization, then scientism is the only church you may advocate with ferocity. Yet the idiom must be policed with vigor and learned by rote. There may exist machines, motors, interchangeable parts and pharmaceuticals only so long as information is exactly repeatable – and only so long as the human can survive in an industrial work site. A modern city is instantaneously recognized by progression from work site, to banal tenements (defaced by graffiti), to final progression to a ghetto of lost souls. In the industrialized West a choice to privilege only a narrow category of data has been made. Modernism is a rogue category of knowledge, since it did not originate from nature.

So long as the machines have fuel, so long as the trucks can deliver their refrigerated cargos to cities of the cationic, the contradictions of modernism are not exposed. The misery and depression of the populace is numbed with state subsidized, processed food, free housing, free pharmaceuticals, and circus-like sport entertainments. There is something wrong with the products made by industrialized information that is exactly repeatable.

What is the issue I am framing? There can be no strong theory of poetry until a society defines what category of data it privileges as prestigious information. The modern assumes that scientism is the most superior idiom yet created. It is hard to argue with an atomic bomb or the power of a nuclear aircraft carrier. Yet an atomic or a nuclear machine does not make all previous human information invalid. The idiom of atomic weapons and nuclear fusion does not make scientism "right" – much less the only possible "right" – it only indicates that scientism was merely one of many possible selections of idiom. So let's not be confused about the necessity of scientism – there is *no* necessity.

Each language embeds its unique sets of prophetic visions. When you desire atomic machines, a new choice of speech is forced to the forefront of the mind. Separate selections of speech lead to different conclusions of the values of human life. Interchangeable prose fits well into a machine age that needs all words to have an exact – if repetitive or banal – meaning. Poetry, on the other hand, does not always function with interchangeable parts – or repeatable sets of data. Words in poems have many levels of meaning – some are metaphoric and not always to be found in a dictionary. Poetry is a one-time event – once for all of time. This is the discussion.

In Story Theory there are two principle indices of information. First, there is a linguistic category of information that is so selected, so limited in its scope, that it may – only because so constrained – be repeatable. A Leviathan linguistic civilization (modernism) has been artificially constructed to ensure that exclusively repeatable indices of information – even if corrupt and fake – are privileged in the public forum. The primary products of scientism are an epidemic of weaponized industrialism and chemicalization. All institutions of modernism must collude in the conspiracy of false information, in order to sell false classes of food and medications that maim and deform. The point? When there is no honesty of information in a society there cannot be any strong poetry.

In Story Theory, therefore, we address a second category of information detectable in human experience. I call this exclusive, unrepeatable information. A few examples of the *un-repeatability of human life* will illustrate the case precisely. No parent loves a child exactly the same way he or she loves another child – each is "just-so." No substitute adult may ever exactly replace the love of a parent, because a child's mother and father may only be approximated with deficiency, loathing, and artificiality. Humans have irrational partialities, that is, they have favorites and attachments having no logical explanation. Likewise, no family history, love, friendship or drama can be exactly repeated. These are actual sets of unrepeatable *human* information.

My point? *No perception within human consciousness can ever be exactly replaced.* The contrast is clear. Human information cannot become obsolescent – only the repeatable data sets of scientism are susceptible to obsolescence. There is no machine that is not immediately obsolete and scheduled to be thrown away. Each machine, in effect, is a delayed crisis. There is no pharmaceutical that is effective for long duration. There is no strain of antibiotics effective in perpetuity. Thus each pharmaceutical is a delayed crisis. No modern seed is able to produce a plant with new seeds. Thus each genetically modified seed is a delayed, but immanent crisis.

At once we detect the fault of a civilization of scientism: *its products are illusionary and momentary.* Each "solution" of scientism, each technology, is a free ticket to a new set of insolvable problems. The products of scientism are sets of slow-release catastrophes. Scientism makes spaces that become emergencies and ghettos in the mind.

In a machine age, all parts that are not exactly interchangeable are eliminated. Thus, a civilization built upon a doctrine of repeatable information has only one philosophical end point – the gas oven. Each idiom that moves to maturity (as scientism) creates self-referent rationalities. Humans, in a civilization run by computers and robots, are increasingly seen as expendable misfits. In WWII, the first modernist technological ideology (fascism) placed humans in the gas oven. That was not happenstance, nor was it an aberration. The modern manipulation of genes will lead inexorably to a selection of "favored" genetic material. The logic of technology, thus, leads eventually to the eradication of all misfits. The gas oven, the ghetto, the trash dump are interwoven into the narrative of modernism.

All technological societies, in my view, secretly contain a hidden, internal logic – *the eradication of all misfits.* The philosopher may insist with eccentricity that modernism shares equivalency with fascism and communism – that is, each is a totalitarian ideology using advanced technology to exercise total surveillance over populations, augmented with biased advertising and propaganda. Scientism is thus a third ideological leg of a troika of originally Victorian technological societies – fascism, communism, and modernism. We can explore this analogy with benefit.

What is the connection between poetry and totalitarian modern states under scientism? There can be no strong poetry in a society that does not have free speech. When only repeatable sets of data (as scientism) are allowed as authoritative information, when there is total surveillance, there can be no strong body of poetry in that society – since speech that is under surveillance cannot pretend to be free. History shows that strong poetry is not a product of modern totalitarian societies – neither under fascism, communism, nor liberal capitalism. We observe that there were no great poets under Hitler or Stalin – nor in the Anglo-American West since the advent of the atomic age in the 1930s. That comprises a reliable test of three technologically oriented civilizations over a significant period of history.

We conclude that the information of modern states is spurious, artificial, and, like fascism or communism, must be maintained by constant propaganda and education, or no one will accept it. We know that the data of scientism is fake – since its false conclusions are eventually exposed: 1) Each decade erases the findings of a previous generation of scientists and academics. 2) The pharmaceuticals advertised in one decade are the basis of litigation in the next one – after the false category of medicines consumed have maimed, deformed, and killed the modern citizen. 3) Only in the West are fake medical studies published in academic journals (funded by the pharmaceutical industry) – and these pass for actual true information. 4) Our landscapes (as our near space) are littered with sparked-out, discarded machines and used products – that is, modernism is a throwaway civilization. Modernism's only claim to "truth" are the lies embedded in advertising and propaganda.

In contradistinction, "just-so," human information does not possess the case, the necessity, the desire, nor the requirement of repetition. Poetic speech is not throwaway. Each story is "just-so"- unlike any other story – each with its own universe and its own unique "time." Each poem, each character of strong narration, is exactly *un*-repeatable. No charged line of Shakespeare can be altered in order to repeat the same effect. No passage of Milton can be improved upon with a new translation. Any strong human speech is exactly unique – exactly untranslatable. And this makes poetry permanent human information – infinitely superior to a throwaway civilization of scientism.

In ten thousand years modern science will be defunct – the machines will all be rusted. All that will remain of *Homo sapiens* is his poetry.

The epic trope is faithful to this perspective.

CHAPTER THIRTEEN

There Is Something Wrong with Homo Sapiens

Any philosophy of man must define its subject. How to define *Homo sapiens*? Since there are no other facts of the origin of the human condition, we may only remark the behavior first identifying the species. As recognized by anthropologists, *Homo sapiens* is that species that carefully buried their dead with hope of futurity – using abstract symbology to decorate objects interred with in the graves. It is a ritual set alien to all other life on Earth. Sacred burial is all that physical science knows of *Homo sapiens'* first origins in the fossil record. It can be confirmed in most early human habitations.

There is something wrong with *Homo sapiens* under modernism. Ritual burial of the dead and the creation of strong (symbolic) poetry are no longer the singularity of modern men. *Homo sapiens,* it may be argued, is consequently no longer extant. Why is ritual burial of the dead so important to our thesis of *Homo sapiens*? Burial of the dead gives us a vital clue about the first use of symbology. It tells us that poetry was the first proof of *Homo sapiens*. How can we be sure? Because there has to be a prior narrative of the afterlife before a human would take care to bury the dead (with objects symbolizing life in futurity). The singularity of our species is the ability to construct religious liturgy (i.e. poems portending eternal life) using abstract symbology.

I propose humans are diminished by the loss of our spiritual and metaphysical heritage. Our rich heritage has been replaced by the prognostications of totalitarian science – and we are poorer for the transition. This is why modernism is a rogue moment in human history. Modernism resembles a dark age of the human spirit. It is a dark age not because we lack intelligence or electricity, but because we have lost the vital rituals of *Homo sapiens.* We have lost the notable speech of spirituality – the sacred wisdoms embedded in religious narratives. We are proud secularists. We do not give prestige or authority to non-scientific speech.

It will be remembered in my argument, that civilizations are made, deconstructed, and remade again by memorable speech. Christianity, no matter what else may be said about it, was powerful speech. Judaism is entirely poetic speech. Islam is exclusively poetic speech. All that ever existed of Moses, Aaron, Isaiah, David, Jesus Christ, or Mohammed was poetic speech. There is no archeology. No bones.

Homo sapiens thus advances by enchanted speech – not by archeology. The Jesus movement, for example, was a rogue gnostic movement – containing a few sets of wisdom sayings – in effect, sets of enchanted speech. The only quality distinguishing Christianity from other gnostic sects is its early single-minded insistence upon faith healings – that faith can be used as a power to correct any physical ill – any danger, any human peril. This power of the mind, by any account a new discovery, only appeared with the use of poetic and religious narrative. The poems of *Gospel* writers led to the discovery of faith healing. Poetry of great power and precision activates the inward agency of mind. Memorable parables were nothing if not precise tools of the inward journey.

Homo sapiens has misplaced his advocacy of spiritual power. In the last century, the enchanted and memorable speech of Christianity has lost the exclusive monopoly to map the human mind. Not because Christianity is defective – but because it cannot compete with the immediacy of electronic communication – repeatable data sets, and the new necessity for archaeology. Christianity, like scientism, is a Church of imaginative speech – yet Christianity's powerful symbols have lost the necessary component of plausibility. Our joys and our manners are blatantly secular.

I say there is something wrong with *Homo sapiens*. Man is not made in the image that modernism portrays. That modern men are civilized, seek peace, and are just – are not correct statements. The human is never satisfied with his condition. He is never at peace. If he has, he wants more; if he wins, he strives to lose it all. In relationships, love becomes, in practice, hate. Shame follows good fortune with sure regularity. Clearly this points to an underlying condition of the self-conscious mind.

The human mind is not made for contemplation. If it was made for sustained contemplation we could correct all disease, all poor judgments, and ensure the health of all our relationships. These are exactly the failures that define our condition. Rather the human mind is suited only to the condition of trouble.

In Story Theory consciousness is at war. The human mind is a locus for a war of good and evil – not of peace or equanimity. Therefore under totalitarian modernism, there will always be something deeply problematic with *Homo sapiens*. He or she will need to be medicated from an early age.

I say, rather, there is something wrong with Western men. Whether we attend a church, temple, or mosque, we have no practice of religious ritual or dogma that corresponds to our daily, modern, secular joy. Some may have an "outward" profession of faith, yet fewer have an inward experience of divine power. In fact, to clarify my point, most Western religious persons walk out of church only to enter modernism again – fully invested in the unique secular idioms of scientism. Something is wrong with a religion that is not a religion.

Westerners, when they face mortal crisis, do not enter the church (or mosque) for healing, they enter secular hospitals for industrial surgeries and pharmaceuticals. This practice blocks the authority, and use, of spiritual correction of all maladies. Spirituality – that is, the distinctive speech of spirituality – is blocked. The true faith of the citizen is in modern medical practice – not spiritual healing that draws upon the unique metaphysical dimensions of Homo sapiens' mind.

Westerners no longer bury their dead with hope for reawaking in a resurrection of futurity of life. Moderns, instead, quickly dispose of the dead with economical cremation and discount any discussion of an afterlife in the public space as unserious speech. Some citizens still may profess a "spiritual church" and a "god," but in demonstration, all are confirmed material secularists in daily life. This makes modern *Homo sapiens* hypocrites by default. With split linguistics, the modern is a bearded lady.

Modernist joys are secular and vicious. Our alternate religious and secular posturing is cringe worthy – and merely represents a parallel, but false, catechism. After all, what is religion? Religion is the belief that spiritual force is superior in all cases to material apparitions (of physicality). Religion is an insistence on a non-material, non-earthly locality of power. Secular materialism, on the other hand, is the belief, linguistically enforced from youth, that man is at the mercy of physical causation. Materialism is linguistically demonstrated to be superior in all cases to a spirituality that cannot be physically detected. Thus, material causality is currently the only human faith taught in state schools and enforced by law.

I advertise the faculty of spiritual attainments to support a strong theory of poetry. I advocate the spiritual sense, exclusively as means of power that I would not wish to be without. As a poet, I ask if spirituality is a human idiom we can dispose of without regret. It is the central question of our time – yet the question is not asked in public forums. There is only the silence of the materialist academic, indicating an embedded secular intolerance of religious thought. There are only whispers in secret of the true believers. The question of Western spirituality concerns *Homo sapiens* intimately. It affects the poetic symbols we use – or do not use.

The insight of Story Theory is to deconstruct human *-isms* to schools of symbology and reduce them all to their final linguistic division. After this transformation, any *–ism* of the modern world can be exposed as mere symbology – poetry. This is how all civilizations are replaced – new people arrive with a new set of linguistic interrogatives – a new set of poems. Modernism will be replaced in exactly the same fashion – by a new linguistic interrogative of human life.

The insight of Story Theory is plausible. One hundred years ago archeology was not a prime component in human understanding of the universe – and in another one hundred years it may also be out of fashion. Why? Because there will be a new human race at that time. That is the narrative of *Kosmoautikon*.

Homo sapiens experiences texts – not archeology. Not every enchanted human narrative needs an archaeology to be operative. There are no verifiable artifacts of Hebrews in Egypt, there are no bones ever dug up of a single person in the *Bible*. All we have are verses of a people of great poetic power. Yet, to the point, these "just-so" poetic narratives of the *Bible* have existed as the plausible reality of the Western civilization. They made conquest of the globe. In Story Theory, this is evidence that archeology, as any form of scientism, is secondary to poetic texts.

This is the challenge Story Theory poses to the modern materialist: is it better to be locked into a fixed, absolute physical materiality – permanently immobile in an aged skeleton – or is it better to choose new forms of life from linguistic innovations – from new fountains of prestigious poetic speech? Divination and prophetic voice go deep in our genome, have survived as long as Homo sapiens has survived, and for that reason are worthy of our attention.

From the perspective of Story Theory, there is something wrong with Western *Homo sapiens.* He has lost his divination bone – his spiritual component – and he fails to communicate with powerful symbols of the afterlife. Sacred texts have no linguistic answer to the constructs of commercialism and industry. Spirits are speechless to judge industrial processes. Christianity's imaginative voice has failed to maintain its race for supremacy. Islam, smelling the death of Western faith, waits outside with a scythe. The churches of secularist Europe are permanently empty.

We age horribly with modernism. Modernism hands out death sentences. In some form, pharmaceuticals are given now to most all Western children at an early period of their life. We daily are schooled about the grisly authenticity of modern diseases. We each accept the finality of the prognosis of new classes of modern cancers. The modern's first act is to make an interrogative of the reality of the disease. Once the case of a disease is linguistically established – the grizzly outcome is prophetically fulfilled. Once the human is gripped with full-bodied materialistic terror – the horrible, crippling, and ghastly material correlative is *unavoidable*. The philosopher would recognize the fully functioning protocol of prophecy. Modernism is its own self-fulfilled prophetic voice.

This is exactly a position in which the human mind should never have found itself – that is, helpless before the materialistic definition of human life. We are cornered – and condemned – by our own self-made, self-referent scientific idiom. Science can prove you are sick, and takes the care to find a sickness for every person. It is profitable and adds prestige to the PhD.

What are the facts of the case? Spirituality gave *Homo sapiens* a superior and accessible resource of power. Again, I speak of a faculty of power – not mere ritual. Spirituality gave humans the imagination to go beyond the limit of their material corporality. By any account, that is an achievement of power unique on the planet. The uniqueness of *Homo sapiens* was first indicated by the treatment of their dead – in burials that looked forward to the spiritual continuation of life. And now this singular uniqueness is to be lost? Is the mind somehow advanced, having forsaken its spiritual audacity?

Modern men have regressed from their *Homo sapiens* ancestors. Modern men are weak and helpless – they cannot call out to powerful gods. They need state care in every category of life. They cannot name the plants in the field, the trees in the forest, and they cannot find their own food. Modernism treats the human as if he is sick – and needs state help and state-funded pharmaceuticals at the earliest age. The Western citizen is only assured he will be handicapped at some time in his life. There is something wrong with *Homo sapiens*. He has lost his purse of images.

CHAPTER FOURTEEN

Modernism In, Modernism Out

No one noticed the day liberalism became totalitarian. It was so implausible – so unlooked for – that it never occurred to anyone.

The Western democracies, in the latter 20th century, used technology to build a Leviathan government apparatus in order to better intervene in the intimate lives of its citizens. After the Cold War, liberalism, for a brief moment, had no more natural enemies. Instead of a right-wing fascist state, it was a leftist, modernist, technological state that embraced the same totalitarian methods of fascist and communist surveillance of its citizens. Few could have predicted that the liberal Western democracies may destroy World War II fascism and Cold War communism, only to use Western technology (finance, surveillance, advertising, pharmaceuticals) to transition to unembarrassed totalitarianism, a civilization propagandizing entire sets of fake or politically correct human data. History is a proverb for the unanticipated.

Technology, finance, and media make modern linguistic choices determinant for the educated. That is, the option not to accept modernism is never a choice for the Western youth. The modern category of "freedom" is thus insidious. Once the citizen is an indoctrinated modern – what other language can he then speak? There is no way to retrace your steps back from modern societies. Any indigenous society making contact with modernist states is made to conform to scientism.

In Story Theory, modernism is one of the three totalitarian ideologies of the 20th century. Communism, fascism, and modernism are, equally, civilizations of technological exploitation of the populace. That is, each is a system leveraging the secularist state with technological innovations to regulate the population into political (or demographic) objectives. Communism and fascism used technology to make surveillance on citizens – as well as to influence their consciousness with repetitive statements of electronic propaganda. Likewise, modernist, capitalistic advertising is supreme in Western media using repetitive phrases, and politically correct speech. Fascism, communism, and modernism are technological totalitarian triplets.

The mistake of Westerners was to assume that liberalism could never transition to a totalitarianism – that is, enforced political correctness, eradication of pre-modern mores, technological dependency, exclusion of spiritual education, enforced enrolment in social medicine, loss of control of private data, and, in state institutions, no sympathetic dialogue of the afterlife.

Advertising makes up new categories of "facts" each week – as well as new classes of marketable food, medicine, and "accepted" social behavior. Modern industrial processed foods (introduced in the 1950s) have killed, disfigured, and made an entire global population diabetic. By 2000, diabetes was epidemic in all newly modern nations (as India). Packaged food is cheap, convenient, profitable, does not perish, and tastes good. Except it is not food.

Modern industrial pharmaceuticals, available to trusting citizens in the 1960s and 70s, have deformed fetuses, maimed healthy citizens, and killed untold numbers. As any good lawyer may tell you, the modern citizen is certain to be pharmaceutically handicapped in some form by age of fifty. For over sixty years, pharmaceutical companies have controlled, twisted, and obfuscated the sets of data in reports and medical studies of new classes of marketable diseases and treatments. New medical journals appear each month selecting only favorable data of skewed studies – and finding a way to hide the negative results of their drugs. Like fascism and communism, modern information is false and corrupted – that is, there are new categories of "food" that are not food, new categories of "medicines" that are not medicines, and freedoms that are under new technologies of surveillance. Modernist information more closely resembles ideological propaganda. Fake information in, fake information out.

The Western citizen is free only so far as he accepts modernist thinking in public and private life. The surveillance of each citizen's electronic communication (and the loss of journalistic independence) ensures that modernism has set the conditions for its demise. When people are harmed by an ideology, the ideology will eventually become a wounded morality.

Is modernism aggressive? It has eradicated every non-Western human culture that it has made contact with – including Indonesia, China, Japan, Vietnam, India and the Plains Indians. Each are urban copies of American skyscrapers, slums, and ghettos – and their cities horribly mock our own industrial wastelands. Modernism has made Europe an ideological American colony – and irrelevant.

Can modernism be resisted, reformed, or replaced? Modernism is unable to reform modernism. No self-referent linguistic civilization (maintained by propaganda) can reform itself. Fascism was unable to reform fascism. It had to collapse. Communism was unable to reform communism. It had to collapse.

What is the point? Moderns are linguistic cowards. They cannot choose their words with free choice. That is, moderns are not free to constitute their own being. Under modernism, as under fascism and communism, sensitive words have become euphemisms for something else. And this is only logical – since we are under surveillance 24/7 to ensure demographic, ethnic, and political correctness.

The West is cowardly in its range of allowable public speech. Under totalitarian monitoring, Western speech gets smaller and smaller each year – until it becomes a whisper. Western public speech, guilty in its vacuity, ensures our poetry is likewise guilty of vacuity. The integrity of words concerns the strength of poetry. Poetry can only portray the truth. If truth is not allowed then strong poetry is not allowed.

To address the integrity of modern speech in society is to address the condition of poetry in the same society. If the information of a society is corrupt or false – then the poetry of that society is also corrupt – or false. Modernism directly affects the poetry we write. Modernism in, modernism out.

There is no separation between the health of society and the health of poetry. There cannot be great poetry in any age where the public voice is controlled. The connection between poetry and the mind of *Homo sapiens* is intimate.

Modernism limits poetry to only whispers.

CHAPTER FIFTEEN

Where Does Science Leave Us?

Every linguistic civilization operates on the faith that its speech is true and sound. When a speech is true and sound, then there are great poets in the land. As modernism propagates fake information, it creates the conditions of human chaos and fear when words are given new ideological meanings – with new categories of shame – where truths have to be whispered. In corrupt civilizations, euphemisms are the norm of common usage and words are only shadows of their original meaning. This is where ideological liberalism leaves the citizen. We are left without a speech able to describe reality.

No civilization has ever made an exact depiction of "reality." That is, no civilization ever plumbs its own illusion. A human civilization is only a linguistic representation of a temporary (and biased) selection of symbols.

Likewise, the problem with scientific civilization is that it never answers its own interrogatives. Science will eternally delay its final answer of "reality" with an unending microscopic investigation of the "physical" universe. Any shortcoming of scientism will be answered with the reply that "we need more time." We know there is no end to that protocol. Scientism leaves us perpetually dependent upon the final promise of a revelation – a revelation that never comes.

Where has the intellectual or philosophic content of science left us? Without an ethnic world, without soul, without prospects for futurity. All our previous sacred stories (of the non-material soul) have been deconstructed as throw away myths. Under modernism Homer, Dante, Milton, and the Shakespeare poet are non-essential - completely irrelevant to manned space travel. *Kosmoautikon* makes a correction.

Science is destroying life on Earth. In our third century of Western science all the delicate constructs of technology are failing – and failing all at once. Industrialism has eliminated the canopy forests and the wetlands – and the species living in these spaces. The antibiotics are failing, the electric grid is failing, scientifically altered food is making entire populations sick. Pharmaceuticals are prescribed for every newly discovered class of human irritation, yet wealthy lawyers are learning that each new artificial medicine is, in fact, killing, deforming, and maiming entire generations.

Significantly, nothing in science can be proven for all time. Every theory of science is a *page-holder* – a temporary and self-referent construct – a narrative of a *throw-away* world. We can test this. Newton and Einstein's universe has been already superseded – by quantum mechanics. This is how we recognize that science is only another *marginal* representation of reality. Newton and Einstein have left behind them only a hypothetical story of imaginable universes—potential laws of multiple material universes. Science is, in the end, only a narrative of possible worlds. Poetry in, poetry out.

What is the result of three centuries of science? Science leaves us suspended, hanging in the air – with no soul to climb back down to the durable roots of life. With science, the human mind ends up located nowhere – no place. This is where we are left.

In scientism, the leviathan, self-conscious human mind has no more value than an advanced ameba. Math and science insist that the Earth and man are only an insignificant comma in comparative relation to the overwhelming body of counted material objects – lost in the greater significance of billions of dust conglomerates. This perspective is a kind of drunkenness – since what do materialists use to imagine the narrative of billions of galaxies – that they never may touch – if not only their mind?

Homo sapiens has one exclusive asset: the *uniqueness* of human consciousness. The human mind is a spiritual aggregation. That is, only the mind is an entity that attempts to reach beyond its material construct. In Story Theory, the human mind is the creator of all that the eye sees. This is our exceptional status in the universe. In Story Theory, as in poetry, man is the measure of all possible things. Math and science teach the opposite narrative. For this cause, we say there is something wrong with the exclusive idiom of math and science.

Science cannot explain consciousness – or what lies beyond space. The *inexplicableness* of space, that is, what "constructs" exist beyond matter, strips the narrative of the "objectivity" of the material universe of integrity and honesty. How may the "limitlessness" of the material universe be imagined? Where is the wall of the sky? There is exactly no physical limit to the universe. An object needs a limit to be an object – or it can't fit within the mind. A limitless vacuum, as a "thing," is an impossible "object" of the mind. Plausibly, then, science does not possess any narrative of phenomena outside of the "small" objects of matter. Science has embarrassing limitations of its representation of human experience.

What does the human mind detect? Are we strictly limited to material causation? No. We experience emotions, prophesy, intuition, miracles, telepathy, foresight, premonition, mercy, charity, love and terror. None of these qualities has material components that can be explained by scientism. So what is the use to continue to believe in secular science? Holding in our hands self-referent electronic devices, we stumble from crisis to crisis like drunkards.

Science does not discuss the ultimate purpose of life; science does not address evil and cannot account for the necessity of consciousness to have a metaphysical origin. Science, in effect, is a poorly designed mechanical arm – a prosthetic. Science, now universally taught to youth as the single supreme category of information, in effect, gets in the way of any further projections of the human imagination. And if science is not the final human idiom – then what is next? Who is working on that *next* projection of the human mind?

To scientists, all phenomena look like a problem of physics—to the man with a hammer, all problems look like a nail. This proves all answers are based on a linguistic configurations. In truth, each language contains its own pattern of observation and interpretation. Science fails to identify itself as only one of many possible linguistic patterns – of data, of proofs, of applications.

Science, consequently a limited idiom, cannot account for its own poetic indispensability. Science depends exclusively on the poetic imagination sustaining its every hypothesis, thesis, exploration, and discovery. Every new invention comes from the imagination. That is, the mathematical equation – as the scientific hypothesis – arrives only after the innovation is already conceived *poetically* in the imagination.

Secular materialism is an artifact exclusively of the imagination – and this fact is illustrated in the genre of science fiction. Science fiction strips modernism of its claim of inevitability. Modernism was never a certain outcome – never inevitable. Modernism was first projected in the literature of "futurism." Science fiction proves that modernism is one of many choice of outcomes – a choice of human speech. Yet Science fiction, as a genera of literature has become passé, a parody of itself – and the Golden Age of Science fiction literature, beginning in the late Victorian age, was over by the 1960s. The canary in the coal mine is dead. What comes next?

This is my thesis. Science explains nothing with completeness; science is a list of corrections without hope of ever giving a full accounting. Thus, only poetry can fill the lacuna of human origins. In his article on Dostoevsky, Freud admitted this very precisely, "Before the problem of the *Dichter* [poet] psychoanalysis must lay down its arms."

Today, we cannot return to the old religious texts any more than we can return to modernism. Nor can we offer oil lamps to the atomic age. Outward Christianity is likewise limited in its range of knowing. How has Christianity left us after two millennia? It has left us suspended in the air with no machine to climb down from religious liturgy to a world of advanced machines. So we reject typical established religions as a solution of human existence.

Every Christian interrogative of life remains unanswered, unfulfilled. Christianity has no competence to address the uses of, say, industrialism, archaeology, taxidermy, astrophysics, or quantum mechanics. Islam does not acknowledge any form of technology. Buddhism does not address the reality of atomic weapons, science, motors, electronics, the existence of modern men, or the possible uses of the sorrows of the human condition. On the other hand, Story Theory finds a plausible way to explain human experience – without ignoring man's spiritual sense.

The gnostic perspective was Jesus' response to the problem of humanity, that is, we should train our mind with spiritual exegesis. For cause, the Buddhists and the Jesus movement rejected the world. The materialist, alarmed at this speech, cries this is the only possible world he may ever have! Story Theory explains the value of both.

We have to continually remind believers of science what science cannot explain. Modernism avoids the question of what science cannot detect. Science cannot detect the origin of love, hate, self-consciousness, nor any charismatic human event – each are not promiscuous to material detection. Clearly, science cannot address its own contradictions, its own limits of detection – it merely ignores its limitations as a forbidden category of interrogative. In fact, no civilization can answer its own interrogatives unless it employs the same prejudices that formed it. The limited scope of modernism is a question, therefore, that is never taken up.

We have to find a way of not being left hanging in the air where science (or previous Roman Christianity) would leave us. We must challenge science with its self-contradictions. Science leaves us with a permanently unanswered riddle: *How can a human, whose mind shows contempt for the limits of matter, consequently, not have a material origin?* Man, alone in nature, exhibits contempt for the limits of its own (apparent) solidity.

Man's imaginative ability to reach *beyond* material constructs has to be explained. That is, a man's mind – his self-consciousness – has to be inwardly explored. Only man attempts to exceed the limits of his own material construct. Only man attempts to be a Caesar, a Caravaggio, a Da Vinci – a maker of worlds that do not yet exist in his own time. He uses symbols to project his art, his still unmade world, his immortal beloved – and his soul.

How to make a world not yet existing? Man becomes a maker of worlds, as the Greek word for poet was "the maker." The human counters the limits of a material world with a further resort to consciousness. What if all possible worlds are already contained within consciousness? Where would a possible world exist if not already inside of consciousness? That is, man makes an additional reach – a new interpretation – into his imagination. Taking inward counsel he recreates his "outward" world. He uses his non-material mind to terraform new horizons of opportunity. He is born under absolute tyranny, yet he makes democracy. He is born ignorant of letters, yet he obtains a mastery of letters. He is born on Earth, yet he attempts space travel. He is weak, yet he transforms every landscape to fit his ease and aesthetic pleasure. He is told by authorities that he is sick – yet he finds a way to heal himself. All the phenomena of his life originate from his mind. The poet claims this enchanted faculty.

How do we find the audacity to counter modernism – now so deep in the modern age? A man may only rise to challenge the information of modernism when he is certain that modernism is not the final idiom of *Homo sapiens*. That recognition is the first step out of modern debility.

It is still unclear which idiom of the human mind shall survive in the struggle for solar-system hegemony. Will it be the modern West still believing in science and liberalism? Will it be China still co-opting Western science and technology? Will it be Islam, when they finally eradicate Israel and the modern hegemony of the West? No, it will be something surprisingly different. The future, therefore, will be a charismatic event.

Why? Because no civilization ever sees what is coming. Every human civilization was always eradicated by the *unforeseeable* rise of a charismatic Mohammad, a Christ, a Hitler, a Stalin, or a Genghis Khan. No destroyer of worlds was ever predicted by the civilizations concerned.

And this is where science leaves us: we have no masters left of prophetic voice.

Modernism is a destroyer of alien worlds. It does not mature – it only replicates – it does not permit transition to a more mature idiom. The entire globe is locked in the stifling and grisly grip of Western modernism.

Yet every hegemony, even a tyrannical one, presents an opportunity for the rogue male within the empire. American English is the only global language that ever existed – across all cultural borders. There are no precedents for American idiomatic hegemony – not with Greek, not with Latin, not with French. In comparison, Arabic and Chinese were never in the race for global hegemony. If global Americanism once enters the outer solar system, our codex will exist for all time. That is the opportunity for *Kosmoautikon*.

I will ride the beast.

CHAPTER SIXTEEN

Vernacular Speakers Degraded by Scientism

No modern poem allows its reader to suspect there is a superior speech of science. Modern prose-poems of the last century have ignored the insights and idioms of science – as if the revolutions of science had never transformed popular culture in the West since the Victorian Age. This is why poetry is so far irrelevant to the modern citizen. Poetry, hiding from the idiom of science, is cowardly and unimaginative.

Modern poetry refuses to face – and face down – a superior idiom of scientism. Modern lyric, prose-poetry has never attempted to challenge the superiority of science for the modern mind. It was a battle worth the fight. Now there is only a cult of vernacular whispers in the West.

The proof? Confronted with the imaginative brut of science, modern vernacular poets are silent. No modern poem has as its subject – or its language – the slightest challenge to the linguistic excellence of science. No modern poet (of the last century) has challenged the self-referent proofs of science – with an idiom superior to the imagination of scientism. Scanning poetry of the last one hundred years, one would not even suspect there existed a robust and omnipresent civilization of scientific men. No modern poem has attempted to explicate a single scientific principle – as if poets are ashamed (or afraid) to meet the dialectics of science head on.

That modern poets ignore the imaginative idiom of science tells us everything we need to know about the failure of poetry in the modern era. The vernacular speaker, the non-PhD poet, cowers before the idiom of a laboratory PhD. The vernacular poet feels unqualified to be in the same room as the scientist. This is wrong. The poet must be a master of his society's idiom. The poet that cannot change his society is not a poet.

We, perhaps, isolate the principle factor limiting a large body of strong Western poets in modernism. Vernacular English has been degraded by the superior linguistic idiom of triumphant science and mathematics. In Story Theory, we are required to tell the truth: science represents the highest imaginative and poetic achievements of the 20th century. This is exactly the period when vernacular poets have been silent and weak performers. They are intimidated by the productive and fertile idiom of scientism. The response? Only a superior counter audacity might reverse the trend. Yet vernacular poets cannot find a way – a charged memorable speech – to challenge the hegemon of scientism.

Modern vernacular poets refuse to integrate the new language of science into vernacular usage. How can there be modern poets if they refuse to incorporate modern linguistic innovations? Modern poets make two mistakes. First, they fail to see that science is just as much a poetic interpretation of phenomena as any imaginative poem. What is more imaginative and poetic than *String Theory, Event Horizons, M theory, quantum physics, black holes, dark matter, pap quintessence,* and *dark energy,* etc.? Science, like poetry, is precisely, exactly a hypothesis, a category of imagination, and thus a sub-set of linguistics. But the modern vernacular poet does not observe the poetic component of science – he sees only a superior idiom he cannot counter-act and cowers from its greater social prestige.

Second, and the most fatal mistake, modern poets do not mount a challenge to the Leviathan. They fail to use their art to construct a complicated narrative recasting the manners of society. They fail to counter the fake prognostications of science and commercialized medicine with new prophetic voices.

It touches the poetry we make. In so far as contemporary poets refuse to integrate scientific innovations, vernacular poets *feel* they have no authority to address the highest concerns of the human condition. Consequently they sense they cannot authoritatively make predictions of the future human condition. It is a calamity of poetic usage that can and must be corrected. Or is nothing more beautiful, more superior than the speech of scientism?

Modern poets no longer craft a compelling human story with their small lyric prose-poems. No single prose lyric may compare advantageously with the more prestigious (and enchanted) narrative of graphic and repetitive cinematic industrial films. Modern (one page) lyric poets fail to integrate a powerful story of modern men, with an enchanted vision of new innovative human manners. In short, with modern prose lyrics, the poetic talent is wasted in trivialities. His work is banal and cringe worthy in contrast to the fertile imagination of science and the wealth-producing cinematic industry.

In Story Theory, the poet alone of all humans is able to give birth to an entire new human idiom – a new human civilization. We can test this. What civilization has ever existed that was not constructed from the edifice of memorable speech? Strong poems make civilizations appear – the *Books of Moses*, the *Iliad*, the Latin and English *Bible*, the Egyptian *Book of the Dead*, and the *Koran* are examples here. Poems each. Verses. Script.

In illustration of the failure of poetry in our time, what are the themes of lyric poets of the last one hundred years? Themselves! Their feelings. Their diseases. Their sadness, their depression, and their insignificance. Their purposeful choice of speech intended to lack all distinction. They have consequently renounced the attempt to make the future story of the human condition. Scientism chooses to use language of distinction. "Survival of the fittest," "Evolution of Species", and "$E = mc^2$" are on everyone's lips. They don't understand the mechanics of any of these speeches – but they believe in them as the liturgy of a great church. A church with a supreme secular, man-made god.

Modern lyric poets have failed to seize the levers of ideational control of human consciousness. Brecht said, "A work that shows itself incapable of dominating the world of events and cannot make its audience capable of dominating such a world is not a work of art." This is why modern prose poetry is difficult to nominate as art.

Who would bother to challenge the assertion that modern poets are insignificant? The mediocrity of contemporary prose poets is so profound that most poems in American journals are translations from poets in other languages. The humiliation of modern English prose-poets is complete.

Kosmoautikon attempts to correct the crisis of the vernacular poetic idiom. My aim is to restore the competence of high vernacular idiomatic speech. At stake is the status and audacity of all vernacular speakers – and vernacular poets who do not possess (or want) PhDs.

The schism between the vernacular and the secret languages (high math, quantum science) should not be prolonged in Western culture. Poets (as powerful vernacular speakers) must seize again the idiom of future men. Modern poets currently have nothing significant to say about what man will face – whether now on Earth or, later – as he attacks into space. Poets must reclaim the social function of prophetic voice, telling complicated and decisive narratives of human manners. With some care, the vernacular poets may regain their usual voice of dark audacity.

Instinctively an epic poet knows his best language must be intimately joined with story – a narrative of power. Prose never satisfies the poet – and he has to be prepared to tell why. He needs to reach towards incantation. Easy to reckon, impossible to force.

It is easy to critique the epic spleen. It may even be amusing. We may rehearse in a few lines the oddity of the epic trope. Homer, Dante, Virgil, Milton, and the Shakespeare poet are honored in the West even though they did not speak the common language of their fellow citizens. No citizen of Homer's time spoke as Homer's characters spoke. Dante constructed a new Italian speech ("The Beautiful New Style") and no contemporary talked to his friend (in meter) as the Shakespeare poet or Milton wrote. No epic poet ever narrated an actual historical event that transpired in his own life-time. No epic poet – of any epoch – made any money from his labor. No epic poet was ever at ease with the political class of his nation. Each was in opposition to the political leadership of their age – Ovid, Lucretius, Dante, Chaucer, Milton, Edward de Vere, and Pound were excluded from the party in political power – each was either in forced exile or expecting momentary imprisonment. Despite the handicap of artificial language, social isolation, political opposition, or economic misfortune they are remembered because they made new and striking speech. (Ezra Pound was in political opposition to a Western liberalist, capitalist civilization – even imprisoned for treason.)

Nothing is as difficult to anticipate as the appearance or, subsequently, the success of an epic poet. No age is more ripe for the anger of the epic spleen than fake, corrupted, lying modernism. He breeds fits of speech on his rage – on the madness of his age. Even Pound may one day be redeemed.

Let another undertake the test before he correctly enumerates the deep foolishness of the epic spleen. Perhaps the idea occurs to a mature critic. How should the poet be maligned for attempting to increase the idiom of a nation's language? Conceivably, after all, the eccentricity of the work is needed.

All poetry begins as a free experiment and only possibly ends as an affirming miracle. The poet always begins with philosophy but ends with theology. There must be so many more experiments than achievements. All poets, as the present writer, are workers in the mines of new selection. No one knows yet what is coming.

All strong poets have to create their own audience. Whitman was self-published. Dickinson was never published; her audience eventually was formed from the mediocrity of American literature, academic boredom, and feminist politics. Donne was unknown until introduced by Eliot in the 1920's. It is not always enough to attain a sufficient personality, a sufficiently original language, a sufficiently heightened achievement of expression, or a sufficient maturity of authority. A century of crystallization of thought is usually required for sobriety. Ideologies have to die out.

Time will have its Mercury, but the work must possess sturdy perfections to outlive the limited sensibilities of one generation. The work must be deeply felt to outlast the narrow personality of the poet. Above all else, the work must contain the sting of an alien mind – a distantly sourced authority. *Homo sapiens* have deep reaching antenna into alien consciousness.

I would encourage a generation of poets to write poetry of wide influence, but they must deeply resent the proscriptions of totalitarian modernity. The essential first step is to recover the audacity of the vernacular speakers. Any possible philosophy – any possible poetics – must place our future condition in a narration that vernacular men can envision and cheer. We want all-in-the-round vernacular narratives – not arcane, cliché ridden fragments of prose lyrics – not obscure wreckages of logic from academics (who only speak to other academics). We don't want yet another banal, modernist, technological dystopia. Modern prose lyric poems are obscure fragments – brick-a–brack of a broken, depressed world – with no effort to charge or distinguish their speech. We want to break out of the technological nightmare.

The second step, as discussed, is to demonstrate that science is only one of many possible poems of "world." Science, being an interpretation of life using symbols, is a poem – and as such is not to be feared by the vernacular speaking poet. An attack should be made from vernacular speaking citizens, fresh from their cribs.

This is the purpose of *Kosmoautikon*.

CHAPTER SEVENTEEN

What New Information Does an Epic Poem Give?

Having established the major outlines of our thesis, we can assemble points so far discussed to illustrate the inevitability – the naturalness – of the epic trope.

What does an epic poem portray? An epic poem reveals the exceptionalism of a hegemonic civilization. What are the conditions for such "exceptionalism?" After all, not every civilization is exceptional in its global scope – or not?

First, modern English is hegemonic. Each nation learns American English in order to operate the idiom of modernism. Modernism is an idiom exclusively promulgated by the 19th and 20th century Anglo-American cultural megalith (drawing Germany and France in their wake). Modernism, as exercised in aviation, industry, business, democracy, medicine, science, cinema, and commerce is essentially conducted in the idiom of English.

Second, in the last two centuries, when an indigenous culture made contact with American modernism, the indigenous culture was forever transformed. The same cultural phenomenon was previously observed in the West only with the example of Greece and Rome. European culture was formerly identified by the hegemonic influence of Greek and Roman institutions. Should American English of scientism decisively enter the Galaxy then English may stand to become the single idiom of a the known universe.

There is a third consideration that establishes English as the vehicle – the indispensable speech – for the epic trope. America is said to be the only indispensable nation.

If any of these arguments may be dramatized in a narrative, then they are possibly themes properly tested by the epic trope.

An epic poem contains no new information. An epic poem contains everything ever known in a civilization. An epic poem tests the unique proofs of a hegemonic civilization's claim to human innovation - in contrast to the claims of other nations. The logic is clear. If there is a distinction of the human idiom, epic speech should be able to test this distinction in a narrative of power and cultural significance. This is the epic art.

What is the nature of an epic poet's contribution to a culture? Everything the culture must face to justify its manners – and its agonistic principles. Epic voice, though unpracticed, yet is not incompetent to address modernity. The modern critic is at a severe disadvantage faced with the unknown and unpracticed epic voice. Few critics can give an accurate report of the labor involved with modern epic composition. What is the proper presentation of a modern epic poem? It is unknown – still untested with decision and force. No critic is qualified to discuss a modern epic poem – since none exists. Let them undertake a similar leviathan struggle, and only then climb down into the pit to speak as equals in the quarry of symbols.

I await the opinion of the tenth future generation, when the politics of this age merely appear pernicious and risible. (As usual, the modern critic, can only decide if he likes the politics of the poet – as if that can be discovered with reliability. In a totalitarian age, ideological purity becomes the chief aspect of the critic's commentary on a new work – ideological zeal usually blinding them to any new attainments of linguistic excellence.)

Epic poets have one overriding purpose: to test life for value using speech. It is recorded in the first Sumerian epics that strange powerful beings appeared to the people of Mesopotamia. These beings taught men civilization, gave them writing, and modified the genes of a primitive humanoid. Yet how, in *Kosmoautikon*, to account for the genealogy of a new class of beings – *Homo faustus*? Certainly, a new form of idiom must be made to retain knowledge of this event. A modern epic speech is developed—from a prescient sense of urgency. Something important has happened – a new discovery was made – and it had to be memorialized for all time.

This is what epic poetry performs. Something important has occurred in a mature civilization—and it must be monumented for all time. A new form of consciousness is made. A flood kills all of mankind. A nation departs slavery. A city falls. A nation is founded. A covenant is made with gods. A species makes Exodus from the home planet.

Humans have a need to broadcast news they feel is significant. A new idiom is achieved that performs the task of epic communication – addressing a century of yet unmonumented attainments of technology and murder. That is, humans cannot suddenly stop making memorable speech in order to announce their highest attainments. In each new discovery of "world," the human still has to make a cultural interpretation of the value of this world —by the means of symbolic speech. This is what the epic trope performs.

Any new, previously unknown, information of the human condition would radically alter the idiom of the species. That is the story of *Kosmoautikon*.

The defect of modernism is that it cannot imagine that – apart from itself – there is any new information of the human condition. If a new form of life could be detected – beyond the cosmos – what would we make with this new formula of human? The answer would disincline many to the experiment. Everything moderns now prize would be eradicated – made useless, dangerous, and toxic – overnight. Any new hegemonic idiom would immediately alter the human living space. Modernism would become a wounded morality.

What would we do with the information of a newly chosen idiom? We would be faithful to the new aesthetics – there would be new machines that would eradicate all other machines. Why? Because each human idiom embeds an exact aesthetics of life. New philosophy brings in new gods. We would eradicate every previous human civilization. We would move to take total control of consciousness. Human populations would be reconstituted to make democracy either unworkable or irrelevant. By that time democracy, with such a long history of corruption and crime, would only be another vicious vice.

We would mandate a unique category of mental rigor. We would make a race of titans and ensure that they do not exclusively seek wealth and self-indulgence. We would ensure that youth are not indolent but challenged to test their character with depravations. There would not only be linguistic rigor of youth but tests of their endurance in nature, uncorrupted by modernist convenience or indolence. All youth would attend outdoor labor camps - until a certain level of maturity is achieved. Work and labor would be a testing ground for the development of young minds. There would be a new class of laborers – and linguists would only rise from this class. We would discourage politically chosen aesthetics (PC) with a severe selection of beauty. There would be a story of thrilling overreach. We would make a race for supremacy.

Is it likewise of concern if scientism becomes supreme on the globe? It all depends – are you a misfit in scientism? Will your children ever be misfits? Is total surveillance a sound basis of freedom – or freedom that a citizen can cheer? Is the idiom of the machine the most supreme human idiom? Gas ovens are awaiting the hour of your miscalculation.

So again we ask, *why is there epic poetry*? Because we are children of wrath – and thus we still seek ferocity. Because we seek to be as the gods. Because we still want to become the unknown. Because language always pursues a further enchantment. Because our minds are weak, so we may bear only the ideal, and therefore being children of wrath, we also pursue a purification of all misfits. In truth, we fear to be the misfit. We barely suppressed the urge to eradicate all others who seek to make us misfits – and when we stand in line at the gas ovens of another's idiom, we ask ourselves, *how did we miss our chance?*

Why is there epic poetry? Because we have mythic code, and therefore there can never be a stasis of peace. Because our consciousness is being tested with peril, dilemma, corruption, vice, and trouble at each instant. All epic poetry is a text of a man in trouble. And, as there is no escape from the test of consciousness, there is no escape from making epic narratives of consciousness.

Why is there epic poetry? Because we seek memorable speech. All that remains of our mind, all that remains of any possible civilization is speech worthy to be retained in the mind. Because we value eternity of expression, more space, and more time, we are careful to discover the correct rituals of power that allow us access to a futurity of eternal monument. Because we want and feel the gravity of charisma, we seek the consequent enchantment of our living space.

Why is there epic poetry? Because we feel rage. Because we have no information of the origin of the human mind – and thus are orphans of wrath. Because consciousness is still unknown. Because the stars in the universe are a projection of our own mind – and we need to tell stories of the unknown – and yet make ourselves, correctly, the center of all possible phenomena.

Why is there epic poetry? Because language is our house of being we thereby strive, at each turn, to grasp at distinctive speech. Because the observer changes the observed. Because we enchant every phenomena we observe. Because we seek prophetic visions from the images of our speech.

There is the epic trope because it is interesting to speak as gods. It is enchanting to remember a speech of great power. The Egyptian priests discovered the urge to enchantment in the *Book of the Dead*, as the Greeks discovered at Delphi, as India remembers in the *Ramayana*, as Islam declares the *Qur'an* to represent the perfect Arabic incantation, the only idol of Islam. The Iranian scholar, Reza Aslan, explains:

> "The ancient Greek bard who sang of Odysseus' wanderings and the Indian poet who chanted the sacred verses of the *Ramayana* were more than storytellers; they were the mouthpieces of the gods. When at the start of each New Year the Native American shaman recounts his tribe's creation myths, his words do not only recall the past, they create the future. Communities that do not rely on written records tend to believe the world is continuously recreated through their myths and rituals. In these societies, poets and bards are often priests and shamans; and poetry, as the artful

> manipulation of the common language, is thought to possess
> authority necessary to express fundamental truths." (*No God
> But God*, p. 156)

In Pre-Islamic Arabia, Mecca's best poets had their verses "embroidered in gold and suspended from the Ka'ba, not because they were of a religious nature, but because they possessed an intrinsic power that was naturally associated with the Divine" (Ibid. p.156-7). There is epic speech since we confirm that what men worship is their language—not an unknowable, unreachable, unnamable god.

There is epic speech because we know no proximate constellation gods. We are epic poets because we are properly men – and do not wish to become as the gods – since they have no idiomatic genius of speech. Language is our closest approach to any divinity we could embrace, since speech embodies our highest, our oldest, and most essential faculty. No civilization, no city, no war, no sacrifice, no peace, no beauty, no god has ever existed without memorable speech following. There is epic poetry because our only church is our linguistically determined mind.

When we enter a mosque, we never see an image of a god—we only see a poetic verse enameled in gold, suspended from the ceilings. Can anything be more evident? Given the choice between god and their linguistic codes—men would choose their language every time. God is embedded in the linguistic code. To change the speech is to change the god.

Why do we write epic poems? Because we possess no absolute facts about the origin of the human mind, we have no choice but to make stories and poems. In the case of the human, everything flows from the unknown. This being so, there has to be a language to exploit the unknown.

Because we have no facts of our origins we make "plausible" narratives of our origins – and call them poems, novels, science, politics, truth, reality, universe, and *Bibles*. In fact, each is only a poem containing prophetic speech. Show me your god or your science, and I will show you the text of enchanted symbols where you found them.

Since we know neither the past nor the future, I conclude, therefore, humans seek prophetic speech. The West is dependent upon the strong poet since observable human phenomena (including the physical universe possessing a still unknown origin) always appear as poetic insight. That is the essential discovery of Story Theory.

Why do we still write epic poems? Because scientism is a school of poetry. The modern, secular, scientific individual is a linguistic straw man – a cypher – made of linguistic assertions. The average human concourse of life consists of alignments of memorable speech. How many speeches begin with, "as my father used to say ...," or "as my mother used to say ..."? Man is ever in retrograde until he finds his distinctive voice. All human acts, all crimes, all acts of beatitude, if examined honestly, are traceable to memorable texts or speech.

With the technique of the American Indian shaman, *Kosmoautikon* casts dice with the future, believing that encoded on the human genome there is more significant texts to be discovered. We chose therefore to try the epic trope – not the prose lyric. Western lyric poetry (as prose) has been misused to the point that it no longer has any cultural authority – no vital content. Today, *prosaic* lyric poetry only references the poet's irrelevant life experience: usually the poet's marginal account of dilatant Eros, disease, depression, or political opinion – thus a kind of nightmarish journalism.

What is missing from an unloved, unread, unwanted, prosaic lyric poetry? 1) A strong narrative (explaining human consciousness). 2) Memorable speech. 3) A new human insight, with new stipulation for human acts (outside of the mediocrity of modernism). So long as poetry is not directly associated with a strong narrative, then the poet, like the philosopher, cannot contend for influence in his or her society.

What would we do with newly discovered speech? We would make poetry important again in the public forum. We would recover the lost faculty of prophetic voice. We would accuse the modern categories of false sets of data. We would build a city set on a hill. The epic poem of its foundation would contain a dramatic device and compel interest with new explorations of the human genome – beyond the banal ghettos of modernism. We would find a device to exorcise Victorian scientism.

Then we would carry the dead wood and rotten limbs to the gas ovens.

CHAPTER EIGHTEEN

Ducunt Fata Volentum, Nolentem Trahunt

The casual reader, as the professional critic, will perceive that my interrogatives are eccentric. They are purposely so. I have promised to follow the logic of Story Theory, no matter how savage or remote the intermediate points may appear, until we reach our end point: a new human landscape. The most accuracy that any prose or poetry (or science) can attain is a plausible fiction – that is, a text may only ever be a conditional statement of truth. That, after all, is only what each story ever written attempts to achieve – a powerful representation of truth.

If a choice has been made to be eccentric, then it is best to enter deeply into the heart of eccentricity with no half-measure. The world already has enough books and pages filled with the accepted attitudes, sentiments, and clichés of modernism. Let there be room for one book that is unlike all others. This nation will not know for a century if there is any actual value.

Kosmoautikon is a pattern of speech never yet used in atomic modernism. Why? What is the point of the exercise? The honor of poetry is the outcome of the test. I make a test of human consciousness using symbols.

Everything human is the case of linguistics. All members of the case of human are the product of language. Thus the poet who makes the future linguistic idiom makes the future human. The language we love extracts the powers of our mind, and as I believe, the receptors on the human genome.

In Story Theory the entire visible universe responds to "yes" or "no." The observer alters the observed. Authority of speech, inviting powerful spiritual exegesis, becomes our uncertainty principle. Memorable speech becomes our range of good and evil. When we travel into space, we meet ourselves – our multi-dimensional mind – with new speech. When we write epic poems, we meet ourselves with new speech – including the visible stars and galaxies.

The photon, as the atom, in my experience, waits upon the intention of the observer, man, to make a choice – *yes* or *no* about the material world.

(Note. The month I made these final corrections I had a dramatic empirical proof of Story Theory. I was given a CAT scan and biopsy showing I had a serious Pancreatic cancer. Four weeks later the VA physician, contacted me to return for a re-test. Perplexed, he then showed me, side by side, that a second set of tests could not find any trace of cancer. Both CAT scans exist as permanent electronic records and can be reviewed by third parties. I will not bother the reader with the mental exertions of the writer during that four weeks, except to say that in small and "great" examples, I have tested that radical spiritual exegesis controls the apparent construction of the material illusion – whether we speak of photons, cells, or stars.)

Our stories of gods, powers, friends, lovers, and enemies are our communication with ourselves. Story is the only language god and man are making to each other. Story is the only missing link to unlock all hitherto unused powers of consciousness. Consciousness is an act of translation. Therefore consciousness operates as a poem. And, this being so, the strong poet should be expected to find authority of speech. We hope he has the talent to outreach his own personality. In this tradition, every poet should ruthlessly seek his own over-reach.

If poetry or myth does not have authority of prophetic speech, then there is no powerful communication across human generations. Only memorable speech may *connect* each generation. We seek a narrative of power that permits each generation to communicate with all future generations. Humans are Balkanized and made miniscule without memorable speech. Poetry makes men the center of all possible time – and all possible worlds.

Modernism ignores poetry and, thus, lacking its own apparent authority, uses prose that must ever be attached to a footnote for authority. Footnotes are crutches of speech. Footnotes are essentially a prosthetics for prose communication. Footnote knowledge (academic science), a category of repeatable information, locks men into a fashion of opinion – into a certain time, dimension, and space.

A footnote only ensures the necessity of its replacement – by a later, updated footnote. A footnote, logically then, contains no authority of speech. A repeatable category of information (as 4+4=8) – only repeats. A civilization of 4+4=8 is a prison from which there is no escape! The answer is always the same! It is mindless! It is useless to infer the most modern information is the most accurate – as a footnote incorrectly implies.

Western men are not allowed to age with dignity since modern commercial societies do not seek or glamorize the mature perspective. There are few American epic poems since there are few writers that waited for maturity before they published. Let us state the truth. Our society is shamed to age past youth. An old man's shoe has no glamor or prestige. *Kosmoautikon* makes a correction. Yet should we not honor the mature perspective of *any* human problem?

If, in the West, the mature poet does not possess authority of speech, who else would undertake a work of maturity? Or should we reverse our project as useless and still wait to hear what the youthful celebrity or the teenager – the pop musician – has to say about human life? That is the deep shame of modernity. Modern culture is ever frozen at permanent adolescence.

Story Theory explains why man has always made myths—not because we are children, but because we are creatures of *Story-Order*—still existing in an age of legend. Story Theory proves the vision of the poets and the necessity of mature poetic achievement. Men are deeply interested in the alien history of the origins of the human mind, of the structure of consciousness, of the cosmic possibility of myths, or there would be no further attempt at literature. The love for literature is the love for maturity of thought – not only youth. Like *Gilgamesh*, modern men want to know if their souls can still be pristine and glorious after their youth and middle age. They want to know if they can survive mortal life. They want to verify that their information cannot be lost.

In the greatest American tradition, I wish to live deliberately. Since we have high European texts, nothing can suppress or defeat us, though we are under attack from alien, non-Western cultures, intending us to fall to our knees. We are dynamic, but not savory. We are audacious, but circumspect. We live in an age of modern midgets, where any distinction of idiom is hailed to the crowd as a species of bigotry. Yet let us take the long view of American letters and I will carry my argument.

Discussing the language of reality, we have made some progressive steps to build a new theory of poetry. Story Theory gives us a tool by which we may locate in macro the actual position of the mind of Homo sapiens – and not just through the myopia of serial and opposed cultural idioms committing random, and narrowly focused, heights of excellence – of random acts of civilization.

I wish to deliberately illustrate that the poet has taken his place again in the public forum. Only an American could undertake this message in a skeptical and jaded Western society. Our time is short. Europe could not do what I have attempted. They would have been subject to too many wounded agendas, fears, shadows, laws, and past histories of shame. Europe now is a museum of wounded moralities. No other cultural man could undertake such an audacious project. America may still braise a voice in the scaffolding of distant futurity. Yet the time narrows on the still broad horizon.

The final conclusion of Story Theory is now, perhaps, clear. What is the language of reality? Every civilization assumes it answers the question of reality with prescience – even with enchantment of idiom – yet utterly fails – one civilization at a time – to describe any actual reality. Every historical civilization is the sum of its self-referent sets of symbols. Each human civilization is simply replaced, in turn, by a new invading linguistic idiom. As any civilization is proven to be a conditional construct of linguistic metaphors, Story Theory demonstrates the only language of reality is poetry - a linguistic encoding using symbols of value. The most a man can do, even if he reaches the Horsehead Nebula, is to realized he reached that location following the path of his symbols (poems).

Therefore, let us reach for clarity. Rational scientism is not the language of reality – it is only one of many – *isms*. Scientism is an artificial idiom for making physical, repetitive, and immediately obsolete machines. Each decade science reverses its previous dictates – and deforms, maims, and debilitates every species it infects. Math is not the final language of reality, since any system of math contains propositions that can neither be proved or disproved (Gödel's Proof). The symbols of math have only the given value that a human may give to the proofs of math.

Religion, paganism, superstition, and romance, have already demonstrated that each idiom is able to make a fully functioning world – without the supposed inevitability of science or mathematics. The modern will insist with righteous passion that they would not wish to live in these other worlds without science or the machines of math. This is only because the modern has not first learned to love these other worlds as a child.

With Story Theory, we answer the question, what is the language of reality? The only tool to explain human reality is to tell a story – using poetic symbols of an enchanted and self-referent idiom – an enchanted idiom, moreover, that persons of the same speech, and time, may cheer. This is as far as a human can enter into the mystery of the metaphor. Outside of newly arriving prophetic speech, poetry, alone, is the only means of comprehension of human consciousness.

This fundamental reality is the basis from which we may build a new theory of poetry.

By my thesis, I break Western society of its illusion of totalitarian science. All the myopic and toxic sciences must be dis-privileged. Scientific speech must be exposed as merely another interpretation of human life using symbols. Scientism, in its ultimate exegesis, is essentially another school of late romantic, Victorian idealism – and thus forever fixed as adolescent in its poetic scope. Scientism is only the last Victorian totalitarian ideology (i.e. leveraging mass technology to control the multitudes) not yet deconstructed – as communism and fascism was recently deconstructed. What is the lesson to be taken? Science, fundamentally a set of poetic symbology, and fiercely romanticized, can be placed in a secondary position by the same linguistic audacity that created it.

This is a conclusion. If all possible worlds are a projection within our consciousness, then all possible worlds can be modified to meet the altered conditions of consciousness we seek. This protocol ensures that the *magus mind* is within reach of Homo sapiens. Until the mind of man seizes control of consciousness itself, the material cultures of men will appear only as passing nomadic tribes – as mere misbegotten children of wrath. After all, take away our many shrill justifications of noble and secular *humanness* – in truth, moderns are embarrassed to be caught in this body – and in this space and time. I know no person that would not trade places with an entity of angelic powers – undiminished by the grizzly hungers, diseases, and defecations of mortality. We have angelic minds – therefore, let us pursue gnosis – and not only knowledge of another person's one-time gnosis. We want direct access to extra-sensory, god-like power. Since, in a place still undiscovered, just over the horizon, we are godlike in power.

As any human text, I consider this work a product of fiction. As any human poem verifies, I understand that human consciousness is still unfinished and I still have to blister my voice on the futurity of life. As any human text, my poem insists upon a "just so" narrative of correct action and thought. As part of this fiction, I nullify and deny all current and previous literary criticism. I can imagine that any achievements of language or idiom I share with the reader have the same faults as poetry may contain, or a man be subject to.

ANNEX

Summary of Philosophic Theses

Main Thesis:

Consciousness is a function of Story Theory.

Since there is no undisputed, absolutely known Deity—no independently verifiable knowledge of man's origin—*Homo sapiens* can only make a story of his existence. When a man attempts to give an account of his life, even in the first syllables, he transitions immediately to story.

Supporting Sub-Theses of Story Theory:

Poetry is the singularity of men.

Anything a man does, any act or discovery—whether he conquers a city, or becomes a millionaire, or discovers a new science, or creates a machine, or expresses love towards others—all he can make is a poem of his consciousness using symbols. A machine can make pictures, prose, predictions, data, DNA matching, language, and tools. But only humans can make, or interpret, poems.

Everything the case of human is the case of story.

There can be no philosophy, no religion—no human quality or value—that is not a product of a story within human consciousness. Consequently there is no actual, objective reality, there is only a human interpretation that can be made of possible phenomena. Human qualities do not hang in the air, they are based on stories containing interactions between protagonists. Modern Western philosophies are barren since they attempt to explore human value without a corresponding story (narrative) of humans. That is to say, modern philosophers explore civilization abstractly—society without a story of society, ethics without a story of men, love without a story of lovers. There cannot be a modern philosophy of the soul, for example, unless there is a story of men with souls – and so on.

No rationalist ever has all the facts of a case to use rationalism.

No human civilization has ever had all the facts of a case to use rationalism as mature philosophy – it may only have the faith that it had all the facts. Any civilization is a linguistic church. That is, every civilization in history has created supporting texts and myths allowing the belief that it possessed all the relevant facts – that it was rational and correct. Yet this is only a linguistic illusion of the correctness of rationalism. Scientism, effectively a linguist church of faith (i.e. believing it has all the facts), is thus no different than medievalism.

Each human contains a pattern of mythic code.

Man has individual value because he contains mythic code. Each living soul has an ancient spiritual origin prior to mortal life. We each enter this sphere of materiality with pre-established issues to face and resolve – a mythic code that cannot be avoided or ignored.

Communication is the only possible manifestation of human life.

There is no evidence of life, except, as it exists in a form of communication. Death, as life, is a protocol of feedback. Thus, there can be no human assertion of quality, life, value, shape, intention, or power without human feedback using symbols. That is, any form of human communication is necessarily an interpretation of human life.

Consciousness is a grid of perpetual spiritual communication.

The protocol of communication reveals that consciousness is so vast that it contains eternal signaling. How, once started, can there be a necessity to end a chain of statement and response? There can be no limit to the imagination – or any human thought. Therefore, no information can be lost (since a full record is required to maintain the integrity of the protocol of communication). Therefore, the act of self-consciousness is evidence of eternal life.

We know nothing of any deity.

Scientism knows nothing about the origin of consciousness – since there is no scientific proofs for a metaphysical Being. All we know of god is the stories we accept from authoritative poems. We only know that where there are men, there are gods. And when found – men and gods – they are only described in sacred texts.

Consciousness is still unfinished, and thus the human mind is the center of all things.

Modern scientists and philosophers have claimed to discover the truths of a material universe that was *already* "complete" and the laws of a *supposedly* final form of consciousness. The protocol of Story Theory, instead, verifies there is still a further value to be tested of life (i.e., the material world is not the final statement of reality). Story Theory, thus, establishes that consciousness is unfinished and man is the sentient agent that is still organizing the future of the human race.

Science and poetry are equal protocols of human information.

The schism between science and poetry is an illusion. Science and poetry are each an interpretation of world using symbols. If we clarify the linkage of science and poetry, then there would be a new human philosophy to unify all disunities – and heal the intellectual schism in Western cultures.

All qualities, all forms of good and evil, originate from story.

Show me your good, or your evil, and I will show you the text (story) where your species of good or evil originated. All concepts, all reality—every value that has ever existed—has a reference to a human text. This establishes the requirement that the poet is the most learned and well-read specialist of human consciousness – surpassing the learning of the scientist.

Western poetry has failed to keep pace with the successes of scientism.

It is nearly impossible to argue with the convenience of technology – until we illustrate with power its harmful and totalitarian effects on the human minds. There can be no further advance in Western poetics until the elephant in the room has been faced. The elephant is the unchallenged prestige of modernism and its twin, rational scientism. We have to place scientism correctly as a sub-set of poetry (symbology). *When we demonstrate that rationalism is no more than another faith – a linguistic church –* we then can proceed to advance the poetic idiom again in Western societies.

There is something wrong with modernism.

Modernism is a rogue civilization. That is, it does not organically arise from nature. Modernism is set to destroy all other formations of life on Earth. Modernism is blinded by reliance on exclusive scientific detection of phenomena. Since life consists of chains of charismatic events, no one in modernism sees what's coming. Liberalism, for example, is always in the case of being surprised by the violence and ruthlessness of human societies or natural disasters.

There is something wrong with Homo sapiens.

The definition of *Homo sapiens* no longer applies in modernism. *Homo sapiens* is that species identified by the anthropologist as one that uses (poetic) symbols and buries their reverent dead with hope of futurity. This is the singularity of our species. Moderns no longer bury their dead with reverence for futurity using symbols to designate their concept of eternal life. We are thus *sapiens minus.*

Only with agonistic struggle with our nemesis can we test the values of our civilization.

The West is defined by its struggle with *other*. We are unable to test our value of life in a vacuum. The greater the enemy, the deeper the language discovered of our code of life. Greece was not diminished by defeat by Persia. Rome was not diminished by defeat by Carthage. Hitler's Germany or the Soviet Empire did not diminish America. All great empires discover the language of their unique virtues through near destruction from their *other*. America must have *other* in order for the national language to achieve a superior linguistic idiom. Our confrontation with *other* is necessary.

Men do not worship god – they only worship their language of god.

Religious ritual is dependent upon language. Judaism does not survive without the use of Hebrew. Islam does not have force outside of the use of Arabic. Catholicism cannot be separated from Latin motifs. Protestantism is directly tied to use of the vernacular translation of the *Bible* (English, German, etc.). When men have the choice between their god and their linguistic identity, they choose to keep their language every time. We worship our language, not our gods. We know our language intimately. Not a single man has met god.

Actual "just-so" human information is not repeatable.

"Information" is a phenomena unique to human consciousness. That is, "just-so" *human* information is a one-time event. No parent loves a child exactly the same way as another one – as no child is exactly repeatable. No family, no love affair, no relationship, can be exactly repeated. Charismatic information, thus, is the only information of the human condition. Scientism, asserting repeatable categories of data, fails the test of human information. Scientism thus misconstrues the human condition with its quickly obsolete information.

Since no object can be perceived outside of consciousness, all possible worlds are a projection from within consciousness

If there was some object in the distant universe, it is *impossible* that this same object lays outside of consciousness. Why? Because it is impossible to perceive an object *outside* of consciousness. Everything a man may recognize is thus a projection from within his consciousness. This cancels the thesis of scientism that there are objects independent from the human mind (i.e. the material universe) that need our investigation. If all possible worlds are a projection within our consciousness, then all possible worlds can be modified to meet the conditions of consciousness we seek.